A Vampire Fairy Tale

Melissa Hansen

TONE
A VAMPIRE FAIRY TALE

iUniverse books may be ordered through booksellers or by contacting:

iUniverse LLC
1663 Liberty Drive
Bloomington, IN 47403
www.iuniverse.com
1-800-Authors (1-800-288-4677)

ISBN: 978-1-4917-4630-1 (sc)
ISBN: 978-1-4917-4631-8 (e)

Printed in the United States of America.

iUniverse rev. date: 09/10/2014

For Dad – the man who knew everything about the past

And

For Matt – the man who knows everything about the present

1. The Great And Powerful

*"I always feel like somebody's watching me.
Tell me is it just a dream?"*

Somebody's Watching Me - ROCKWELL

Once upon a time I believed in magic. Now I was learning to trust in it. The little girl in me was gone. The young woman yearning to unveil the truth was gone too. I was different now—more than human and vampire. I was power; a searing embodiment of power and I had absolutely no idea what to do with it.

Changed by my beloved Christian into a vampire only a few short months ago gave me a sense of confidence I'd never dreamed of. Life, or more aptly *afterlife*, was good, but it was fleeting. When I discovered that my family tree included a legacy of witchcraft dating as far back as the Salem witch trials, everything changed. *I* changed. The power beneath my skin felt more real than ever and it scared the hell out of me.

Witch. The word was weird. I didn't feel like a witch, but then, what exactly was a witch supposed to feel like? I wasn't cackling or urging to ride a broomstick and no houses had fallen on me yet, but I felt the power—and it was strong, so strong in fact that I worried it was consuming me.

I thought eternity with Christian would be filled with sunsets and seduction. I was wrong. Time became our keeper and us its reluctant prisoners. The only sun-oriented event we shared was an awe-inspiring sunrise about a month ago. Sitting outside his tattoo shop, La Fuente—the fountain as it translates from Spanish, we watched first light cast its gilded sheen upon Key West. It was beautiful indeed, but short-lived.

That was the morning Christian told me he'd taken a cure to reverse his condition. I didn't even know there was a cure for vampirism (well there wasn't until Christian and his brujo BFF Marco concocted one in secret.) And choosing the cure was choosing to live without me. I knew that Christian had grown tired of slowly living as an irreverent teenager over the last two centuries—I just never figured he could actually do something to change it. He was a perfect vampire. He was beautiful, smart, and worldly and oozed with sophistication and charm. Christian was Bela Lugosi's Dracula and Rob Pattison's Edward. He was vampire exemplified. And choosing to become human was as stupid as an angel choosing to sever his wings.

As time passed, my anger eased. It was hard for me to stay mad at Christian. He was pretty incredible. Even as a stupid human he still managed to amaze me. He was still charming and unbelievably funny to watch. Seeing him eat, even the dumbest of foods, and drool over the taste was arguably adorable. And nothing compared to the way he looked at the sunrise. Watching him stare at that damn sun as though it was the most inspirational thing he'd ever seen was admittedly kind of endearing.

"There you are!" a voice shouted.

I jumped and pivoted on my heels. It was Eradan—my time shifting guardian angel of sorts.

"Where the hell have you been?" he snarled.

"Me?"

"Yeah, you. I've been looking for you everywhere."

I hadn't seen Eradan in weeks and was starting to think that I never would again.

"Have you been hiding?"

"I didn't think I could. You always seem to know where to find me!"

"Well not anymore."

He pressed his lips in a hard line. His dark hair gleamed. He looked as strange and as stunning as ever. His brow furrowed. I could tell that he was mad. Eradan was a lot of things—odd, young and real cute too, (although he always hid behind a pair of darkly tinted spectacles,) but he was never mad.

"What's wrong?" I asked.

"I'm not sure exactly."

"Is it residuals?" Residuals were the outcome of my actions from traveling into the past. I was a time-shifter, albeit a bit of a sloppy one, and I was certainly no stranger to residuals, but they were dangerous and possessed the magnitude to change the world around me in the past, the present and the future.

"It's not residuals," he said.

"What then?"

"Something has changed Hope. Tell me all that's happened since I last saw you?"

I shrugged.

"When did you last shift?"

I shrugged again.

"Tell me!" he insisted.

"Fine."

"Tell me the truth."

"Okay."

"When did you last shift into another person's blood?"

I bit my lip. Ever since my sweet Christian became human again I'd been working hard to resist the urge to travel into his past through his blood. Christian hated my power; its unpredictability and the constant threat of causing change.

"Was it Christian's blood?" Eradan asked.

"No."

"Who then?"

"Mr. Salazar." He was the beast that tried to kill us not so long ago—and the ancestral sorcerer I didn't know I had. I wasn't lying. Mr. Salazar really was the last person's blood I had shifted through.

"It's not him," Eradan groaned.

"There's been no one else. I swear."

"There must be. Think Hope."

"I don't know."

"Try. What else has happened?"

"Eva's baby—"

"No."

"Baptiste corked—"

"No."

"La Fuente was—"

"No."

"Henry and Rosa—"

"No!"

"Damn it, Eradan. I've just mentioned everyone and everything that's happened since I last saw you! What are you searching for?" And then I stopped myself. Like a bolt of thunder I knew exactly what he was looking for. The only thing of real significance that had changed since I last saw Eradan was the fact that Christian had discovered a cure for vampirism. I parted my lips to speak.

"Don't," he said pressing his gloved index finger to my mouth. "If you think it, you'll authenticate it. And there's still a chance to—"

"To what," I barked, pushing his finger away.

He shook his head and for some strange reason, I felt as though he was helping himself to my thoughts the same way Christian used to.

"Eradan," I insisted.

"I've said too much already. I must go now."

Just then the sound of Christian's motorcycle resonated in the distance.

"When will you be back?"

Eradan licked his lips and grinned, but he didn't reply. And with an incredible inky bolt he suddenly disappeared. A warm wind swept past. My cotton dress billowed in the sunlight as I watched the remains of Eradan fade away. I stroked my arms and liberated myself from the dusting of my own ashes. The continual cremation was admittedly gross, but at least I'd finally built a tolerance to being out in the sun again!

"Hope!" Christian shouted. His voice was just louder than the rumble of his engine. I looked ahead and as I set my sights upon him, all thoughts of Eradan instantly vanished.

Christian was everything to me. He was the beautiful stranger of my childhood and the seductive paramour of my afterlife. I zoomed through the air at the speed of light toward him. I jumped on his bike facing him, even before he had a chance to hit the kill switch.

"Hello to you too," he greeted, in his fading English accent.

I smiled; gingerly inhaling his usual tin-cinnamon scent and melted at the hints of sweaty—human, teenage boy that roused my sensibilities. God, I hated that I found him so attractive as a measly human.

"I have a present for you," he said.

My eyes lit up.

"Don't get too excited."

"Too late."

"Close your eyes."

I closed my eyes.

"Give me your hand."

I extended my palm to him. A moment later I felt something falling into the recess of my hand. I closed my fist.

"Open your eyes, Hope."

"No."

"Why not?"

"I like this."

"You like what?"

"They mystery of not-knowing."

"Oh c'mon. It's not that great a gift. Just open your eyes."

"No," I giggled. "I'm waiting."

"Waiting for what?"

"True love's kiss," I teased, puckering my lips.

"Oh Hope," he sighed, suddenly pressing his warm mouth to mine. "Satisfied, Sleeping Beauty?" he said pulling away.

"Always."

"Now open your damn eyes!"

I opened my eyes and stared at the item in the palm of my hand.

"It's just a silly necklace," he said.

"It's beautiful," I replied eyeing the delicate silver chain and quarter-sized, heart shaped pendant.

"I bought it from a street vendor at Mallory Square. It's not like it cost much or—"

"I love it. Put it on me," I said handing it over.

He smiled, took the necklace and draped it around my neck. "You really are the one who holds my heart you know."

"I know," I said, feeling the weight of the pendant fall against my chest. I touched the heart with my fingertips, when suddenly my eyes began welling with wetness.

"Not again," he uttered, concerned.

I wiped the wetness from my cheeks. It was blood. I'd started crying tears of blood again.

"What's wrong Hope? Are you feeling okay?"

"Everything is fine. I'm just a little emotional."

When Christian divulged that he'd taken the cure, I revealed a little secret of my own too. I was pregnant with his baby. The truth was we didn't even know we could procreate, but when our good friend Eva gave birth to her shape-shifting vampire son a few weeks ago, we knew it was a reality. None of us imaged that the little life which lingered deep within our icy veins was enough to propagate, but apparently it was.

"The last time you cried tears of blood you were shifting through time...have you—"

"No! I promised you I wouldn't and I haven't."

He ran his fingers through his scruffy, dark hair. "Oh how I wish I could still read your mind."

"Me too," I replied eyeing the stubble that framed the line of his jaw. Christian never had stubble when he was a vampire. He was always very clean shaven, pale and pristine looking. But now that he was human, there was an undeniable unkemptness about him. It was a real rough and readiness and I liked it. I liked it a lot.

He laughed.

"What?"

"I might not be able to read your mind anymore, but I definitely know that look."

"You do?"

"Uh huh," he grinned, grabbing me by the thighs and pulling me on his lap. He wiped the bloodstains from my skin and smirked. "You want me," he whispered. "You like me like this. Admit it."

"No."

"Tell me that you like me better as a human."

"Never!" I shouted, shoving him off.

"Oh Hope," he groaned.

"You've really become an arrogant ass since you turned human, you know."

He laughed. His whole face suddenly enlivened with colour. I hated that he could be ridiculously charismatic and gorgeous even when he was being utterly egotistical.

"You think I'm arrogant?" he teased, pulling me back.

"*And* an ass, don't forget."

"But it's a nice ass, wouldn't you agree?" His voice was soft and alluring. He leaned in close and kissed my earlobe. I was helpless under his touch. I closed my eyes and smiled. I grabbed a fistful of his T-shirt and pulled.

"Hope!" he shouted.

"What?" I said, realizing that I'd accidently tore the shirt straight off of his body!

"I really liked that shirt."

"Sorry," I laughed, ogling his sculpted, naked chest.

"You're strong."

"I know." I tossed the remnants of his shirt to the ground. "And don't you forget it."

A moment later we exploded in a kiss. Like fire and ice our lips merged in a charged union of passion. I was lost in Christian. His lips were soft and affectionate and his tongue was skilled and felt like heaven inside me. Everything was perfect, when all of a suddenly the motorcycle engine came alive from beneath us!

"What the...?" Christian muttered. "How did you do that?"

"Me?"

"Yeah you," he said reaching into his pocket and dangling the keys.

My body heaved with energy; fiery currents coursing through me like waves.

"Do it again," he insisted, killing the ignition.

"I-I can't."

"Just try."

"But I didn't do anything," I said, still feeling the intensity from the flow of energy within me.

Christian sighed, running his fingers through his hair like usual. I stared him in the eyes, panic palpable in my expression.

"C'mon," he said, empathetically. "Let's get outta here."

I nodded relieved and watched as he slipped the key into the ignition. The engine roared again and like a rocket we were off. I straddled him tightly, wrapping my legs around him. I leaned my head against his shoulder and let the air caress my back. The open road ahead gave me the momentary freedom from reality I needed. I'd almost forgotten about the baby, Christian's humanity, the cure and even seeing Eradan again. Everything was perfect.

"Looks like rain," Christian said. "Sorry baby, but I have to turn back."

"No," I pleaded.

"I have to, Hope." Then all of a sudden the rain began descending in hard, heavy drops. "Shit," he groaned.

I looked up to the sky, and where I should have seen clouds and raindrops, I saw eyes instead! Hundreds and hundreds of glowing eyes stared down at us like a celestial tribunal of sorts. My heart thumped in my chest, when all of a sudden the eyes turned into flashes of fire!

"STOP!" I shouted, thrusting my hand in the air.

Time abruptly slowed to its most infinitesimal measure. The world around us decelerated to a stop. Fireballs and raindrops hung in a stagnant, lethal patterning before us.

"Hope?" Christian mumbled, anxiously.

An instant later everything changed. Fireballs imploded into nothingness and time resumed its normal speed again. We were hurling down the wet road at an unimaginable velocity. Fate and fear twisted like an ill-fated tango and I knew that impact was imminent. My body swelled with power, but I was utterly helpless in knowing how to use any of it!

"Damn it!" I shouted. "Damn me!" I continued, disgusted with myself. A deluge of bloody tears streamed from my eyes and all I could do was contemplate that Christian was about to die simply because he was human again and I was incapable of saving him.

2. Poor Unfortunate Soul

*"The boy that you loved is the monster you fear,
Peel off all those eyes and crawl into the dark."*

Man That You Fear – Marilyn Manson

I tried forcing my limbs to move. I was paralyzed with fear. Then, suddenly, and most unexpectedly, Christian managed to gain control of the bike. We screeched to a halt. The bike hit the pavement and so did we. Our bodies flew though the air like fireworks before slamming against the pavement.

"Christian!" I shouted, springing to my feet. I rushed toward him. He was pale and deathly still on the ground. I pressed my ear to his chest. *Thump-thump. Thump-thump.* "Heartbeat," I mumbled. "C'mon baby." He was alive! The sweet sound of his heartbeat was music to my ears. I stroked the side of his face, when suddenly he moved.

"What...what happened?" he moaned.

"We hit the road. We flew off the bike!"

"Feels like it."

"You okay?"

"I don't know."

"Anything feel broken?"

"Everything," he joked. "This human thing hurts."

I laughed, checking his body for injuries. "You're a little banged up, but nothing a bit of blood can't fix."

I let my fangs cut through my gums. I bit into the skin on my wrist and drew some blood. I pressed my bloody wrist to Christian's lips and he started drinking immediately. In an instant his injuries began mending.

"What happened back there?" he said, withdrawing. "You nearly killed us, Hope!"

My eyes widened. I watched a trickle of blood drip down his cheek from the scrape on his face.

"Hey. Are you even listening to me?"

I reached out and caught a droplet of his blood in my hand.

He sat up. "Why the hell did you wreck my bike and practically get me killed?"

"I didn't!" I barked, tightening my fist over the droplet.

"You can't play games like this anymore. You can't keep showing off."

"I wasn't showing off. I was saving us!"

"Saving us from what? The rain?"

"The eyes Christian! The fireballs!"

He rolled his eyes at me.

"Don't pretend like you didn't see it. It was right there above us, in front of us, all around us damn it!"

His expression contorted.

"They were like grenades! C'mon Christian. You really didn't see it?"

He shook his head.

"What?" I barked.

"Oh how I wish I knew what you were thinking."

"Well you used to, but then you *chose* to take a cure to do away with all of your gifts."

"Gifts?"

"Yes, gifts."

"The only gift that means anything to me is you."

"And had you not had those gifts then you never would have lived long enough to have met me."

"Hope..."

"It was your gifts that let us be together."

"You wanna philosophize?" He ran his fingers through his hair.

"It's not philosophizing if it's fact. And don't ask me whether the chicken or the egg came first either. We're not having that conversation again. Ever!"

"And why not?"

"Because the answer is simple."

"Enlighten me," he said, groggily.

"It was the egg." I grinned, cockily. "It will always be the egg."

"Then tell me this, where'd the egg come from? Was it sent from the sky along with your glowing eyes and fireballs?"

"Christian!" I shouted.

"That was in poor taste, I admit it."

"You really didn't see it?"

"No. But that doesn't mean I don't believe you didn't."

I nodded.

He pulled me close into the circle of his arms. His bare chest was warm and I could feel my icy, apathetic heart melting against him. I felt safe in Christian's arms. I always had, even when I was a little girl and he saved me from falling into the mangrove estuary. There was something almost magical about being in his arms.

"My heart hurts when I'm without you," he whispered.

"Mine too."

"Never leave me."

"I wasn't planning on it."

"Good."

I looked around. The lush green foliage was blissful, the blue sky was heavenly and the breeze was tranquil and smelled of gardenias. "Besides," I smiled, "where would I go? Perish Key is our paradise."

He smiled and kissed me on the cheek.

"It scared me today," I muttered quietly.

"What you saw?"

I nodded.

"Was it after us?"

"I guess. But I waved it off."

"You did?"

I nodded again. "Why couldn't you see it?"

"Maybe because I'm human?" He tightened his hold on me. "You must be careful Hope."

"I'm always careful."

"Not your kind of careful. I mean really careful. I might be mortal, but I'm no fool."

"Are you implying that it's after me?"

"I'm suggesting that what you saw was meant for your eyes only."

"How do you figure?" I asked, intrigued.

"This isn't the first time I've heard of something like this happening."

"It's not?"

He nodded with reluctance. "Long ago, when your mother was alive, something similar happened."

My eyes widened.

"Your mother and William—your father, they were messing around out back by the forest."

"Okay..."

"And William...he saw something."

"Like the eyes?"

"He described it like a vision—an apparition of sorts with eyes staring down at them. It concerned William tremendously. He became convinced that someone was on to us...watching us from afar."

"Oh my god!"

"Your father was never the same after that. He wouldn't let it go. He *couldn't* let it go. He'd ramble incessantly about those damn eyes all the time. I hate to admit it, especially after all these years, but now after today, I'm beginning to believe that maybe William wasn't wrong."

"Did my mother see them too?"

"No."

"And neither did you."

Christian nodded. "What you saw—I don't think any of it was real."

"Like hell it wasn't!"

"Hope," he uttered, "I believe you saw it just as William did. I'm merely suggesting that I don't believe it really happened. I think that someone or perhaps even something inserted this into your consciousness."

"Like a veil?"

"Yes."

"But who...and how? And why would they want—"

"I don't know," he interrupted. "But that doesn't mean we can't find out."

"How are we gonna find out? I mean if William couldn't—"

"Rosa."

"Rosa? That old bitch of a witch doesn't agree to favors very easily."

"I know that."

"Plus, I thought you hated her."

"That's irrelevant."

"Well it might be irrelevant to you, but she hates you more than life itself right now, Christian."

His expression hardened.

"She blames you for losing her grandson Marco."

"Well that's ridic—"

"After you guys concocted that stupid cure—"

"Stupid cure!" he exclaimed.

"She won't help us!"

"You don't know that."

"Her grandson disappeared. She thinks it's punishment for using black magic in making that damn cure. Believe me Christian. She hates you and by hating you that means she also hates me!"

"Just so you know I didn't force Marco to do anything he didn't want to do already."

"Rosa doesn't care. And to be honest, I don't either. You've pissed off a very old and powerful witch. You're an idiot if you think she's gonna be all Hermonie Grangier with us."

"Well Mrs. Potter, I hate to enlighten you, but you're wrong. I know that she'll help us, *you* in particular."

"She won't."

"She will."

"Why?

"Henry."

"My grandfather?"

"She's still in love with him."

"But I thought that ridiculous love triangle between him and her and my grandmother ended years ago."

"Real love never ends—it merely hibernates for a while."

My brow furrowed.

"She'll help us. I'm telling you." He moved away from me and toward his bike. It was busted up and sat on the hot, black asphalt as a reminder of the strange events we'd just experienced. Christian leaned down and struggled to pick it up.

"Here," I said, lifting the weighty bike from the ground with virtually no effort.

"Don't think I'll ever get used that," he complained.

I grinned.

With a bruised ego intact, he straightened his bike and started walking it along the road.

"You never did give me an answer," he suddenly implored.

"To what?"

He smirked.

"Oh god, are you still on about the chicken and the egg?"

He smiled a giddy, boyish smile.

"Fine," I scowled. "The chicken shifted though time into the past and laid the damn egg. Okay?"

"Oh Hope. There really is so much fire in you."

"Fire?"

"Fire! Vigor! Life!"

"Life? You're the human. Not me."

"So right you are," he replied with a smile. And while he fixed his eyes on the road ahead, I kept mine glued to him. He was just so damn pretty to look at: defined, tanned and beaded with sweat. I really hated that I was so attracted to him in his stupid human form. I wanted nothing more than for him to be like me again—a strong, confident, powerful vampire, but the sweet stink of his humanness continued taunting me. I pulled my eyes off of him and set them on the road ahead. The undulating mirage of heat waves in the distance relaxed me a little, but wasn't helping ease the potency of his damn smell any. I cocked my head to the side and stole another peek. I brought my hand to my lips and licked the drop of Christian's blood that had dried to the centre of it. It tasted like heaven; he tasted like heaven as a human. I sighed inside knowing that it would be a long walk back home to Ambrose House.

3. There's No Place Like Home

"I put a spell on you."

I Put A Spell On You - Screamin' Jay Hawkins

Ambrose House was old, immense and named after the ship that brought my beloved Christian to Perish Key. It amazed me that Christian and William—my biological father, actually built the house from the wood of their fallen vessel.

"Finally," Christian said, relieved.

I nodded and eyed the grand silhouette of Ambrose House in the distance. It was quite beautiful, like a fairy tale castle surrounded by a kingdom of woodland.

"My bike's gonna need a real overhaul."

"Yeah," I replied, barely listening. My thoughts drifted to the last time I'd begged Rosa for help. It was to free an innocent human woman that had been cursed to live in a wooden mast-head for over two-centuries. Her name was Alexandra and she had been posing as a young man aboard the HMS Ambrose when she was cursed. Alex was a friend of my father's and for that reason alone I felt a certain onus to both free her and protect her here in Perish.

"Haven't seen Ambrose House this alive since...well since ever," Christian uttered, approaching.

The porch was ornamented with women. My buddy Ryan and her new friends had also recently joined us in Perish. Reawakening from a curse of a different kind in Mexico following the destruction of their vampire leader, gave them all a second chance. Ryan's friends were militant girls, some vampires and some human, and came to us seeking refuge. In exchange for room and board they vowed to protect us and our secret existence. Considering the amount of trouble we'd recently encountered, their offer seemed too good to refuse.

"Hope!" Ryan shouted. "You okay?" She was tall and slim with jet black hair cropped right at her jaw line. She was extremely pale and wearing a black dress reminiscent of Winona Ryder in Beetlejuice.

"Yeah. I'm fine," I said, approaching.

"Well that bike doesn't look fine," she said, eyeing Christian's motorcycle.

I hadn't known Ryan long, but I had known her from my so-called normal life up north when I lived in the city. She used to work for the Society (an enigmatic group of powerful vampires that seemingly ran the world.) Ryan was employed to study me; a half-breed—born half human and half vampire, but things changed. She became like a sister to me and chose to go rogue. She cut out her sustenance-implant (a highly complex feeding device) and fled the Society. She ended up in Mexico caught in the middle of a black-market, blood-trading ring.

"Did Hope do that to your bike?" she teased.

"How'd you guess," Christian replied.

Ryan shrugged and smirked when suddenly the front door swung open. Alex appeared in the doorframe holding two steaming cups in her hands. Alex was the woman that Rosa helped me free from the wooden masthead. She was literally the most androgynous looking person I'd ever met. Dressed in her tattered, navy uniform coat with a pair of modern jeans didn't help matters either. Her short tufts of blonde, pixie-like hair, thin, wiry frame and rather genderless features made it easy to see why my father and the rest of the crew on the HMS Ambrose thought she was a boy.

"Aye!" Alex barked, in her thick English accent. "What happened to that there machine?"

"It's a long story," Christian replied.

"I likes the long stories," she said, handing Ryan one of the cups.

"Well you won't like this one," he continued.

"Try me mate." She sat down in the old rocking chair next to Ryan.

"Some other time," Christian replied. "We're looking for Henry. Have you seen him?"

Alex smirked. Her face lit up like a child's on Christmas morning. She was without a doubt the most enigmatic relic salvaged from the wreckage of the HMS Ambrose. And I felt like I'd known her all my life and rightfully so as she'd hung encased in a pretty wooden masthead in my hallway for centuries!

"Henry's inside," Ryan interjected.

"Fallin' in love with that old bag of a lassie!" Alex snorted, hot soup spraying from her lips as she laughed. She was so unusual; gruff and guttural.

"In *my* house?" I snapped.

"Aye, Angel," Alex continued. "But no sense gettin' your knickers in a bunch about it."

Christian grabbed my hand. He pulled me up to the porch toward the front door. My body was limp, but I could feel the swells of power coursing again under my skin. The thought of facing Rosa kind of terrified me. She was a tough old broad and a very powerful sorcerer. I knew she blamed Christian for Marco's disappearance. What I didn't know however, was how far she'd plan on taking her vengeance.

"Hey," Ryan whispered as I approached. "What kind of trouble are you in?"

"Definitely not the good kind."

Ryan's eyes sparkled. She wasn't stupid. As a former intelligence operative for the Society she knew a thing or two about reading situations. Just then Christian tugged on my arm, pulling me through the front door.

Had it not been for inheriting this damn house half a year ago when my estranged grandmother passed away, none of this would have happened. I would have still been naïve, sort-of human and living my somewhat normal life up north in the city. But here I was, living a freakish afterlife, deep in the Florida Keys, on a mysterious Island named after death itself!

"Henry!" Christian shouted. He grabbed a hoodie that was hanging near the front door and put it on.

"In here," Henry replied.

Before coming to Perish I didn't remember anything about the maternal side of my family; my so-called step-father Richard did his best to protect me from any and all ties. But once my late grandmother's will was read and I discovered there was still a link to my mother's side of my family, I was eager to learn everything I could. I packed my bags and embarked on a journey that literally changed my life forever. Along with her house my grandmother bequeathed the brood of motley vampires she'd been living with—which also included my biological, blind, twenty-five year old, vampire grandfather named Henry.

"You in the kitchen?" Christian asked.

"Yes."

"Is Rosa with you?"

"Yes Christian, she is."

Christian pushed open the kitchen door and dragged me through. A mix of unusual smells immediately imbued my senses. I started coughing.

"There you are," Henry greeted. The family resemblance between Henry and I was incredible. Our fair-skin, blonde hair big, bright blue eyes and soft features were nearly identical. He definitely looked more like my brother than my grandfather. But there was a timeless quality about him; something that made him seems both modern and old-fashioned looking at the same time.

"We need your help," Christian insisted.

Rosa grunted. Her back was turned to us and she continued stirring something in a large black pot on the stove. She was heavy-set, olive-skinned and very wrinkly. Rosa was old and she looked it too.

"What kind of help do you need?" Henry pried.

"Always needing," Rosa mumbled in her heavy Spanish accent. She had long black hair that hung in a tight braid down the center of her back. Her clothes were out of style and always a little too tight for her hefty frame. Thankfully, for her sake, Henry was blind!

"Why is she here?" I asked, abruptly.

She grunted again.

"Dinner!" Henry said, eagerly.

"You planning on eating us?" I teased.

Rosa kissed her teeth before turning back to her pot.

"She's cooking for us Hope," Henry replied. "Isn't that wonderful?"

"Well unless there's a really rare steak in the bottom of that pot I don't—"

"Hope had a vision," Christian interrupted.

"What?" Henry inquired.

"She saw eyes...eyes in the sky."

"Dios mio!" Rosa exclaimed. She slammed her wooden spoon against the counter. "No! No! No!"

"William was different," Christian snapped.

"No different. He her father!" Rosa shouted.

"But she is much stronger than he was. I know it."

"No," she grunted.

"What happened with William?" I interjected.

"It's complicated, Hope." Christian's voice was edgy.

"Poor child don't even know," Rosa snickered.

"Tell me!" I insisted.

Christian groaned. "Rosa did a recollection spell on him to reanimate the vision so that maybe we could make some sense of it."

"And?" I continued.

"And it didn't work."

"Spell work fine," Rosa barked. "He was loco before spell."

"Willy was not loco," Christian snarled.

"I not care. I still not do again!"

"Why can't you just be nice for once?" he shouted.

"Nice?" she grunted. "Ha!"

"Stop!" Henry pleaded. "You're getting ahead of yourselves. Hope," he said, concerned. "Can you tell me what you saw?"

"I saw eyes. They were glowing in the sky."

"Anything else?"

"Fireballs. But I managed to fend them off."

"You did? How?"

"With my hand, I waved them off, I think."

Rosa grunted.

"Did you see anything else?" Henry added.

"No."

"And the eyes," he continued. "How did they make you feel?"

"Like I was definitely being watched...by *them*."

"Them?"

"The Society," I said. "It has to be them. I knew that feeling. I remembered feeling it before when I lived in the north with my step-father Richard."

"No!" Rosa interrupted. "I not do it!"

"Why do you have to be so damn obstinate all the time?" Christian snapped.

"You make my Marco leave!"

"I didn't make him leave."

"You make him do black magic!"

"I didn't make Marco do anything he didn't want to do already. Jesus!"

"Diablo Blanco!" she hissed, suddenly.

"Did you just call me the White Devil?"

"Stop!" Henry hollered. "That's enough! Hope needs our help and I don't think either of you have the luxury of denying her at this point." He cleared his throat. "Any danger we face, we face together. Rosa, I know you've lost your grandson, but we will get him back. Christian, I know you love Hope, and so do I. We won't let what happened to William happen to her."

"I still not do spell," Rosa insisted.

"You might not have to," he continued. "Hope, your friend Ryan worked for the Society right?"

"Well yeah. She lived and worked among them for years."

"Do you think she would be willing to share her knowledge and experience to help us shed some light on what this damn Society wants?"

I grinned. "I have a feeling she'd jump at the chance."

"What do you have in mind Henry?" Christian's tone was full of skepticism.

"Hope uses her ability to shift inside Ryan's blood—"

"Forget it!" Christian exploded. "She promised me that she wouldn't shift anymore."

"I understand that Christian, but it's the lesser of two evils here. You know the danger of performing a spell."

"Residuals are dangerous too Henry. And the shifting alone is killing Hope. You're not considering—"

"Don't I get a say in all this?" I interrupted.

"No," Christian replied. "Because I know exactly what you're going to say."

"That's not fair," I whispered, touching his arm. "I know I made you a promise, but sometimes promises need to be broken."

"Promises never need to be broken," he snapped.

"You broke your promise to me."

"I didn't."

"You promised me eternity Christian. You broke that promise the moment you decided to become human again."

He exhaled noisily before running his fingers through his hair.

"I can't continue living everyday as though it's our last. I hate the thought of being watched. I hate the thought of feeling like someone is coming for us. Isn't our life here in Perish worth protecting?" My eyes narrowed. "Isn't our freedom worth fighting for?"

"You make it sound like a revolution!" Christian exclaimed. "It's just an island Hope. It's only water and wood and sand. Nothing more."

"Well it's more to me. Perish is my home."

"And mine too," Henry agreed.

"It's different for you now," I insisted. "As a human you can leave here. You can live anywhere in the world. We're still bound to live in the shadows and Perish is that shadow for us."

"But you can be human again too," he insisted. "If you just—"

"The cure is gone Christian. Even if I wanted to take it, which I don't, I can't. It vanished along with Marco. It's over."

"It's never over."

"If Hope does this for us," Henry interjected, "she'll only be looking for answers that may shed some light on what the hell this Society wants. Nothing more."

"They want world domination!" Christian scoffed. "She doesn't have to risk travelling through Ryan's blood to know that."

"Perhaps," Henry replied, "but as more and more of them tear out their implants and defect towards our shores, their throngs will grow angrier. Perish will inevitably become a safe haven for these lost and hungry rebels."

"So it really is a revolution!" Christian insisted.

"And now that you're human," I added, "you won't even be on the front lines with us."

"Like hell I won't!"

"Enough!" Henry shouted. "I understand your concern for Hope. I don't want her to suffer either, but we must do something to thwart this threat."

"Then let me go to them," Christian offered.

"What?" I exclaimed.

"You said it yourself—I'm human now. I'm free to go anywhere I want in the world."

"But not right into the enemy's hands!"

"And yet it's okay for you to do it?"

"I'd be going through Ryan's memories. It would be different."

"But if you get caught or worse killed, Hope, you still die." Christian's phone rang. He pulled it from his pocket and eyed the screen. "I've got a television interview in an hour, I have to go."

"Right now?" I snarled. "This conversation is far more important than your stupid TV interview."

"You don't think I know that? Look, these interviews are what's keeping this so-called safe haven of ours operating. I've got to keep up appearances Hope. Always." He leaned in close. "I'll be at La Fuente if you need me. I trust you." He kissed me on the cheek. "I love you."

"I love you too," I replied, watching him leave. I bit my lip, regret weighed on my conscience like a rock. "He's gonna kill me," I muttered under my breath.

"You're already dead," Henry teased, poignantly.

"In that case," I laughed. "What the hell are we waiting for! Let's get Ryan."

4. Down The Rabbit Hole

"I got a black magic woman
Got me so blind I can't see"

Black Magic Woman - SANTANA

A trip into another's past wasn't exactly first class. There were no hot towels and leather seats. It was a turbulent molecular thrill-ride through a suffocating concave wormhole. But I was ready. I'd done it more than a few times and was starting to get used to it.

"Rosa," Henry grinned. "Can you get Ryan for us?"

"Si."

"Tu eres mi luz en la oscurida," he whispered.

Rosa smiled before waddling through the kitchen door.

"You love her Henry, don't you?"

"Love is complicated, Hope."

"What did you say to her?"

"I told her that she was my light in the dark."

I grinned.

"I loved your grandmother, Hope."

I shrugged. "I didn't really know her."

"Can I ask you something?"

"Of course.

"It's about Mexico."

"Mexico?" I said, intrigued.

"Why haven't we heard anything on television, the radio or in any social media about what happened in Mexico?"

"I've wondered that myself."

"You changed history, Hope. You destroyed the leader of the blood-trade ring in ancient Mexico even before she became a vampire!"

"Believe me, I know. And it should have caused monsoon-sized residuals on a global scale!"

"Yes. The dead should have risen from the ground all around the world. Vampires should have burst into flames in the middle of crowded shopping malls. Mass hysteria should have ensued."

"But it didn't."

"The ripple effect—the residual, of what you did in ancient Mexico should have forced an exposure of our kind to the human world. Vampires should have been breaking news by now! Humans should have been in a mad-panic!"

"I don't understand," I confessed.

"We already have empirical evidence proving that residuals did in fact take effect."

"You mean Ryan's friends?"

"Yes. The fact that some of them did become human again validates the outcome of your actions in the past."

"Do you think the Society had something to do with covering it up?"

"Yes." He scratched his chin. "I'm beginning to wonder whether this Society is even more powerful than we initially imagined."

"They'd literally have to veil the entire population of humans and control the media...control everything! Do you really think they could be that powerful?"

Henry shrugged, when suddenly Rosa opened the kitchen door. Ryan was standing beside her.

"Are we taking down the fanged-man or what?" Ryan said, smirking.

I laughed. "Rosa filled you in?"

"Well sort of—but my broken-English is pretty rusty."

"Sit with us," Henry said, warmly.

Ryan sat beside him at the kitchen table and listened attentively as Henry took great care in explaining what we needed from her. The moment she realized that she really would be helping us bring down the Society so-to-speak, she was totally on board. Ryan resented the Society and who could blame her? They took her human life away from her, turned her into a vampire and made her forget most of her human memories. She'd spent years living by their rules in their world working for them and was hungry to destroy them.

"It won't be so bad," I pleaded, tenderly.

"Oh, I can so tell when you're lying to me," she replied.

"Drink." Rosa handed her a mug. It was steaming hot.

"What is it?" she asked, taking it from her.

"Sleeping potion."

"No," I snapped, snatching the mug from her hand. "I don't want anything clouding her memories. We must do this cold."

"I trust you," Ryan said.

"Thanks."

"Just bite her already!" a familiar, whiney voice shouted from the doorway. "I've got a hungry immortal kid here and I need the kitchen to warm him a bottle of blood."

It was Eva. She was an Ambrose House original. Eva and her strong-man, Spaniard boyfriend Baptiste lived with Christian, William, Henry and my grandmother for many years. Eva was a surly, shape-shifting vampire with fiery red hair and a bitchy attitude to match. She was like the sister I wished I'd never had. And now she was mother to an immortal baby vampire-shifter named Stromboli.

"We're kinda in the middle of something," I insisted.

"So," she countered. "I'm kinda in the middle of raising a child."

"Stromboli is welcome to drink what is left in my cup," Henry offered.

"No thanks," she replied flinging her crying, hefty newborn from one side of her curvy body to the other. "I only serve him organic."

"Organic?" I laughed. "What's that?"

"Organic is clean and pure and a lot healthier than that dirty mixed-mess the rest of you drink."

"And where do you get this organic blood?" I continued.

"It's Amish."

"Amish?"

"That's why he cry," Rosa scoffed, quietly.

"Don't start with me," she snapped, pushing her way into the kitchen. She began rummaging through the cupboards. She was loud and clumsy and totally intolerable. Stromboli started crying even louder.

"Eva!" Henry shouted.

"I told you," she barked. "I need to warm a bottle!"

"Now?" he pressed. "In here?"

"Yes now! Yes in here!"

"Dios mio!" Rosa snarled. She got up from her seat and waddled toward Eva. "You not hold baby right."

"Don't touch him!" she gasped.

"Ah," Rosa grunted taking Stromboli from Eva's hands and nestling him in the cradle of her arm. He stopped crying instantly. "See," she said. "You not hold baby right."

Eva scowled and snatched him back. She flung the child on her hip again. He started crying instantly.

"Eva!" Henry shouted.

"What?"

"Either hold the baby the way Rosa showed you or please get out of this kitchen!"

"Fine," she replied, flinging the baby into the boney crook of her arm. He stopped crying. She eyeballed Rosa. "I hold baby right? Happy?"

"Yes!" we all exclaimed in unison.

She grabbed a dirty, old pot from the top shelf and put it on the stove. "What's going on in here anyway? Am I missing out on some kind of feasting orgy or something?"

Rosa removed Eva's dirty pot from the stove and replaced it with a clean pot instead. Eva glared, but continued using the clean pot. She turned to the fridge and took out a margarine container labeled *Organic*. Rosa watched her like a hawk. She snapped open the lid and poured the bloody contents into the pot. Rosa passed her a wooden spoon. I had to laugh. It was difficult picturing Rosa and Eva being besties once upon a time, but I knew that they had been. They were so different. Eva was young, immortal and beautiful. Rosa was an old witch with more wrinkles than a Shar Pei. To me, the only thing they seemed to have in common was the fact that they were both bitches!

"Hope is going to travel inside Ryan's past to observe the Society," Henry explained.

"Oh," Eva answered, nonchalantly.

"Do you know what the Society is?" he continued.

"Yup."

"You do?" I patronized.

"Uh duh."

"Well doesn't their presence concern you?" I continued.

She shrugged.

"How can you be so casual?" I exclaimed.

"What do you want me to do? Slap on some armor? Bring in the tanks? We've been in constant danger since you came to live here Blondie!"

"Well this danger is like the frickin' genocide of dangers," Ryan interjected. "So can we please get on with it already?"

I nodded. I looked down at Ryan's wrist, at the site where she had ripped out her sustenance implant. Looking at her scar was like looking at the X on a treasure map. It was the perfect place to dig in. I pulled her wrist close and let the smell of her skin invigorate me.

Drinking vampire blood was entirely different from drinking human blood. It was intoxicating, high-inducing and even perilous in large quantities, but I needed her blood. It was the simplest way of getting an inside look at the Society.

"Do it," she whispered.

My fangs were already sharp and pierced through her skin with ease. Blood quickly flowed against my tongue. It was bitter and cold and a little like how I imagined the taste of sadness to be. I lapped it up quickly and swallowed it down, inundating myself with her cells. With every drop I knew the doorway to her past would soon open up to me.

Then, the familiar coercive pull began drawing me inside. I opened my eyes and filled my lungs with a deep breath of air. Inhales moved me backward through time. *Inhale.* I was on the move deep inside Ryan's past. I saw Mexico, her friends on the beach in the moonlight, the first time she visited me in Perish and even her attempt at extracting her own implant. Images moved like a freight train zipping past. I saw myself and my apartment, I saw where I used to live in the city in the north, I saw Richard—the father I'd grown up with and then suddenly I saw something else. *Them.*

Light and color merged together in a seamless unification while sounds began to blur into a numbing stream of static. I knew what was coming next-the concave time tunnel. Images from her life arched around me into the most unimaginable passageway; a wormhole of Ryan's memories.

Exhale. Exhales pushed me back to the future, but also had the ability to cease shifting when executed with great care. Gingerly, I forced a breath of air from my lungs. The concave time tunnel collapsed, shattering into millions of pieces. Everything went dark and a deafening boom reverberated. I closed my eyes and when I opened them again I knew I had arrived.

I was standing in a long, empty corridor. It was white and went on for miles. I began looking around when suddenly I felt a hand on my shoulder. I froze.

"What are you doing here?"

"Eradan?" I exclaimed, turning around.

"Leave! Leave now!"

"No."

"Damn you!" he insisted grabbing my arm with his gloved fingers. "This is beyond dangerous." He dragged me down the strange, sterile corridor toward what looked like a narrow trash bin. Just then the sound of footsteps resonated. "Holy hell! he mumbled shoving me inside. "Don't come out until I call for you. Got it?"

"Got it," I replied, reluctantly.

He closed the lid. It was dark and smelled of cardboard. A moment later I heard the footfalls nearing. I stayed quiet and listened.

"You're pushing your limits Eradan," a soft male voice said.

"I know and I'm leaving."

"You're damn right you are."

"I'm not here to make trouble."

"Whether you make it or not," the voice laughed, "trouble always follows you."

"Will you report this?"

There was a long drawn-out silence.

"No."

"I owe you," Eradan replied.

"I'll add it to your tab." Just then the footsteps resumed, fading as they distanced.

"You're the damn trouble that follows me," Earadan said, opening the lid.

"Me?" I replied, hopping out.

"Yeah you. Now go, Hope!"

"But I just got here."

"And now you're just leaving."

"No!"

"This isn't negotiable."

"Well I'm not leaving!"

"Then I guess you give me no other choice." He took off his gloves and planted his bare hands on mine. The touch of his skin electrified me instantly, searing my flesh like fire! I closed my eyes and doubled over with pain. Not a moment too soon I opened my eyes again and found myself back in the kitchen at Ambrose House.

5. Make a Wish and Take a Bite

"I heard about your lessons, but lessons are so cold."

Hot For Teacher – Van Halen

I looked around. The pain was gone and I realized that I was grasping Ryan's bloody wrist in my hand.

"What happened?" Henry asked, concerned.

"I-I'm not sure."

"Did it work?" Ryan inquired.

"I don't know," I said withdrawing from her wrist. "I was there and then suddenly I was here again.

"Your nose, Hope!" Ryan exclaimed. "It's bleeding.

I wiped my skin. It was dripping with blood.

"Are you alright?" Henry asked.

"Yeah...no...I don't know." I sat back in my chair. "I feel faint."

"Maybe Christian was right," Henry admitted. "This is far too dangerous for Hope. We should have used the spell."

"Bad idea," Rosa snapped.

"Oh sure," Eva replied, "easy to judge from the peanut gallery."

"You were there weren't you?" Ryan said, suddenly.

I nodded. "I saw a white, sterile corridor. Almost like a hospital."

"Is that the Society?" Henry asked.

Ryan shrugged. "Everything was always very sterile at headquarters." She touched my shoulder. "Do you want to go back?"

"No!" Henry exclaimed. "I won't risk her health again."

"You need spell," Rosa suddenly grunted. "Fancy vampire trick will not give meaning in vision."

"So you'll do it for me?" I asked, eagerly.

"No."

"Oh Rose," Eva chirped, dangling the blood-filled bottle from Strombo's mouth. "Just do it for her. What's the big deal?"

Rosa kissed her teeth.

"C'mon, Rosa." I smiled "I don't know what happened with William, but I can assure you, I'm much stronger than he ever was."

"No."

"Rose," Henry charmed. "Please."

"No! I tell you. I not want to get mix up in this again. Besides, she don't need witch to do this for her."

"What do you mean?" Henry asked.

"I mean she don't need witch because she is witch!"

Rosa was right. I was a witch—a pathetic mess of legacy and power which I didn't understand and couldn't seem to reign.

"You can help her," Henry said, elatedly.

"Noooo!"

"Rose," Henry flirted. "You are the most talented conjurer I know."

Rosa grunted.

"And Hope is the only family I have left. She is my granddaughter and yet I have no way of helping her myself."

"Dios mio," she groaned. "I so old and so tired. I can not take another apprentice. I try with my grandson Marco and look what happened."

"Please?" he pressed.

"I cannot."

"Rose..."

"No! I too old, I tell you!"

"Rosie..."

"No!"

"Chica bonita," he continued.

"Dios mio!" she blushed, flattered.

"Great!" Eva cackled. "It's all settled then. Obi-Wan has her little Padawan. Everyone is happy now."

"Well technically," I interjected, "Obi-Wan's Padawan was Anakin and you likening me to Darth Vader is basically saying I'm Satan."

"Sorry," Eva replied. "I don't speak nerd."

Ryan laughed.

"Hey," I said, swatting her in the arm. "Whose side are you on?"

"Satan's," she replied.

"Rosa has agreed!" Henry exclaimed.

"I only agree if you follow rules," she insisted. "You do as I ask and you not question instruction. Si?"

"Si," I replied. I bit my lip, a sudden jolt of excitement rushing through my veins. "So how do we start? A locator spell to find the leaders of the Society? A hex? Or maybe a curse?"

Rosa laughed.

"What's so funny?"

"You!" she replied.

"But I thought you agreed. I thought you were going to teach me witchcraft."

"I teach you yes. But this not witchcraft." She put her hand on my forehead. "It come from here."

"My head?"

"Si." She moved her hand to my chest. "And here."

My heart?"

"It come from within you, child."

"And so it begins," Henry whispered, proudly.

I grinned. It was rather exhilarating—my first lesson.

"Blah," Eva grumbled. "I liked it in here so much better when I thought it was a feasting orgy." She stood up. "I can't force my child to listen to this any longer. We're out!" She flung the baby up on her hip again and left the kitchen.

"Manana," Rosa uttered, ominously.

"Manana?" I asked.

"Tomorrow. We begin then."

"Why not now? I'm ready now."

"Manana," she stressed. "You need time to prepare, child."

"I do?"

"Si. And I tired."

"But Rosa—"

"You have Fairchild grimoire?"

"Grimoire?"

"Si. Book of—*how you say*—spells and secrets."

I shrugged. "I don't know of any spell-book."

"I cannot help you with no grimoire!"

"Henry?" I exclaimed. "Where's Moira's spell-book?"

"I don't know," he shrugged. "She never told me anything about that sort of thing. She kept all that tomfoolery very hidden from me."

"Tomfoolery..." Rosa grunted.

Henry smiled, teasingly.

"I don't know how I help with no grimoire," she stated, matter-of-factly. "Grimoire like...bible for witch."

"She had journals," I divulged, hopefully.

"Que?"

"Journals," I continued. "Maybe there's something in them...something that might lead me to where her grimoire could be."

"Okay. You look then. Si?"

"Si," I replied. "I mean...yes. I look right away."

Rosa cracked a smile. Her accent was totally infectious. You could hardly blame me for wanting to talk like her. I rose to my feet. Ryan and I left the kitchen together.

"Are you sure you're alright Hope?" Ryan's voice was laced with concern.

"Yeah."

"But the bloody nose...I had no idea your ability was physically affecting you."

"My body can't seem to keep up with my powers these days," I laughed, sloughing it off. "Hey," I said, changing the subject. "What do you think of Rosa?"

"Me?"

I nodded.

"Personally," Ryan replied. "I think she's a total whack job."

"So you think I'm stupid for getting her to train me?"

She put her thin, pale hand on my shoulder and grinned. "Truth?"

"Truth."

"I think only a whack job like her could train you!"

I laughed. Ryan laughed too. Her dark sapphire eyes shimmered like stars in a velvet sky. A moment later she moved toward the front porch to be with the other girls again.

"Aren't you coming?" she asked.

"Can't. I've got homework."

"And homework you do, young padawan." Her voice was mocking.

I smiled. Ryan smiled too before joining her friends on the porch. The heavy hum of girlish giggling was a little too upbeat for the mood I was in, so I made my way upstairs to the bedroom. I really did need to get reading those journals after all.

As I reached the second floor landing, I contemplated the devastation poor Ambrose House sustained. Reawakening Alex from her wooden tomb really did wreak havoc on the place. A mammoth gust of wind tore an ungodly hole straight through the roof. The foyer was like an open-air patio—and a constant reminder of the open-ended trouble I seemed to be spurring.

"Homework," I mumbled, under my breath, creeping inside my room.

I jumped on the bed, slipped my hand beneath it and tickled the edges of Moira's journals with my fingertips. I extracted the pile and scattered them across the satin, white sheets. I grabbed one and opened it.

September, 1958.

Today we watched the moonrise again. I'd long since forgotten the days when Henry and I could sit outside and watch sunrise together. I digress. Even with his sightless eyes he still manages to know when the moon is at its fullest. My Henry, blinder than a bat, but smarter than a crow! I suppose even this life of moonrises is better than no life at all...

It was always the same: ranting about Henry being a vampire, ranting about how much her life changed after he lost his sight and even ranting about how my mother refused to embrace her potential...*her potential.* Could that potential have meant her potential as a witch?

I continued reading, but still no mention of a grimoire anywhere.

October, 1958.

Audrey refuses to learn her lessons. If only she would embrace her potential. That girl is so damn stubborn—Fairchild stubborn.

Stubbornness definitely did run in the family. I smiled to myself and flipped ahead a few pages. A moment later I heard a peculiar ruckus coming from the dark end of my bedroom.

"Who's there?" I called out.

"It's just me," a voice replied.

"Eradan?" I said, watching him step foot into the light. He was still wearing his weird circular sunglasses and white gloves.

"Glad to see you're okay Hope."

"I nearly wasn't. What the hell did you do to me? When you touched me, I—"

"You nearly got caught."

"By whom?"

He grinned, but he didn't reply. He moved toward the bed. His strides were long and imposing. He was making me nervous. I recoiled and started gathering up my grandmother's journals.

"What are you doing?" he asked.

"Homework."

"Homework?" he laughed, sitting on the edge of my bed. Eradan was strange, but stunning all the same.

"You can't just show up all the time, you know." My voice was edgy.

"I realize that."

"Do you? I mean what if I was taking a bath...or what if I wasn't alone. What if I was with—"

"Enough!" he insisted rising to his feet. "I just came to check on you," he said matter-of-factly.

"Well you've seen me. Please leave."

"I will."

"Good."

He stepped back into the shadows again. "May I just say one thing before I go?"

"Is it an apology?"

"For what?"

"For nearly killing me with that lightening blot of a touch you have!"

He smirked. "I'm sorry."

"Fine. Now go."

"Are those Moira's journals?"

"Yeah," I replied, skeptically. "What do you care?"

He shrugged. "Have you read them?"

"That's what I'm doing!"

"Not the words." He grabbed one of the journals and thumbed through the pages. "Haven't you ever studied Japanese painting?"

"Do I look like I've studied Japanese painting?"

"Well no," he snickered. He opened the book with the water stains on it to a blank page and showed it to me. "It's about what you don't see Hope—the negative space. It's all right here."

I reached out to take the journal from him when suddenly, with an inky flash, he was gone.

"Japanese painting?" I sighed, confused. Maybe there was something to what Eradan was saying. Maybe there really were clues hidden in the journals. Rosa wouldn't teach me without my family grimoire. I had no other option. Any lead was a good lead. I knew absolutely nothing about Japanese painting, but I knew someone that did. I grabbed my purse, tucked the journal inside of it and bolted through the house at the speed of light.

6. With Just One Prick

"Really got a lot of lovin' that I wanna give,
Baby I'm a mystery but you know I gotta live."

Bloodsucker – Deep Purple

La Fuente was the hottest tattoo shop in all of Florida. It was a tiny shop nestled in the heart of downtown Key West, but it was always busy. Articles in both local and more widespread publications were definitely helping make the shop an even bigger success. I loved reading about the shop's hot and talented owner, my beloved Christian. And I suppose the fact that he was kind of genius with ink didn't hurt either.

Last month, an article in *The Weekly Examiner*, quoted some of Christian's clients. Apparently they described their sessions at La Fuente as *serene*. Some even went so far as to compare the experience of being inked by Christian to being *touched by an angel*.

It all made me laugh. Not because I didn't think Christian was an amazing artist, but because I knew that the *serene* feeling these people felt was nothing more than being veiled. Humans were incredibly gullible and using our powers of persuasion to make them forget or even remember was part and parcel of living as a vampire in a human world. And while we continued using La Fuente to pinch blood from these unsuspecting clients while they were being inked, I often wondered whether some of them really did return for the art itself.

"You did it. Didn't you?" Christian snarled.

"You knew I would."

He bandaged up a young brunette. I watched on intently.

"And what happened?"

"Let's talk in private," I said.

"And you're all finished here," he said patting his pretty client on the arm.

"Oh my god, thanks!" she giggled.

Christian nodded.

"It's all totally true, you know," the brunette continued.

"What's that?" he asked, bashfully.

"What they say about you."

He smirked and ran his hands through his unkempt hair.

"You're amazing," she gushed.

Christian laughed. I wanted to vomit. It did get nauseating watching lowly human women swoon at Christian's feet all the time. I mean yeah he was hot, and he certainly hadn't lost any of that hotness when he became human, I just found his effect on women utterly ridiculous. Was I jealous? Hell yeah! But then that wasn't the only reason it bothered me. *We* were supposed to be a team. I was supposed to be his and he was supposed to be mine. We were supposed to be together forever! But that damn cure ruined everything.

"If this is about you time shifting again—"

"It's not."

His expression hardened. He grabbed my hand and pulled me to the back of the shop.

"There is another way Christian."

"Another way to what?"

"Understand my vision—the Society."

"Rosa?" he asked, as we approached his office.

"No. She won't do the spell."

"Then what?" he demanded, opening the door.

"Me."

"You?"

I slipped inside his office. He followed behind, closed the door and fastened the deadbolt locking us in.

"What do you mean—you?" he asked.

I sat down on the firm black leather couch in the corner of the room and smirked. He sat down next to me. I stole a cautious whiff of his scent. He smelled delicious, like tin, cinnamon and sweat mixed together.

"Look," I said. "I don't need Rosa to do the spell. I can learn to do it myself," I explained. "Rosa has agreed to teach me."

"She has?"

"You were right about her. She's still in love with Henry. She'll do anything for him. Even take me on as her apprentice!"

"Wow."

I touched his chest and stole another inhale of his divine aroma.

"And this makes you happy?" he asked, perplexed.

"Well, yeah."

He heaved a sigh. "I hope you realize what you're getting into."

"You mean with Rosa?"

"Rosa. The power. All of it. You already have the power of a vampire and now you'll be learning how to harness your power as a witch too. It's a lot of power for one person, Hope."

"You jealous?" I teased.

He laughed and leaned his head against the couch. His neck was elongated and I could see the steady thump of his pulse though his skin. My insides began to churn. Hunger coursed through my veins like wildfire. My fangs inadvertently cut through my gums. My eyes widened and the only sound I could hear was the steady rhythm of his heartbeat. It was thunderous and seductive. It was irresistible—*he* was irresistible. I leaned in close, a fragment of a second from tasting him when suddenly there was a loud banging at the door.

"Busy!" Christian shouted.

"We need you up front!" a deep voice insisted.

"Not now! Go away!"

I withdrew from him at once and buried my urge.

"Can't bro. There's a situation."

"Is that Baptiste?" I asked, resuming composure.

"Yeah, he's been pulling double duty at the shop. I think he's scared to go home."

Baptiste was huge like the incredible Hulk only he wasn't green; he was a French Spaniard by descent. He was tough and strong and definitely unafraid. He was baby Stromboli's father and Eva's main squeeze. He was a vampire, changed by my biological father William many years ago and lived with us at Ambrose House. He was the insanely intimidating older brother I always wanted.

"Christian!" Baptiste continued.

"Okay. I'm coming."

"Why's he scared to go home?" I whispered.

"Eva's mood swings."

"Or maybe because she'll make him change that kid's diapers!" Christian laughed.

"Have you seen what he eats?" My eyes widened. "Organic."

"What the hell is organic?"

"Amish blood."

Christian laughed, jumped to his feet and unlocked the deadbolt. He swung the door open. Baptiste's colossal body blocked the entire doorframe. His bald, tattooed head and dark, deep-set eyes were menacing to say the least.

"Esperanza," he greeted. "I didn't know you were here?"

"Hey B. Seems like I never see you anymore."

"Yeah. I've been working."

"What's this situation?" Christian asked.

"This guy," Baptiste explained. "He's freaking out about his tattoo... makin' a real scene."

"Who did the tattoo?"

"Gabe."

Just then the sharp sound of hollering echoed. Christian pushed past Baptiste and rushed toward the front of the shop. I followed behind.

A skinny, dreggy looking client was thrashing around shouting and yelling at the top of his lungs.

"That guy cut me!" he barked.

"What guy?" Christian asked.

"Him!" He pointed at Gabriel.

Gabriel was one of the few human tattooers we employed at La Fuente. He was incredibly talented, but meek and nerdy. He'd been veiled dozens upon dozens of times. He was a sweet guy and totally sincere. I did always wonder how many times he could be veiled before finally becoming a vegetable.

"He's a bloody butcher!" the client shouted.

I looked at the inside of his wrist, at the half-finished tattoo of a Asian inspired dragon and the stream of blood that dripped from his arm. I froze. It was a blood-waste indeed, but it was also a lawsuit waiting to happen.

"I'm telling everybody this place is nothing but a god-damn butcher shop!"

I grabbed a handful of first aid crap from a nearby shelf and the mickey of Jack Daniels that Eva kept hidden behind the filing cabinet. I pushed up my bra a little, plastered on a pretty smile and sped to the front of the shop.

"Excuse me," I said, sweetly. "Maybe I can help. Here," I whispered beckoning the irate client closer. "Don't be afraid."

"Now that's more like it," he said, grudgingly.

A moment later he even managed to give me a half-smile. Then, when he stared me square in the eyes, I veiled him. I projected an unyielding screen of calmness around his thoughts and voila, he was *serene*. Veiling rocked!

"I dunno know what came over me," he sighed, groggily. "I was so mad," he laughed.

"It's okay," I replied. I wiped his bloody wrist with a spray of green soap.

"There was so much blood," he said concerned, but still calm.

"Well, it is a tattoo. Sometimes there's blood."

"You sure are a pretty girl."

"Thanks."

"Now what's a pretty girl like you doing in a place like this?"

"Oh, I'm really not that pretty."

"Like hell!" he laughed. "I'd give my right arm to have a woman like you."

I looked down at the bloody mess on his right arm and laughed. "You nearly did," I joked.

He smiled.

"Here," I whispered handing him the mickey of JD. "I snagged this from the boss's office. It'll help with the pain."

His eyes lit up like Times' Square at sundown. He unscrewed the cap and took a swig.

"What's your name?"

"Earl," he said, downing another swig.

"Well Earl, it's nice to meet you."

"Likewise."

Between veiling and drinking this guy was putty in my hands.

"Mind if I tape you up Earl?" My voice was steady as I spoke.

"Tape me, cuff me, chain me!"

Christian mouthed the words *thank you* from across the room. I batted my lashes and grinned.

"I ain't paying for this tattoo," Earl muttered.

"Of course not!" I replied. "Now hold still. I just need to finish cleaning you up."

I looked down at his arm again. Something wasn't right. A small piece of plastic tubing was wedged under his skin.

"Christian," I whispered, signalling him closer.

He stood beside me and together we both noticed the visible broken off end of a bloodsucker sticking straight out of Earl's arm!

"I'm the manager here," Christian said, calmly.

"Well, Mr. Manager," Earl said, "this has been a really shitty tattoo."

"Yes. And please accept my apology."

Bloodsuckers were the tubes attached to our tattooing machines that we used to pinch blood from humans while they were getting inked. Christian and I both knew that the very presence of a bloodsucker out in the open like this was beyond detrimental—it was catastrophic!

"Forget an apology," Earl stuttered. "I need a freebie."

"And you shall get one indeed," he replied.

I reached in close and carefully extracted the severed piece of tubing. I hid it within the dirty towel I was holding in my hand.

"Hope is doing such a fine job cleaning you up Earl." Christian's voice was soothing.

"Damn straight. Shoulda had her tattooing me!"

"Nearly done Earl," I said, smiling. I took a pad of gauze and placed it against Earl's wrist. I taped him up and grinned "All done!"

"Thanks angel."

"Anytime."

"And you said that Gabe did this tattoo for you?" Christian asked.

"Yeah, the weasely-looking guy over there."

"Gabe," Christian insisted. "Come here please."

I watched Gabriel snap into action. He was like a child walking to the principal's office as he approached.

"Is this your client?" he asked.

"Yeah."

"And what happened?"

"The needle," Gabe explained. "It was running hard. I went to swap it out and it got stuck."

"The needle?"

"Yeah."

Christian's eyes narrowed. "Go back to your station."

Gabe nodded and followed Christian's orders.

"Please accept my deepest apology for your inconvenience today Earl. The tattoo is of course free. Once your skin heals come back and I'll finish it for you myself."

Earl nodded, pleased. Christian escorted him to the exit. He opened door and patted him on the back as he sent him out into the street. The moment Earl left, Christian b-lined strait back to Gabriel's station.

"You're done for the day Gabe," Christian said. "Please pack up and go home."

"I'm sorry Christian. Nothing like that has ever happened to me before."

"I know," he replied, sternly. "We'll talk about it tomorrow."

Christian moved toward Baptiste and me.

"To my office," he said, icily. "Now!"

7. What Big Teeth You Have

"I fell into a burning ring of fire,
I went down, down, down as the flames went higher."

Ring Of Fire – Johnny Cash

All hell broke loose once we got inside the sanctity of Christian's office.

"What the hell was that?" Baptiste growled.

"That my old friend," Christian replied, "was the beginning of the end of our secret life here."

A bloodsucker visibly stuck in a human's arm was bad, but I had my own crap to deal with. I needed to talk to my Japanese watercolour expert before he left the building for the day.

"Hey," I said touching Christian's shoulder. "I gotta do something."

"Right now?"

"Yeah."

"What's more important than lamenting the fall of our paradise?" he mocked.

"How about trying to save it."

His eyes narrowed. He was pissed. I knew he wished that he could still read my mind. But he couldn't. He simply had to trust me.

"Go," he whispered.

I kissed him on the cheek and left his office. I looked around the shop. I couldn't find Gabe anywhere. I looked ahead, toward the exit and spotted him stepping into the street.

"Gabe!" I shouted, following behind. He didn't hear me. I ran after him. "Gabe!" I shouted again. This time he stopped.

"Hope?" he said turning around.

"Hey," I continued, catching up to him.

"What are you doing out here?"

"I needed to talk to you."

"Look, if it's about what happened—"

"No. It's got nothing to do with that."

"Oh," he said, intrigued.

"It's something else entirely." I smiled. "It's actually something for me."

His eyes lit up from behind his oversize, wire glasses.

"Do you have a second to talk?" I continued.

He swept his straggly hair behind his ears and smirked out of the corner of his mouth. I always knew Gabe liked me and now seemed like as good of a time as any to take advantage of that.

"Um..." he said, hesitantly.

"It won't take long."

"Well..."

"Please?" I begged.

"I suppose I've got some free time," he smiled, "particularly now that your boyfriend told me to leave the shop!"

"I know. Christian can be pretty hard-headed sometimes."

"Sometimes?" he teased.

I grinned. "I'm sorry about that."

"Don't be. It wasn't your fault."

"Well, I don't think it was yours either."

"You don't?"

I shook my head. "Weird shit happens every day. We can't be responsible for all of it—can we?"

Gabe sighed. He seemed incredibly relieved.

"Christian is...well...just being Christian!"

His expression contorted and his beady eyes narrowed.

"He's just looking to protect the best interest of the shop."

"I suppose," he replied. "I just didn't like the way he yelled at me in front of everybody. Like I was a little kid, you know?"

"I know. And trust me he thinks you're the bee's knees."

"Bee's knees?" he replied, laughing.

"The cat's pajamas...top shelf...I don't know what I'm even saying anymore!" I grinned.

Gabe bit his thin bottom lip and stared at me as he laughed. I felt incredibly awkward. His stare was intense and making me uncomfortable. I stopped smiling and cleared my throat.

"You're his best employee Gabe," I said, diverting. "And La Fuente wouldn't be what it is today without you."

"Well, Christian sure has a funny way of showing that."

"I know," I agreed. "Especially lately," I mumbled under my breath.

"What's up with him?" he asked, intrigued. "He seems really different all of a sudden."

"Christian?" I said, playing dumb, "different?"

"Yeah."

"What 'cha mean?"

"Well I've worked with him for years." He shook his head. "I don't know it's just lately he seems different."

"Oh yeah? I guess I hadn't really noticed," I lied. I couldn't just come out and tell him that after two centuries his boss suddenly took a cure and became human again!

"Even his whole look is different," Gabe laughed.

"His look?"

"He was always so pale and now he's rockin' a tan?" Gabe laughed. "I don't get it."

"I know," I shrugged.

"He's way more uptight lately, and disorganized too." Gabe looked around for a second. "Do you wanna sit down some place and continue this chat?"

"Yeah. Cool," I replied. I still needed to ask him about Japanese watercolor.

"How 'bout that place?" he replied, pointing up the road.

There was nothing up the road except for an old dive-bar at the end of the street.

"That place?" I asked, apprehensive.

"What's wrong with that place?" he laughed.

I shrugged, unsure whether to say that even I—a parasitic immortal, had standards!

"I know it ain't The Ritz but..."

"Um..." I debated, scanning the area for a Starbucks.

"And I know it ain't the cleanest and it definitely isn't up to code like La Fuente, but—"

"It's fine."

"It is?"

I nodded.

"Great!" he beamed. He was giddy and a little too excited with my reply.

"C'mon," I said, eagerly. I grabbed his arm and pulled him along the street.

"Wow," he mumbled, eying my hand on him. I withdrew immediately and continued walking. Gabe was without doubt a little weird.

"Where is this place?" I said, desperate to fill the awkward silence between us.

"Just a little farther." He kept his eyes on me the entire time we walked.

"You've been there before?"

"Yeah," he laughed.

"No rats or roaches right?"

"Maybe a few," he teased.

I shook my head.

"What's with Christian's hygiene obsession anyway? His shop is spotless—I mean like squeaky clean. Is he one of those OCD guys?"

"Naw, he's way too paranoid to be obsessive compulsive."

Gabe laughed. I laughed too. A moment later we'd reached the bar. It was an old, crappy hole in the wall, but it was good enough for right now. He opened the door for me and I walked inside.

"Welcome to The Whet Willie," he said, pleased.

"The wet what?"

"Whet Willie," he corrected. "I take it you've never been here before?"

"No."

"You live in Key West and you've never been to the Whet Willie?"

"No."

"Ah," he said, knowingly. "Now I get it."

"Get what?"

"Why you haven't been here."

"You do?"

"Christian. He wouldn't dare let you come to a place like this."

I looked around. The interior was dark and dirty. There were a few tables and a huge bar lining the back end of the room. The décor, if you could call it decor, was most definitely shitty-chic. With lots of old, worn-out, wood everywhere I felt like I was at the bottom of the ocean inside the HMS Ambrose!

"Gabe!" the barmaid shouted. "Here in the afternoon?" She was young and curvy with red hair and a crooked nose.

"I've got the day off," he said, reluctantly.

"The day off?" She looked me up and down.

"Yeah. Bring me the usual, Justine."

"Of course," she smiled, "and your girlfriend?"

"Oh, I'm not his girlfriend," I exclaimed, a little too eagerly.

"In that case," she said happily, "I'll bring you both a double—on me!"

As the barmaid left I nudged Gabe in the arm.

"She's cute," I teased.

"I hadn't noticed, besides, she's not really my type."

I stayed silent.

"C'mon," he said, leading me to a table at the back.

We sat down at the small wooden table.

"Why'd you go and say you weren't my girlfriend?" he asked, suddenly.

A chill ran down my spine. "Because I'm not your girlfriend Gabe." My tone was edgy.

He nodded. His eyes were hard and I could tell that he was a little pissed.

"Why are you with Christian anyway?"

"What?" I replied, taken aback. His tone was firm and his approach was assertive. It was utterly Jekyll and Hyde of him to be so forward.

"I'm sorry," he suddenly apologized. "It's none of my business."

I pursed my lips. I felt a sinking feeling in the pit of my stomach. Maybe this was a bad idea. Maybe I shouldn't have come here with him.

Just then the barmaid returned.

"Gabe," she said putting his drink on the table. "Gabe's not girlfriend," she continued, placing mine in front of me.

"Thanks," I said, watching her return to the bar again. I eyeballed the drinks. The glasses were small and filled with a yellowish looking liquid. It definitely wasn't coffee.

"Tequila," he said.

"Shots?"

"You drink Tequila?"

"In Mexico I did."

Gabe laughed, excitedly. "I prefer to sip it. I like the burn as it goes down."

He liked the burn? If Gabe had been a vampire he would have been in seventh heaven! Nothing burned better than a shot of freshly brewed blood from a bottle of Baptiste's private reserve.

"Ladies first," he insisted.

I smirked, grabbed the glass and took a sip. It did burn. He watched me like a hawk.

"Do you like it?"

"It's not awful!"

He laughed.

"Look Gabe, the reason I brought you here is because I need to know about Japanese watercolour painting."

"Whoa! That is *so* not what I thought you were going to ask me about."

"Can you help me?"

"Yeah...but..."

"But what?" I asked, perplexed.

"What do I get outta this?" His tone was cheeky. I'd never seen him act like this before. In fact, I didn't realize that squirrelly-nerdy Gabe was even capable of this kind of bravado!

"Um..." I replied, uneasily. "What if I talk to Christian about what happened at the shop today? I can tell him to ease up on you and start showing you a little respect."

His brow creased. "That's not exactly what I had in mind, but alright." He smiled.

"Cool," I replied. "So can you tell me about Japanese watercolor?"

"Why didn't you just ask Christian? I'm sure the almighty great and powerful Christian knows something about it?"

"Probably, but you're the best. I've seen your work. You're incredibly patient and precise. You really put your whole heart into your art."

He smiled, flattered.

"Does your boyfriend agree with that?"

"Yeah. I think he does actually. Christian might be the almighty great and powerful, but you're what's behind the curtain Gabe."

"Are you saying I'm a little nerdy conman pretending to be great and powerful?" he laughed.

"No," I replied. "I'm saying you're the backbone of La Fuente. You're a really talented artist and you've helped make the shop what it is today."

He smiled.

"So, can you help me?" I asked again.

"How could I say no after all that ego-stroking!"

I half-smiled.

"Where do you want me to start? I mean it took me years to learn—"

"I don't have years. I have like twenty-minutes. Let's go with the basics."

"Basics," he pondered. "There's Japanese aesthetics to consider and subject matter..."

My eyes were already glazing over. I was bored and his insight wasn't helping any.

"And then there's negative space," he continued.

"Stop!" I said, elatedly. I remembered Eradan talking about negative space. "Tell me about that," I implored.

"About negative space?"

"Yeah."

Gabe's eyes widened. "Ma."

"*Ma*? Like what a cowboy calls his mother?"

"No! *Ma*—it's the negative space. It's about the consciousness of place in composition."

"I'm totally lost. You're gonna have to dumb it down."

"Why do you want to know all this anyway?"

I froze. I couldn't tell him the truth. "I'm working on a project...an art project," I lied.

He nodded and leaned in close. "*Ma* is not created. It's what occurs in the mind's eye of the artist."

"I'm still not getting it." I took another swig of Tequila.

"It's experiential, Hope. Think about it in terms of choice and rhythm. Like music. It's about how the musician chooses to interpret the spaces in notes."

"Okay."

"In what *I* do, *Ma* is used to enhance the overall piece of the artwork being created. It's part of the whole. Think of it as how the artist decides to interpret an interval in time and space."

I downed the last of my drink.

"It's quite philosophical and rather simple really."

"Maybe for you!"

"Look," he said. "Once you accept that space doesn't necessarily mean empty—as in blank space then—"

"Stop!" I shouted. My heart thumped in my chest. My mind exploded with revelation. "Blank pages!" I uttered, excitedly.

"What blank pages?"

I smiled, got up from my chair and kissed him on the cheek. "Thanks for the drink!" I said turning to leave.

"Where are you going?"

"I've got homework to finish. Thanks for your help!"

I pushed the door open and left The Whet Willie. I had to get back to Ambrose. I needed to find the journal with the blank pages. *Ma* was telling me that maybe those pages really weren't so blank after all!

8. The Lost Boys

"Cry, little sister, thou shall not fall,
Come to your brother, thou shall not die,
Unchain me, sister, thou shall not fear,
Love is with your brother, thou shall not kill."

Cry Little Sister - Gerard McMann a.k.a. G Tom Mac

Ambrose House was alive like never before. Since Ryan and her pals had come to live with us the place was almost cheery. Giggles and whispers were constant and the smell of perfume tickled my nostrils every time I neared the place. I didn't mind. I liked having people around—even if they were militant-ex-vampires. Christian, on the other hand, hated it. He equated fun with attention and if we were having fun, then we were generating attention and failing to keep our life on Perish a secret.

"Hope!" Ryan shouted, the moment I arrived.

I rushed toward her. She was standing on the veranda. There was a bright look her dark, sapphire colored eyes.

"You missed them," she exclaimed.

"I missed who?"

"The visitors."

"What visitors?" I asked, afraid.

No one ever visited Perish. The last few so-called visitors we had were lethal and destructive. If someone really was visiting I needed to know about it.

"Relax. They're cool."

"Cool?" I exclaimed, my fangs suddenly bursting through my gums.

"Chill!" she insisted. "Don't get all vampy on me!"

I widened my eyes, enraged. Energy surged through my body again. I was getting way too frenzied.

"Hope," she insisted. "I'm sorry. I wasn't trying to upset you."

"Visitors *are* a big deal around here!"

"I'm starting to get that."

"People just showing up on our shores is a bad thing, Ryan!"

"But these aren't just people. They're my friends."

"What?

"Andy, Sara and Pedro. I knew them when I worked for the Society."

"Shit, Ryan. Their defectors?"

"Yeah. Like me."

I ran my hands along the sides of my face.

"Don't worry. I know them. They're good people."

"It doesn't matter!" I shouted. "Ambrose isn't some wayward vampire-backpacker hostel and it isn't a safe haven either."

"I didn't think you'd mind, seeing that you let me and the other girls stay here with you."

"I mind."

"I see that."

"Jeeze!" I exclaimed, frustrated.

"I saw their scars," she said. "They really did defect and I really did know them." She looked me in the eyes. "Not everyone is an enemy, Hope."

I shook my head at her. "Where are they now?" I asked, through gritted teeth.

"In the forest...at the boathouse."

"How did they know where to find you?"

"I don't know," she shrugged. "They said they just kept moving south. Coincidence maybe?"

"No such thing as coincidence."

"I really didn't think I was doing anything wrong by letting them stay."

I turned away from her and walked down the porch steps to the grass again.

"Where are you going?"

"Away from you. I need some space."

"Damn it!" she shouted, upset. "I'm sorry. Don't be pissed at me. Please!"

I didn't reply and I didn't turn back to face her either. I marched across the grass to the backyard. Every bone in my body was telling me to zip through the forest to the boathouse and meet those sons-of-bitches, but I didn't. I had to find my grandmother's grimoire. I needed Rosa to agree to teach me how to harness my power before I did something I'd likely regret. The newcomers would have to wait.

I rounded the corner of the house and headed toward the back door when suddenly I heard a baby crying.

"God," I mumbled, under my breath opening up the door and slipping inside. That poor baby didn't have a chance of a normal life with Eva for a mother.

I tried sneaking past the kitchen and up to my bedroom, but the pathetic sound of Eva failing uselessly was gut wrenching. I decided to lend a hand. Eva was such a pain in the ass, but still like family to me. I moved toward the kitchen and went inside.

"Hope!" she shrieked. "You scared Strombo!"

"Nice try, but I heard him crying even before I got here."

"I just don't know what to do with it!"

"It? It's not an *it*. He's Stromboli and he's your son!"

"You don't think I know that?"

"Well he needs to know it too."

Eva glared.

"Hold him like you mean it." My voice was soft. "Cuddle him," I said guiding her arms into position. "Show him how much you love him with your touch." She brought Stromboli close to her chest and within an instant he stopped crying. I smiled.

"How do you know so much about babies?"

I shrugged.

"Maybe you're just one of them idiot servants."

Knowing she really meant *savant*, I rolled my eyes. "Did you meet the new visitors?" I asked, changing the subject.

"What visitors?"

"The ones that Ryan let shack up in our boathouse."

Eva's eyes glowed with scarlet iridescence. A moment later baby Stromboli started whimpering again.

"Relax, Eva. He's reading your mood. Calm down and he'll calm down too."

She looked daggers at me, but took my advice. Within seconds Stromboli was at ease again in her arms.

"They're friends of hers," I replied, in an airy sing-song voice, "from her days working for *them*."

"Do they have a scar from their implants?" Her voice was so high and light it sounded like she'd been sucking on helium!

"Ryan says yes."

"How'd they find us?" she sang, pleasantly through gritted teeth.

"No clue. Ryan says its coincidence."

Eva's eyes narrowed.

"I don't like this. Not one bit," I sang, in my best happy voice. "It's like we're reliving Maxim and Sakura and—"

"You're preaching to the choir, Blondie!"

Eva was getting riled up. A moment later Stromboli started full-out crying again.

"Jeeze boy!" she complained. "Won't you ever give your mama a break?"

Stromboli gurgled and then suddenly, he vanished!

"Where'd he go?" I asked, alarmed.

"Playing," she shrugged, relieved.

"It doesn't bother you not knowing where he is?"

"He's a shape shifter. And he's a baby. How much trouble could he possibly get in?"

I bit my lip. Eva really was the worst mother in the world. But she looked pretty worn-out and it was clear that she'd been through enough today. I didn't need to fill her head with more concerns.

"When Baptiste gets wind of these newcomers," she said, reclining in her chair, "all hell's gonna break loose!"

"Maybe don't tell him."

"I have to tell him."

"Maybe just don't tell him today."

"And why not?"

"They had a big set-back at the shop this afternoon. I don't think the sudden arrival of these new expats will go over very well."

"What do you mean a set-back?"

"There was a situation."

"Pray tell," she implored.

"A blood-sucker broke off in a client's arm."

"What the—"

"I dealt with it. I managed to veil the client, but it was a close call."

"A close call? Shit that's like suicide! Our entire existence relies on what we do at La Fuente!"

"I know."

"In all the years...nothing like that has ever happened!"

"Now don't go saying it's all because of me again!"

"If the shoe fits, Cinderella."

"Nothing bad ever happened in Perish until you got here Blondie!" I said, mimicking her voice.

She grinned, reluctantly.

"Like I said, it's was only a close call. We're still in the clear."

Eva nodded. "Was it B that broke it off?"

"No. It was Gabe."

"Gabriel? Squirrely, art-nerd Gabe?"

"Yeah."

"Well did he see it? Did he wonder what some freakish plastic tube was doing concealed inside his needle?"

"I don't think so," I said, shaking my head.

"Did you veil him just to make sure?"

"Um...er..."

"You didn't veil him?"

I shrugged.

"You idiot!"

"Christian kicked him out of the shop right away. It was awkward and—"

"Don't speak anymore." She took a very dramatic deep breath.

"But—"

"Shh."

"Eva—"

"Stop."

"Listen!" I shouted. "Do you know where my grandmother would have kept the Fairchild grimoire?"

"What?" she said, her face contorting with confusion.

"The grimoire...spell-book. Do you know where she kept it?"

"Why would I know?"

"I don't know, but I had to ask."

"Why do you need her grimoire?"

"Rosa won't agree to take me on as her apprentice until I find it."

Eva laughed. "Maybe that's a blessing! Do you really want that old bitch telling you what to do?"

I cracked a smile. Eva smiled too. All of a sudden the harrowing sound of screams resonated.

"Strombo!" Eva shouted.

The sound was definitely coming from the porch. We rushed toward the front of the house at super-sonic vampire speed. When we arrived, baby Stromboli was sitting on the porch. He was surrounded by the women.

"Strombo!" Eva exclaimed, picking him up. "Are you okay?"

"What happened?" I uttered.

"He happened," Ryan replied, pointing at Stromboli.

"But why all the screaming?" I continued.

"The baby...he just suddenly appeared!" Ryan, explained.

"You girls screamed because he appeared?"

"Well yeah!" Ryan laughed. "It's not every day a baby just suddenly appears outta thin air!"

I watched as Ryan and her friends continued fussing over him.

"We have to be more careful," I whispered, leaning close to Eva. "Especially with these newcomers around."

She nodded and there was a bonafide look of dread in her eyes. Eva might have been a terrible mother, but from that look alone, it was clear that her mama-bear instincts were fully in-tact.

9. A Dream Is A Wish

"Strange as angels,
Dancing in the deepest oceans,
Twisting in the water,
You're just like a dream."

Just Like Heaven – The Cure

As nightfall approached so did my anxiety. Christian hadn't returned home from La Fuente yet. I still hadn't searched through my grandmother's journals for the one with the blank pages and tomorrow was supposed to be my first day of training with Rosa. If that wasn't enough, I was completely preoccupied by the presence of these precarious visitors and was starting to wonder if maybe I really was the catalyst for the fall of Perish.

I was totally unsettled. My head felt like it was going to explode. The little bit of tequila I downed at the Whet Willie didn't help any either. Was I even supposed to be drinking alcohol while pregnant with my inhuman baby?

My stomach churned like a stormy sea. Nausea was enveloping me. All I really wanted to do was down a warm bottle of blood and go to sleep. Why was I so damn tired all the time? I wondered if it was because of the baby.

I contemplated making a trip to the kitchen for some blood, but was just too exhausted. I unzipped my hoodie and tossed it to the floor. I slid off my jeans and let them fall to the ground too. I grabbed one of Christian's white T-shirts from the nearby dresser and pulled it over my head. I stole a cautious whiff of his shirt. It smelled like him. I grinned. I fastened my long, blonde hair into a tight braid and climbed into bed with a head full of questions and an empty stomach.

A loud groan resonated from within my abdomen. I put my hand against my belly and stroked it. I thought about the feeling of that funny rock deep inside of me. *A baby.* I still had a hard time processing it. *Pregnant.* It was all so incredibly weird. I simply couldn't imagine thinking of my body like a machine; working on overtime creating a new life inside of me. I briefly contemplated what I'd be like as a mother, but the thought of it scared the hell outta me! At least I knew I'd never be as terrible as Eva was to poor Stromboli. I speculated whether I could even handle the next six years or so of pregnancy—*six years*, that was a long time to be pregnant! I sighed inside. Why couldn't I have been a normal human; their pregnancies only lasted for about forty weeks!

My stomach growled again. I laughed. It was like I was communicating with the baby.

"Hungry?" I uttered, wondering if it could even hear me. "Me too," I insisted.

I closed my eyes and waited for sleep to seduce me. It didn't take long to doze off and when the soft tenor of *his* voice echoed through my thoughts, I knew I'd arrived on dream's doorstep.

I loved dreaming of Christian. My dreams of him were always sensational. Ever since I was young I'd dreamt of him. Back then, my slumbers were filled with vision of him as the dark prince of my enchanted life in Perish. As I grew older, my dreams matured. Thoughts of him became much more intense. My dark prince became my paramour and my dreams of him became incredibly passionate and lucid.

"Hope," he whispered, in my ear—*in my dream.*

"Yes?"

"Good morning."

I smiled with delight.

"My sleeping angel," he uttered.

I grinned and open my eyes. We were still in bed, beneath the sheets. I had my back to him and could feel the icy tingle of his breath against my neck.

"You're skin," he said touching me, "it's so soft."

He stroked the palm of his hand along my leg. It felt amazing and so incredibly real.

I reached for the sheet and clung to it.

"Don't," he implored, tugging the sheet away. "I love seeing you like this."

"Like what?" I asked, releasing my grasp on the fabric.

"Like this...so fresh."

"Fresh?" I giggled.

"Unsullied," he teased, drawing circles on my skin.

I melted inside. The touch of his fingertips and the tone of his voice sent shivers down my spine.

He leaned closer and kissed my earlobe. "Hope," he whispered.

I shifted and began turning towards him.

"Don't," he implored. "Stay as you are." His voice was persuasive.

I keep my eyes ahead and sank my face back into the sheets again.

"So clean," he flattered, continuing to stroke the length of my leg.

"But I haven't even showered yet!"

"Mmm," he purred.

"But I'm dirty!"

He moaned in response before grabbing me by the thigh. His grip was hard and my skin puckered between his fingers.

"I'm still sleeping," I said, responding to the intensity of his touch. I'd only just awoken. I really wasn't ready for any hard-passion yet.

He released my leg and drew down the sheet. I could feel his eyes on me from behind. "You're so perfect."

"I'm nowhere near perfect!" My voice was swollen with insecurity. I reached for the sheet again and pulled it up.

"Stop," he muttered, tugging the sheet from my hand. He drew it back down again, exposing my bare skin. I could feel his gaze intensify. He traced his fingers over my hip. "Perfect," he maintained. He massaged my hipbone for a moment. His touch was softer and much gentler now. "And your skin is like velvet," he said.

I closed my eyes and let the feeling of his fingers elate me.

"You're faultless," he continued.

"I'm *not* faultless."

"Shh," he implored.

His touch was unreal and quickly filled me with exhilaration.

"You're so...pure," he uttered.

"Pure?" I laughed, playfully.

"Pure as the freshly driven snow," he replied, caressing the skin between my thigh and my groin.

I moaned.

"You're so beautiful."

I smiled and let the feeling of his fingers continue teasing me.

"I love to watch you," he confessed.

I giggled.

He traced his index finger along the edge of my panties until he met with the waistband.

I grasped the sheets tighter. "Oh," I uttered.

He slipped a finger beneath the fabric and then drew it back out again.

I moaned, wantonly.

"I really do love watching you," he said, stroking my skin again.

"Chris—"

"Shh," he implored, "especially when you're just waking."

His fingers felt like heaven against me.

"Do you like this?" he asked. His tone was ardent.

"Yes!"

He moved his hand along my skin, up my shirt.

I giggled. "It's too early for this. I'm barely even awake!"

He ran the heel of his hand against my mid-section and traced the circumference of my bellybutton with his pinky finger.

"I can't do this," I sustained, teasingly.

He groaned and whisked his hand over my ribs and up to my breasts.

"Don't," I pleaded. His fingers were cool, skilled and virtually irresistible, but I was exhausted and my body still craved rest.

"I want you," he said. "No more sleeping."

I planted my face in the fluffy, satin-cased pillows.

"Hope," he snarled. "I don't want you sleeping!"

I perked up. Christian wasn't usually so bossy. I shifted to look at him, but he quickly forced me to continue facing away.

He leaned close to my ear. "I want you awake for this." His voice was hard and stubborn. "I want you to feel this," he continued. Abruptly, he moved his arm around my abdomen and heaved me against him! My backside hit him with a thud!

"I'm awake!" I exclaimed.

I could feel him grinning. "You belong to me this morning!" His voice was strong and mighty and scaring me a little.

I struggled to move, but he had me pinned. His arm was fixed around my middle, keeping me in position like a seatbelt! I stopped struggling and gave into him.

"That's a girl," he whispered, pushing against me from behind. "Just surrender...surrender to me."

This wasn't like Christian. Sure he was confident and assertive, but never pompous and aggressive.

"Stop!" I shouted.

He laughed.

I struggled to free myself again, but my effort remained futile. "Please," I pleaded.

"Please?" he laughed. "I love hearing the *tone* of desperation! Beg me again!"

"Let go of me!" I demanded, still fighting against him.

"Not today. Not ever!" He was forceful and his hands were unbreakable.

I opened my lips to speak. "Chris—"

"Shh!" he growled.

"S-t-o-p!" I shouted again, only this time at the top of my lungs.

"No!" he raged, continuing to grasp me and pressed himself against me.

Something was wrong—*this was wrong*! Christian was *never* like this in my dreams, in reality—ever! I couldn't take it anymore. I summoned my fangs to extract through my gums. I brought my mouth to his arm and bit down into him!

"God!" he shouted, releasing me instantly.

I flew from the bed and turned to face him. I froze. It wasn't Christian—it was Gabe! He was so squirrely and nerdy, but violent and overconfident. What the hell was Gabe doing in *my* dream?!

My eyes flew open!

My body shuddered with an icy chill. I felt sick inside. I felt violated and undeniably sordid for having dreamt of Gabe! I sat up in bed and looked around the room. It was empty. I was indeed totally alone. It really had been a dream—thank god.

I fell back to the bed again and pulled the covers way up over my head. All of a sudden I heard a tapping at the window. I sat up again. I looked around. I was vexed with concern.

Tap-tap. Tap-tap.

I heard it again. Who was it? Was it Christian coming home for the night? Or maybe even the strange visitors staying in my boathouse?

Tap-tap. Tap-tap.

10. Bibbity Bobbity Boo

"I don't practice Santeria,
I ain't got no crystal ball."

Santeria - SUBLIME

I perked up immediately. I scanned the room carefully. I didn't see anything unusual. I waited for the sound again. It never came. I fell back to the bed.

TAP-TAP. TAP-TAP!

I heard it again. This time the tapping was even louder than before.

I got out of bed. I looked toward the large window at the end of the room. The sun hung like molten gold on the horizon. It was dusk and the light was fading fast. I moved closer.

"Eradan!" I exclaimed. "What are you doing here again?"

"I couldn't come in the front door—there's a fortress of women out there!"

I watched as he fumbled around on my bedroom floor when the cloying aroma of vampire blood entered my nostrils. There was a fresh cut on the side of Eradan's neck.

"You're bleeding," I exclaimed.

"I am?"

I moved closer and touched him.

"Don't!" he barked, stopping me. "I'm fine."

"It's gushing. What happened?" I moved close to touch him again.

"I said don't!"

"But you're bleeding."

"You mustn't touch my skin. Ever."

I recoiled at once. I looked at the weird, white gloves on his hands and remembered the horrific pain I felt when he'd taken off his gloves and touched me in Ryan's past. If that's what touching his skin felt like, then I was happy to appease his request.

"Did you interpret the journal?" he asked, abruptly.

"Interpret?"

"Yes, Hope."

"I haven't," I admitted, "but I think I know what to look for."

"Do it then."

"Right now?"

"Time is always of the essence."

I hated when he said that. Despite the fact that I knew he was right, I really loathed how much it sounded like a corny time-shifter joke.

I moved across the room, reached under my bed and grabbed the stack of journals. Hastily, I tossed them on the bed, fanning them out.

"You should really take better care of these."

I drew my eyes upward and glared.

"I'm merely suggesting that these are mementos...heirlooms if you will. You should consider taking better care of them."

"Thanks for the advice," I replied, unimpressed by his lecture on the preservation of heirlooms.

I drew my eyes back to the journals. It had been a long day and I definitely wasn't in the mood for Eradan's strange and snobbish attitude.

"I am not a snob," he suddenly, sputtered.

My jaw dropped! He could read my mind! I knew it!

"I mean...um...er—" he stuttered.

"How are you able to read my thoughts?"

He took a deep breath.

"Eradan!"

He shrugged.

"Can you read other people's thoughts too?"

"No."

"Only my thoughts?"

He nodded.

"Why?"

"I don't know," he said, aggravated. "But clearly I can. May we move on to the journal now?"

"No," I replied, frustrated, "we may not move on to the journals! I wanna know why you can read my thoughts?"

"I told you. I don't know."

"And you don't think it's weird?" I asked.

"No. Yes. I don't know!" He was exasperated.

"Look," I said. "There's only been one other person that could—"

"Christian," he interrupted. "Yes, I'm well aware that he could read your thoughts too, now can we please move on?"

Eradan was complex; his clothes, his vocabulary, his behavior. He was without a doubt the most frustrating person I'd ever met.

"I can still hear you," he reminded.

I rolled my eyes.

"I can see you too," he continued.

"Fine," I snapped. "I'll find the damn journal and pretend like it's not weird that you can read my thoughts."

"Thank you."

I turned my attention back to the journals again. I sifted through the pile until I found the one I needed—the one with the water stains. I flipped it open and turned to the last entry at super-sonic speed.

September 20, 1935.

FATE IS A DARK SORCERER!

The half-dozen pages that followed were entirely blank! It wasn't like my grandmother to leave any blank space in her journals. I turned to Eradan and shrugged.

"So," he said. "Do it."

"Do what?"

"Your magic."

"You expect *me* to do magic?" I laughed.

"Well how else did you think you'd be able to translate what's written on the page?"

"Why do you care so much anyway?" My tone was skeptical.

"I don't know," he shrugged. "I...I want to help you is all."

My brows furrowed in the centre of my forehead. I was stressing out and to make matters worse I could feel Eradan inside my head helping himself to my thoughts like I was an all-you-care-to-eat buffet.

"Performance anxiety," he concluded.

"Excuse me?"

"You're scared. Aren't you?"

I glared at him.

"I can't imagine you being scared of anything!" he muttered. "You're so powerful and confident in the future. Especially when you—"

"The future?" I interrupted, intrigued.

He smirked.

"Tell me! Tell me please?"

He shook his head. "Forget the future Hope. Focus on the present."

"Easy for you say," I said, shutting the journal. I tossed it to the side. "It's useless. I'm useless. I have no idea how to do anything with this stupid power inside of me."

Eradan picked the journal up and opened it. He turned to the last entry again and placed it in front of me.

"You really are stubborn when you want something," I said.

"You have no idea," he laughed.

"I can't do it."

"Search your heart for the answer, Hope." His tone was dove-like, almost anesthetic.

I lowered my gaze and focused on the page. I re-read my grandmother's last entry again:

September 20, 1935.

FATE IS A DARK SORCERER!

I looked at the words. It was clear that they were about magic.

"Don't be so literal," he whispered.

I looked back at the page again. I read the date. September 20, 1935. It didn't mean anything to me.

"Much too literal" he insisted. "Go deeper."

Deeper, I contemplated? How much deeper was he talking—puzzles and ciphers?

"Perhaps," he replied in response to my thoughts.

I straightened my posture and tried again. I concentrated on the words this time. I read them over and over in my head. *Fate. Is. A. Dark. Sorcerer. Fate. Is. A. Dark. Sorcerer. Fate. Is. A. Dark. Sorcerer. Fate. Is. A. Dark. Sorcerer.*

"Oh my god," Eradan pleaded. "Please stop reading that entry over and over again!"

"Fine," I replied. "I just don't know what you want me to do here."

"*I* don't want you do anything. You must want to do this for yourself."

"For myself? I don't even understand why I'm doing this in the first place!"

"Has it not bothered you that your grandmother left this journal blank—when all of the others are filled completely?"

"Well, yeah."

"Don't you feel as though you're missing something—a key perhaps to unlocking all the unanswered questions you have about your past... your heritage?"

"Eradan, my whole after-life has been about unanswered questions!"

"Search your heart."

"I still have no freakin' clue how I'm going to—"

"Forget logic. Think with your feelings.

I tried getting in touch with my feelings, but they were twisted in knots.

"Don't see with your eyes. See with your thoughts."

I focused on the words again. I looked at each letter and contemplated whether it was an anagram or something.

"Your feelings Hope," he reiterated, calmly. "Use your feelings—not your head."

I tried harder. This time instead of focusing on the words, I focused on the blank space instead.

"Good," he encouraged.

I looked harder, but all I saw was emptiness.

"Forget your eyes Hope. See the page with your emotions. Think about *Ma*..."

"You know about *Ma*?"

"Don't lose focus," he interjected. "Keep looking with your feelings. Eventually you'll see it."

I continued looking. I tried remembering what Gabe—*ugh, Gabe*, had told me about *Ma*. I struggled to make sense of his explanation and how it was the creator's choice to interpret intervals in time and space. I closed my eyes and focused on seeing with my feelings. Flickers of light and color flashed before my eyes inside my thoughts. I opened my eyes again and immediately everything had changed.

I watched awestruck as the letters began moving around the page in an orchestrated ballet of sorts. Like leaves in the wind, letters scattered until finally taking a permanent position. I realized that the jumbled letters from FATE IS A DARK SORCERER actually served as the basis for whole words!

All of a sudden, right before my very eyes, new letters appeared, filling the formerly blank spaces. Old letters and new letters blended together until the entire page was filled with writing! Before long the whole journal was filled with writing too!

"Amazing," Eradan uttered.

"But what is it?"

"Something she didn't want anyone but a witch to see!"

11. Poison Apple

"But Oz never did give nothing to the Tin Man,
That he didn't, didn't already have."

Tin Man -America

The journal didn't look like a journal anymore. It was more like a textbook, an album or even encyclopedia. Its pages suddenly thickened, browned in color and filled with words and illustrations. I thumbed through the many pages with awe.

> Protection...LOVE...Recourse...
> shielding...awakening...BLEED,
> Purifying...CURING...delusion...
> DrEAm...HEX WARD...ill OMENs...arrow
> healing...Altruistic Blessings... Peace
> Bonding...summoning...

Words stood out like rays of sunshine and I beamed! I'd found it; the Fairchild grimoire! All of a sudden the bedroom door swung open. I jumped! Eradan disappeared instantly. I closed the grimoire and froze.

"Christian!" I exclaimed, nervously.

He was standing in the doorframe with a bag in his hands.

"What's going on in here?" he asked, suspiciously.

"Nothing."

He stepped inside the bedroom. He spotted the open window at the far end of the room.

"Hot?"

"Don't be silly. Vampires don't get hot." My voice was shaky.

He looked around, his pretty green eyes dilating with doubt.

"What's the matter?" I asked.

"Someone else was in here."

"Don't be ridiculous!"

He moved across the room and peered out of the window. "Who were you talking to?"

"I wasn't talking to anyone."

"I heard voice in here—a man's voice."

"Christian!" I scolded.

"I'm human Hope—not an idiot."

"Well you must have heard me talking to myself." I held up the grimoire, except it didn't look like the grimoire anymore. It looked like the journal again; plain and thin.

"Hum," he mumbled, disapprovingly.

"There's no one here but me. What's in the bag?" I asked, changing the subject.

He reached inside of it and pulled out a green, glass wine bottle.

"Bordeaux or blood?" I asked, wide-eyed.

"Guess," he said, handing it to me.

"Better than flowers!"

"It's fresh."

I tore out the cork with my teeth, spit it across the room and downed a gulp.

"Baptiste just corked this one at the shop."

"At the shop?"

Christian nodded.

"It's really good. God, I was thirsty!" I said, taking another drink.

"That's not what I heard."

I froze mid-swallow. The delectable taste of blood hung on my tongue as I tried to process what he was getting at.

"I heard you were at the Whet Willie today."

I swallowed what was left in my mouth.

"Were you there?"

"Well I..."

"Just because I can't read your thoughts anymore doesn't mean I can't tell when you're lying."

"I'm not lying!"

"Well you're not telling the truth either!"

I took the bottle from my lips. "Look, the truth is I did go to the Whet Willie today. I went with Gabe." Even speaking his name made me queasy—particularly after that disgusting dream I'd had with him in it.

His expression toughened. "You went with Gabe?"

"Yeah."

"Why the hell would you go anywhere with that guy?"

I shrugged. "I needed to talk to him."

"At a bar?"

"I know it looks bad..."

He ran his hands through his hair and groaned.

"I wasn't trying to make you angry...or jealous. Don't be mad."

"I can't believe you'd do that Hope, especially after that fiasco with the broken tube at La Fuente today!"

"I'm sorry, but I needed to ask him something. It was research."

"Research? What kind of research?"

"I don't know, stuff about Japanese painting."

"Painting!" he exploded. "You turned to that snot-faced, little weasel instead of me for advice about art!"

"I would have asked you, but you were busy."

"Yeah," he scorned, "busy cleaning up the mess that *he* made!"

"That's hardly fair."

He heaved a noisy sigh. "What did you need to know about Japanese painting that was so urgent?"

"It's not important..."

"You met with another man in a bar today—it *better* damn well be important!"

I cupped my face with my hands and groaned aloud with frustration. I wasn't happy about the way the situation looked any more than Christian was and clearly my subconscious agreed! I was still reeling from that horrible dream I'd had!

"I hope you realize the seriousness of what happened at the shop. Gabe broke a bloodsucker off in a client's arm. Everything is spinning out of control...and without control our life here is done!"

"But we fixed it. We regained control. The client was veiled and Gabe... it's not like he did it intentionally. He's not even aware of the bloodsuckers!"

Christian shook his head. "We were lucky and luck isn't something I like to live by." He ran his fingers through his hair again and started pacing.

"I know you've lived a very long life. *A very careful long life.* I'm sorry that things are spinning out of control. I'm worried that it's all because of me."

His brow furrowed. He looked me in the eyes and almost smiled. "Don't be ridiculous."

"I'm not. Perish was safe before I got here. Ambrose House wasn't in ruins, your job—La Fuente ran flawlessly. Eva and the others never had to live looking over their shoulders. I changed all that."

"No."

"Yes. My very presence drew danger out of the woodwork. Now expats are flocking to Perish in droves. It's almost like we've posted an ad in some anti-Society newspaper somewhere!"

He smiled.

"Glad I amuse you."

"*You* don't amuse me," he said grabbing my hands and pulling me toward him. "But your imagination certainly does."

"I wish I could agree." I pressed my head against his chest. The steady thumping of his heartbeat eased my distress almost immediately.

"Oh Hope," he said, tightening his hold. "I wish I wasn't so mad at you."

I recoiled from his chest and looked him in the eyes.

"Don't give me that look," he threatened.

"I'm not giving you a look."

"You went behind my back!" he replied. "You met with another man at a bar!"

"It wasn't a man," I insisted. "It was Gabe! And the Whet Willy is the crappiest hole in the wall ever!"

"Well I don't like it. I don't like it at all."

"So you are jealous?"

He smirked.

"Well I'll be damned. The great and powerful Christian Livingston can get jealous!"

He ran his hands through his hair yet again and sighed.

I grinned from ear to ear and pressed myself against him. I wrapped my arms around his body and squeezed.

"I'm gonna miss you this weekend," he whispered.

"Miss me?"

"I was meaning to tell you earlier but—"

"Where are you going?" My tone was icy.

"I've got another interview. It's a television interview this time...on some big, late-night show."

"Where?"

"New York."

I froze. I could feel my heart breaking inside my chest. I couldn't go to New York with him. It was in the north—in the Society's domain.

"The Big Apple," he gloated.

"The Poisoned Apple!"

"I have to do this."

"Send someone else!"

"I was considering sending Gabe, but after the incident today..."

"Cancel it then."

"I can't."

"Anywhere but New York. It's their territory Christian. It's dangerous. If they found you...if they caught you—"

"See, that's the thing," he said. "They won't find me because they aren't even looking for me. I'm human, remember." He stroked the side of my face with his long fingers and smiled. "You said it yourself; I've been hiding in the shadows for centuries. I don't have to anymore."

The blood in my veins froze like ice.

"Nothing confines me any longer. Not the south, not the sun—"

"Only me," I interjected. Tears of blood abruptly welled in my eyes.

"Hope," he consoled, wrapping his arms around me. "You give me reason to want to live again. You make me want to do things I never imagined that I could!"

"Like going on a big TV show in New York?"

"Yeah," he laughed. "Like going on a big TV show in New York!" He held me tighter. "I'll be back on Monday at the latest."

"Not soon enough."

He kissed me on the forehead. I could tell that he wanted to go. I could sense the anticipation in his voice.

"You won't even notice I'm gone. You're starting your training tomorrow. Rosa's gonna have you so busy you won't even notice I'm—"

"Please stay!" I begged, collapsing on the bed. I was tired just thinking about what Rosa was probably going to make me do.

"Everything will be fine," he assured, lying down next to me.

"But all the dangers are in New York."

"Like what? The muggers? Getting Broadway tickets?"

"I'm serious. The Society runs that city. It's not safe—even if you are human. I've got a really bad feeling about this Christian. Don't go. Please."

"Shh," he whispered, kissing me. I melted inside. With the absence of our inner voices, it was easy to get swept away by the moment. Soon, I was like putty in his hands and all that mattered was the moment itself. I dug my nails into his back and held on tight—like I never wanted to let him go.

12. Drink Me

"So drink me in,
Like tainted wine,
Come bite down on my sharpened cup,
And taste the dreams that numb the mind."

Silver – Moist

I woke to the melodic chirping of birds in the nearby trees. Sunlight sparkled against my eyelids. It was morning and I was alone. Christian had left for New York—without saying goodbye.

I stretched out. I ran my fingers along the pillows when unexpectedly I felt something. I opened my eyes and spotted a beautiful red rose sitting upon the pillow next to me. I picked it up only to discover a matching red envelope hidden beneath. My name was scrawled across the front of the envelope in Christian's handwriting. I tore it open and began reading.

My Hope,

Never wake a sleeping angel...or is it sleeping baby?

You looked lovelier than ever this morning, making it harder than ever for me to leave you!

Please stay safe. Trust Rosa. I know she's old – and certainly not my most favorite person, but I'm confident she will be able to help you along.

Never doubt the wonderful things you have done for me...Eva, B, Henry...for all of us. You didn't draw danger out of the woodwork—you carved a new future full of potential from within it.

I've been doing a lot of thinking lately...about us—about our future and there's something that I want to ask you, but it will have to wait until I return.

Until then,

Your Tin Man

Tears welled in my eyes. I pressed the letter to my chest—to my heart. It pained me to read his words. Christian was so romantic and so ridiculously old fashioned and I loved every corny bit of it!

Just then there was a knocking at my bedroom door.

"Who is it?" I shouted.

"Only me, Henry."

"Come on in."

The door swung open. Henry was standing in the frame holding a steaming cup of tea in his hands. He was nearly naked!

"Henry!" I exclaimed. "Why are you wearing one of Eva's silk robes?"

"I—I um..." he stuttered.

"Oh god, if this is some sex-thing with Rosa I'd rather not—"

"No," he laughed. "I shifted into a monkey to bring you this drink." He extended the cup. "I would have spilled the whole damn thing had I walked it up here blinder than a bat!"

"Thanks" I jumped out of bed and took the cup from his hands. "You really didn't have to go to so much trouble to bring this to me."

"No trouble. Rosa needed you to have it right away."

"So why didn't she bring it to me herself?"

He shrugged, gentlemanly. Rosa was old. I suppose the thought of her hauling her hefty behind and pair of tired legs up two flights of stairs was somewhat overwhelming.

"Try it," Henry insisted.

I brought the cup to my nose and gingerly inhaled.

"Smells like 1969 if you ask me," he teased.

I laughed. There was a specific skunky aroma to it.

"It's not tea."

"But apparently I'm supposed to drink it right away?"

He shrugged.

"And you think I should?"

"I don't see why not."

"Henry," I said. "Can I ask you something?"

"Of course."

"Do you trust Rosa?"

"Of course!"

"I figured you'd say that."

"Why do you ask?"

"She's so angry and stubborn and she hates Christian."

"Well," he laughed. "I suppose I can't really argue with you there."

"But you trust her."

He nodded and placed his hand on my shoulder. "Rosa might be a little prickly and experienced—"

"Try bitchy and ancient."

He shook his head and grinned. "But she's always been there. She's kept our secret for decades. She's helped us when we needed her most. She was best friends with Eva for many years. She cares about us—all of us, even if it doesn't seem that way. She's like family, Hope."

"I guess."

"You don't sound convinced."

"I just can't keep from feeling as though she's going to curse me in my sleep." I eyeballed the liquid. "Or poison me with a drink!"

"Rose is a lot of things, but two-faced isn't one of them. Now, taste that damn drink already, poison or not! Otherwise, I'll be the one she'll be cursing in their sleep tonight."

I laughed, brought the piping hot cup to my lips and took a sip. *Everything went black.*

The next thing I remember was waking up in the living room to the screeching whistle of the teakettle. Like an air raid siren, the scream echoed from the kitchen. My eyes flew open. I looked around. I was sprawled across one of the antique, red, velvet couches wearing nothing but panties and Christian's white T-shirt.

I looked ahead, to the large window in front of me. The sun had already set and it was dark outside. Henry was standing over me. He was wearing his normal clothes (thankfully) and holding yet another steaming drink in his hand.

"Oh no!" I said eyeing the cup. "I'm not drinking another one of Rosa's—"

"It's only coffee," he promised.

I was relieved. The bigger question remained: why in the hell had I been unconscious all day?

"Felling okay?"

"No. She poisoned me! I knew she would. And here I believed your emotional heart-to-heart about trusting her."

"She didn't poison you—well not really."

"Not really. How do you not really poison someone?"

"Rose is taking a big risk agreeing to train you, Hope."

"Risk?"

"The craft is not something usually taught by an outsider. It's a gift, meant to be passed through a family from generation to generation."

"Well great," I lamented.

"By agreeing to do this, Rosa's agreeing to reveal her family secrets to you. It's a big deal." He reached for my hand and stroked it. "She needed to know that she could trust you."

"By poisoning me?"

"She was testing you."

"And you knew that?"

"I knew that the only way she'd agree to help you is if I let her hypnotize you."

"Hypnotize?"

"Well, it was more of an entrancement.

My eyes bulged.

"She needed to see how much you really knew about magic and..."

"And what, Henry? I'm feeling a little mind-raped right now. Tell me."

"And she also wanted to know your exact involvement in creating Christian and Marco's cure."

"I had nothing to do with that! In fact, I didn't even know—"

"Yes," he interrupted. "She knows that now."

"So I passed her little test then?"

"With flying colors."

Rosa suddenly appeared, waddling across the living room toward me.

"Ah," she muttered. "Sleeping Beauty finally wakes."

"No thanks to you Maleficent," I replied, cheekily.

She kissed her teeth.

"So what's on the agenda for today?" I joked. "Exorcism?"

Rosa scowled at me before turning to Henry. "I not do this if she act like clown."

"I'm not acting like a clown. Pissed off maybe, but definitely not a clown."

"Hope is a little bitter from the entrancement is all." He grabbed her weathered hand. "She needs you. I need you."

"You hypnotized me Rosa!"

"I entranced you," she defended.

"But you don't just do that to someone!" I scolded.

Rosa grunted. Henry tightened his hold on her and suddenly she succumbed with ease.

"No more tests," I said "Unless you tell me it's a test and I agree to take it. Okay?"

Rosa scowled. Henry squeezed her tighter.

"Si. But if you keep making silly joke and act—"

"No more clown," I added.

Rosa tightened her lips. "So you find Fairchild grimoire."

"Yeah. How'd you...oh right...the hypnosis."

"Si."

"So we're cool then? You'll train me since I have the book?"

"Si. We cool."

I smiled.

"Come." She began walking toward the front door.

"Where are we going?"

"No question."

"Can I put on some—I mean I need to put on some pants first."

Rosa smirked. I wondered whether she actually appreciated that I was such a quick learner. I zoomed up the stairs at super-sonic, vampire speed to my bedroom and slid on a pair of jeans. I desperately wanted to look at the grimoire again, but I knew Rosa would have a hissy-fit if I took too long. I got back to the hallway even before she had a chance to grunt again.

We walked to the door together.

"Henry," I said. "You coming?"

"I think I'll sit this one out."

"You will?"

"You'll be fine. You're in good hands."

I bit my lip and continued walking.

"Is this gonna be a long walk?" I asked.

"No question."

"Right," I replied, frustrated.

"Sit," she said, pointing ahead, toward the big tree in the centre of the yard.

"The tree?"

"No question!"

"I mean—the tree."

She nodded.

I began walking; suddenly realizing that she was barely following behind. She was panting and struggling to waddle across the yard. I stopped and turned back to help her.

"My mind is okay...but mi body...viejo...not so good no more."

I took her arm and started escorting her. She removed my hand and continued struggling to walk on her own. Rosa was a pain in the ass. She was super-independent and undeniably prideful—I guess I couldn't argue with that.

"La juventud se desperdicia en los jóvenes," she mumbled.

"My Spanish isn't great. What did you say?"

"Youth is wasted on young."

"Apparently."

Just then she stumbled. Her hefty body lunged forward, through the air toward the ground!

"Rose!" I shouted, waving my hand through the air in an effort to grasp her when abruptly she froze! Everything froze! The world was silent and cold. Very, very cold.

13. Frozen

"Got a strange magic,
You know I got a strange magic."

Strange Magic - ELECTRIC LIGHT ORCHESTRA (ELO)

Time was at a literal standstill and Rosa hung in mid-air like a dirigible. I reached out to touch her, waving my hand slightly, and suddenly she moved. My interest was tweaked. I waved my hand again, ever so slightly, and she moved a little more.

"My god," I uttered, shocked. Did I now possess the power to both stop life and rearrange it?

I swallowed hard and waved my hand again. Rosa's body shifted.

"Unbelievable..." I muttered, amazed.

She was like a doll; at my disposal to rearrange and adjust. Quickly, I waved my hand backward. Rosa's body returned to an upright position. I waved my hand downward. Rosa's feet sank to the ground. I started waving my hand again when suddenly an inexplicable, icy chill began cutting through my body. I fluttered my eyelids and the world resumed instantly.

"Lord!" Rosa shouted. "What on earth—"

"You stumbled! You were falling! I was helping."

"Helping?"

"You would have face-planted if I hadn't—"

"What you do exactly?"

I shrugged.

"I no think I can train you."

"What?" I exclaimed. "But I found the grimoire!"

"I think it not matter. You is vampire. I not—"

"I'm a witch too," I implored. "Please."

She heaved a sigh.

"Please," I continued. "You're my only hope."

Rosa suddenly reached for my braid. She held it in her hand and studied it.

"What's wrong with my hair?"

"Blanco," she uttered, perplexed.

I took my braid from her fingers and eyeballed the ends. My hair was white! Just below the elastic, the golden blonde tips had actually tinted a bright white color!

"You not do this to yourself?"

"No!"

"Young people today do so many strange things to hair."

"Well not me," I defended. "I didn't do this and it certainly wasn't white this morning!"

She grunted. "I *will* try to help you."

I let my braid slip through my fingers and smiled.

"But remember," she said. "I old. I not do all I once could."

"I understand that."

"I thought Marco be my last apprentice. I not ready for this."

"I know."

Rosa mumbled. "Come," she said, urging me to walk with her again.

As we continued toward the tree I couldn't help but wonder why Rosa hadn't tried an anti-aging spell on herself. I started laughing.

"What funny, child?"

"Well if the love of my life and your grandson can create a cure that makes vampires human again, then why in the hell can't we create an anti-ageing spell?"

Rosa grinned. "It has been tried. Many times."

"It hasn't worked?"

She heaved a sigh. "Nature is...almighty."

"Nature?"

"Si. Nature. Life. Energy. Even time. Nothing stop it. Not even *magia*." She licked her lips. "Now sit."

"Here?"

She glared.

"No questions. I forgot." I cleared my throat. "I'll sit right here on these roots." I crossed my legs and pressed my back against the big tree trunk behind me.

Rosa placed her hand against the trunk too and struggled to sit down across from me.

"Let me help—"

"No."

"Why are you so damn prideful?"

She laughed and strained to lower herself to the ground. It was unbearable to watch. I reached out and helped her anyway, despite her protest.

"Gracias," she muttered, grudgingly.

"If magic can't cure old age," I insisted, "then why can't you just accept it?"

"You give up," she muttered, "you die."

"Fair enough."

"Si," she said, sitting on the roots across from me. "Now, close eyes."

I closed my eyes.

"Empty thoughts."

"That shouldn't be too hard."

"No clown," she barked.

I cracked a smile.

"Breathe."

"I can't."

"Why you can't?"

"Deep inhales send me back in time. Deep exhales move me to the present again. Breathing is...tricky for me."

"Okay. No breath. Just listen."

My brow furrowed.

"Corazon...listen to beat of your heart."

I tightened my lids and focused my hearing. At first all I heard was ambiance: nature and giggling, but then, when I listened closer, specific sounds illuminated. A nearby blackbird shaking its feathers resonated like hurricane winds. A long-legged grasshopper chirped like a mechanical piston. I'd nearly forgotten what it felt like to listen—really listen. I licked my lips and listened harder and there it was—the completely unsteady, lethargic thump of my undead heart.

"*Magia* is in you," she whispered, "and you is in everything."

I nodded, eyes still shut.

"What you feel?" she asked, intrigued.

With eyes closed, I tried absorbing my environment through sensation. At first, all I could feel was the tickle of the wind caressing my skin, but then, past the wind I felt so much more. I could feel the minute legs of a tiny insect crawling up my arm and the prickle of tree bark jabbing at my back. I felt sound waves moving past my ears and moonlight penetrating through my skin. I felt the energy inside of me—*the power*—coursing through every fibre of my being. And for once I felt almost in control of it!

I tightened my lids and imagined I was free! I pictured Christian and me together on the beach. The sky was bluer than a sapphire and the sea was like turquoise. I saw us running and laughing and I saw our child there too. Everything was perfect. Life was perfect, maybe for the first time ever, when all of a sudden a menacing darkness appeared. Ominous thunder clouds hung overhead. The blue sky was gone. The beach and the water were gone too. And then *they* appeared. *The eyes.* They were glowing and staring down at me from above, just like before. It got cold. Really cold. I waved my hand in the air in an effort to send the eyes away when suddenly everything collapsed around me!

"HOPE!" Rosa shouted, in a distressed voice.

My eyes flew open. I saw Rosa and myself hanging several inches above the ground. We were floating...levitating...when unexpectedly we plummeted to the roots below us!

"Rosa!" I shouted, rushing to her aid.

She was toppled over on her side with her head against a large root.

"Are you okay?"

"I warn you child. I too old for this."

Her voice was shaky and weary. I eyed her head. There was a large gash stretching from her temple to her cheekbone. Blood streamed down the side of her wrinkly face.

"Rosa," I uttered, concerned. "You're cut."

"Forget cut. My arm. I no feel my arm!"

I reached toward her and tried moving her.

"NO!" she wailed. "Can't move."

Gently, I touched her body, scanning her frame for fractures.

"You must let me take you back to the house," I implored.

"No!"

"You must!" I insisted, the smell of fresh blood streaming from the cut on her face was distracting me entirely. "Your arm feels broken. And maybe your shoulder too."

She groaned, with pain.

"I need to take you back to the house whether you like it or not!"

"No," she shouted, grabbing my hand and squeezing.

"Just accept my help for once, damn it!"

"No!"

"Fine," I snapped, fluttering my eyelashes. The world came to a standstill again. I extended my hand toward Rosa and waved it upward. Just like before, her body obeyed my command. Her hefty frame elevated in the air. I waved my hand forward. Her body followed again. I walked toward Ambrose House, signalling for her body to follow and before long we were back at the porch. I moved Rosa through the front door and into the living room with the simple flick of my fingertips. A moment later I had her laying on the couch in the living room. I fluttered my eyelashes and suddenly the world reanimated again.

"Rose!" Henry exclaimed, rushing toward us. "Is that you?"

"She's hurt," I said. "And it's all my fault."

Henry hurried to her side. He examined her briefly with his hands. "Broken arm...broken ribs...my god, Hope! What happened?"

"I don't know! She was helping me channel my energy...this damn power of mine...and then *they* appeared again...staring down at me just like before."

"The eyes?"

"Yes."

"We were levitating, but then we fell. It was the fall that injured her."

"Oh Rose," Henry said, stroking her leg.

"Maybe she was right," I said. "Maybe she really is too old to help me."

Henry exhaled noisily. "I suppose it's my fault too. I urged her to agree to train you. Clearly, it was just too much."

"Can we fix her?" I asked.

He nodded. "But it won't be easy. Witches tend to refuse vampire blood."

"Yeah, but we have to try. She's in so much pain."

Henry extended his fangs, brought his wrist to his lips and bit down. Blood dripped from the cut instantly. He brought his wrist to Rosa's lips and forced the blood to drop inside her mouth.

"No!" she wailed.

"Drink it," he implored.

"No. Stop!"

But Henry was unrelenting and as his blood continued streaming inside Rosa's mouth the healing effects began manifesting. Her arm slowly straightened. Her torso elongated and I could hear bones snapping back into place.

"It's working!" I exclaimed.

"Good," Henry replied.

Suddenly a surge of blood rushed from Rosa's mouth!

"Oh no," I shouted. "She's spitting it out!"

"Damn, it" Henry muttered.

"Do something!" I pleaded.

"Like what?"

"Force her to drink. Make her drink."

"I can't Hope. I told you it was difficult to get a witch to take our blood."

"C'mon, Henry. Keep trying."

He moved closer and pressed his wrist even nearer to Rosa's blood slathered lips.

"That's it," I encouraged.

"Is it working?" he asked, anxiously.

I widened my eyes and watched. Rosa appeared to have latched tightly to Henry's wrist.

"Yes! I think she's drinking."

A moment later, yet another surge of blood abruptly spewed from her mouth.

"Shit!" I shouted.

Henry withdrew his wrist.

"Don't stop!"

"I have to. If continue Hope, I'll be hurting her even more."

Suddenly, Rosa's arm contorted with a vigorous flick.

"Her arm!" I exclaimed. "What's happening to it?

A moment later her torso contracted too. The sharp snapping of bones re-breaking echoed through the corridors of Ambrose House with a harrowing sound.

"God!" I hollered. "Why isn't she mending?"

"I told you. She's strong. Her body—her blood, it's rejecting our help. You can't force a witch to do anything, let alone drink!"

I bit my lip. "What do we do?"

"We wait."

"For what?"

"For her to heal...naturally."

"But what about my training? What about my—"

"It was because of your training that she ended up like this!" Henry's voice was hard. "No more, Hope. Your training is officially over."

"Over? But it barely began!"

"We made a mistake. We put Rosa's life in jeopardy. There is nothing more we can do right now except wait."

"I can't accept that."

My body suddenly came alive from within. My senses were on fire. I felt the power surging, like waves in the ocean, beneath my skin. I widened my eyes and let the peculiar scent of Rosa's blood beckon me. I gingerly inhaled. My fangs shot through my gums and hunger voraciously swelled in the pit of my stomach. I was aflame with power and nothing could stop me.

"Hope," Henry exclaimed. "What are you doing?"

"The only thing I know how."

My voice was unwavering. My expression was resolute. I leaned over Rosa and bit down into the thin, creased skin on her neck.

14. The Fairest

"I've got to keep control,
I remember doing the Time Warp.
Drinking those moments when,
The blackness would hit me."

The Time Warp – Rocky Horror Picture Show

Rosa's howl was louder than a crack of thunder. I knew that it would inevitably draw the attention of everyone in Ambrose House—including the precarious newcomers, but I didn't care. I had one thing on my mind: power.

I needed to learn to control it. I could feel its potential growing within me. I had to find a way of harnessing it before it took over.

Rosa really was my only hope. It was unorthodox, dangerous and totally exploitive, but I simply had no other choice. This was the only way I could imagine having her help me; by travelling inside her blood and into her past to a time when she was younger and healthier.

And as her strange-tasting blood slipped between *my* teeth, I momentarily contemplated the depth of the shit-storm I was causing. I knew the residuals would be awful. I was well aware that yet another journey into the past would inevitably wreak havoc on my health. I'd been crying tears of blood for weeks and was beginning to wonder if the sudden whitening of my hair was merely the tip off the iceberg. Plus, I couldn't deny the fact that both Christian and Eradan would be furious with me for shifting through blood again—let alone a bruja's blood!

Immediately I felt the familiar pull of something fighting to take over. *Inhale.*

With a deep breath I triggered the shift and began my descent into Rosa's past.

Light and color merged together in a seamless unification while sounds began to blur into a numbing stream of static. The concave time tunnel opened up and suddenly I was traveling inside the wormhole of Rosa's memories.

The only other time I'd ever been inside a witch's past was when I travelled inside the beast's blood, my ancestor, Mr. Salazar. As an aged sorcerer cursed to live as a beast for many years, his memories were endless and cloaked in a nearly indescribable darkness. Rosa's past was rather vivid, cheerful and incredibly short by comparison. She hadn't lived extensively and really wasn't that old—except by human standards of course. It didn't take long for me to reach my final destination.

Exhale.

I released a breath of air from my lungs. Everything slowed to a stop. The wormhole of Rosa's memories shattered into millions of fragmented pieces right before my eyes. When the air cleared I knew exactly where I was.

It was hot. The sky was blue. Gardenias and hibiscus were in bloom. The sweet sounds of songbirds and cicada's resounded. Ambrose House was much less dilapidated in Rosa's past. The window trims were freshly painted. The shingles were clean. The porch was decorated with new iron furniture. Even the pool outback shimmered with icy blue water. This was Ambrose in her glory days.

The front door swung open. I hid behind a grouping of verdant yuccas. It was Henry. He looked exactly as he did in the present, only his clothes were like something out of a Frankie & Annette movie. The loud sounds of Sinatra resonated from the small transistor radio in his hands. He sat in the large chair on the porch. He stumbled a little and wobbled as he moved. He was blind and obviously already a vampire.

"Henry!" a vaguely familiar voice called out.

I hid a little deeper.

"Frigidaire on fritz," the female voice continued. "You is busy now?"

I widened my eyes. It was a woman. She was curvaceous and statuesque. Her skin was olive colored and her hair was shiny and black and hung in soft curls at her jaw. Her bombshell figure was wrapped in a wild leopard print dress. Her shoes were black stiletto and she even had a red scarf tied around her neck. She smelled of roses and limes as she neared. She was beautiful; like a Latina Marilyn Monroe!

"Rosie!" Henry exclaimed.

"Si senor!"

I froze, my eyes nearly bulging from their sockets. Rosie! This is what stout, wrinkly, old, Rosa looked like in her prime? It was no wonder that Eva hated her.

"What can I do you for today?" he said, excitedly.

Rosa crossed the lawn in her tall shoes and clip-clopped up the stairs to the porch. Her curvy body swayed in just the right way as she moved and despite the fact that Henry was blind, I knew he could feel her sex-appeal; it was unavoidable.

"Frigidaire?" he said. "I think I can fix that."

"Gracias," she purred.

"No need to thank me yet."

"Ciao," she giggled, clip-clopping her way back down the stairs.

"I'll be over a little later," he said.

"Si senor."

That devil! That temptress! I couldn't believe her audacity; luring my newly blind vampire-grandfather into her wicked den of *magia*! I wanted to scream, but I didn't. Just being in Rosa's past was dangerous enough. I didn't need to start completely re-writing my own family history while I was here. Plus, I needed Rosa.

The moment she moved away from Ambrose House I followed her. And when she opened the door to her late 50's fire engine red, finned Impala and slipped comfortably into the driver's seat, I knew my chance had presented itself. She was alone. She was contained and no one was close enough to hear her scream.

I leaped out of the brush, opened the passenger door and jumped into the car with her.

She screamed!

"Shh!" I shouted, silencing her with the palm of my hand.

Her pretty brown eyes bulged and she fought heartily to remove my hand from her face. Rosa was young and full of fight—she was exactly as I needed her, but she was no match for my strength as a vampire.

"Rosa," I insisted. "I'm not here to car-jack you. I just need your help."

She stopped fighting.

"I'll take my hand away if you promise you won't scream. Okay?"

She nodded.

I removed my hand.

"Who is you?" she asked, in her even thicker, Spanish accent.

"My name is Hope and I need your help."

"I not know any Hope." Her voice was hard, and resonated with the same edgy bitchiness she used with me in the present.

"Please," I insisted.

"Get out mi car!"

"You have to trust me."

"Trust?" She grunted. "I not even know you. How I gonna trust you?"

"Because in a long time from now, you and I...we become like family to each other."

Her eyes widened. "Who is you?" she demanded.

"I told you. My name is Hope."

"How you know me?"

"I'm from the future Rosa—your future."

She laughed.

"Laugh all you like, but it's true."

"True?"

I nodded.

"You come in spaceship?"

"I'm not an alien Rosa! I'm a time shifter. I have powers—just like you do."

"No such thing as—"

"Witches?" I interrupted, "vampires, shape-shifters and—"

"Enough!" she exclaimed. "How you know all this?"

"Like I told you. I'm from the future."

Just then the loud sound of a motorcycle engine resounded.

"Mierda," Rosa uttered. "Get in backseat. Hide under blanket. Si?"

"Okay," I replied, jumping in the backseat and hiding beneath her red, crocheted afghan.

The rumble of the motorcycle drew louder. A moment later I heard someone approaching.

"What are you doing here?" a sweet, male voice said.

It was Christian! I knew it. My body tingled, swelling with waves of passion and power. I pulled back the afghan and stole a glimpse.

"Frigidaire," she snapped, coolly.

"Leave Henry alone, Rosa."

I pulled back the afghan a little more.

He sniffed into the air. "Geeze," Christian said, spotting me. "Who you got hiding back there?"

"Dios mio!" she exclaimed, suddenly turning the key and pressing on the gas. We bolted away and flew down the road like a freight train!

"Why you not listen?" she shouted, pulling over into a ditch. "Why you not hide like I tell you?"

"I'm sorry." I hopped back into the passenger seat again. "I just had to see him."

She stopped the car and turned off the ignition. She jumped out the car and slammed the door behind her.

"Who is you?" she barked, enraged.

"I'm not an enemy," I said, getting out the car too.

"Why you need see Christian? He you father or something in future?"

I shrugged, unsure as to what to divulge without causing too many devastating residuals. "He's the love of my life," I said, diplomatically.

Rosa groaned, slid a cigarette out from aside her ear and lit it with the tips of her fingers.

"Oh my god!"

"What?" she uttered, inhaling.

"You just lit that with your fingertips!"

She shrugged and elegantly blew circles of smoke from between her scarlet, stained lips.

"You really shouldn't smoke."

"Why? Cigarette is bad in future?" Her tone was mocking.

"Actually yes," I said, pulling it out of her mouth and stomping it out on the ground.

Her eyes narrowed. She glared at me with a harrowing intensity before pulling another cigarette from within her cleavage.

"Geeze," I shouted, frustrated. "You never change. So damn stubborn."

Rosa smirked and lit the new cigarette with the tips of her fingers again.

"How do you that?" I asked, intrigued.

"Fire?"

"Yeah."

She exhaled three large rings of smoke from between her lips and grinned. She took her free hand and lightly rubbed her middle finger against her thumb like she was snapping. And voila; fire appeared.

"That's freakin' awesome!" I shouted.

"Que?" she replied, confused.

"It's amazing! I have to try it." I extended my hand and gently rubbed my middle finger against my thumb and suddenly—it sparked!

"Again," she said, grinning.

I continued trying a few more times and with each attempt the spark grew in size and intensity.

"So you is bruja," she said, with a deep exhale of smoke.

"I told you. I have power." I rubbed my fingers together once more. "I just don't know how the hell to use any of it." Suddenly, a flame emerged from the tip of my thumb. My eyes lit up elatedly.

"Look like you know more than you think." Her voice was swollen with pride.

"I need you to help me," I said, blowing out the flame.

"Me?"

"Yes."

"I not help nothing." She took the cigarette from her mouth and flicked it across the road.

"I need you to train me how to be a witch."

Rosa laughed, more of a cackle than a laugh really, and opened the car door.

"Please," I begged. "You are literally my last chance."

Her eyes narrowed again. "Who you—really?"

"I can't tell you everything. If I do, it may change things in the future—for the both of us."

"Then why I not help you in the future?"

"Well," I said, cagily, "the you in the future..."

"Si?"

"You're..." I stared her up and down. "You're just not the same."

"Muertos?" she panicked.

"No! Definitely not dead—more like stubborn and bitchy, but definitely not dead."

"Vieja."

"Vieja?"

"Old lady, right?"

I nodded.

She got back in her car and slammed the door shut. She turned the key and started the engine.

"So much for young Rosa," I muttered, running my hands through my hair.

"Chica," she shouted. "You coming?"

BOOM! A jolt of adrenaline jumped started my heart. Rosa had agreed! I opened the passenger side door and leapt inside the car.

"Thank you," I said, excitedly.

"No thank me yet."

She smirked and lit another cigarette.

"You really ought to quit those," I insisted. "It's bad for the skin."

She blew smoke in my face and slammed her foot on the gas pedal. We flew down the road like a bullet. And when the smooth baritone vocals of Sinatra singing none other than *Witchcraft* suddenly came over the airwaves, I knew for certain that everything was going work out perfectly.

15. The Dark Prince

"From her snow white throat fill a space,
In which two bodies float operatic by voice."

Blood Sugar Sex Magik - Red Hot Chili Peppers

"Hope."

I groaned and hid beneath the woolen serape.

"Wake up."

"No."

Rosa's house was cozy and dark. It was perfect for sleeping.

"Hope!"

"Can't you see I'm sleeping?"

"Wake up, damn it!"

I pulled back the serape. "Eradan?"

"You must go. Get out of here and back to your future."

"No."

"You can't stay here."

"Why not? The 50's are so much better and simpler."

"Hope, you can't live in another person's past."

"But Rosa has finally agreed to train me!"

He shook his head and glared at me from behind his weird circular spectacles.

"Don't judge me."

"Why not?"

"Because...you're not the boss of me."

"How right you are," he snickered.

"And she's already showed me how to make fire with my fingertips! I'm staying."

"At what cost? You're killing this poor woman in order to stay here."

My face paled. I'd completely forgotten about present-day Rosa and what I'd done to get here.

"Time is of the essence."

"Oh god, stop saying that! What are you—the time police?"

"I've been called a lot of things, but never the time police."

"So you are," I exclaimed, distressed.

"It's not what you think."

"And you would know," I said, feeling him inside my thoughts again.

"My work has absolutely nothing to do with the fact that I can read your mind."

"Oh that's comforting."

"You are not my charge, Hope."

"Your *charge?*"

"My responsibility."

"But you have been sent to keep me in line?"

"Yes...I mean no."

"Who sent you? Tell me."

"No one sent me!"

"Then why are you here? Why do you care?"

"I care because..."

"Because you work for them—the damn Society, don't you?"

"No!" he shouted. "I don't work for them. And no one sent me to keep you in line."

"Bullshit."

"Trust me."

"Why, because you've been so honest with me until now?"

"That's not fair."

"What's *not* fair is the fact that you seem to know everything about me and I know absolutely nothing about you. Hell, I don't even know what you look like!" I stared at the strange spectacles covering his eyes and scowled. "Take off your glasses," I ordered.

"I'd rather not."

"Take them off."

"Hope, please don't ask—"

"If you want to earn my trust, do it."

"It's not that simple."

"Do laser beams shoot out of your eyes?"

"I'm not Scott Summers!"

"Who are you? Tell me."

"I'm from the future."

"How far?"

"Almost sixty years from your present."

"And you work for *them*?"

"No. I told you that already. You're wasting time interrogating me. You need to go—for Rosa's sake."

"I will, but not before I see your face. Take off your glasses."

He groaned.

"Do it!"

"Fine." He removed his spectacles with reluctance. His eyes were large and the most beautiful green color I'd ever seen. In fact, he was virtually the most beautiful man I'd ever seen! And as I stared at his face—his whole face, I was taken by his familiarity. His dark hair, his sculpted jaw, his full lips, straight nose and lovely green eyes.

"Who are you?" I shouted.

"Eradan."

"That's not good enough."

"We don't have time for this," he implored.

"Why do you care so much?"

"Don't do this, Hope."

"Tell me! Why are you so interested in me...my friends?"

"Please," he begged.

"You always know where I am. You're always telling me where to go and what to do.

"Hope. Stop."

"Why can you read my thoughts?"

"I don't know."

"I think you do. Tell me!"

"No!"

"But you've already said I'm not your job. I'm not your responsibility. Why do you give a shit where I go or what I do?"

"Because!"

"Because why, Eradan, tell me!"

"Because, I'm your son!"

BOOM! My face paled. My heart thumped with a thunderous thud inside my chest. Power surged through my veins and suddenly everything turned black.

When I opened my eyes, I was back in Ambrose House again. Had I fainted? Had I inadvertently shifted back to the present? Had my ears played tricks on me; had Eradan really confessed that he was *my son*?

"Holy hell!" Eva shrieked.

Eva, Henry, Ryan and Baptiste hung above me like a creepy mobile of angry faces. I widened my eyes and stared up at them when without warning a shockwave of tremors occurred! The ground pulsated intensely. Everyone stumbled and struggled to grab hold of something. I grasped the arm of the couch and steadied myself.

"What's happening!" Baptiste shouted, in his deep, Spanish voice.

"It must be residuals," Henry replied. "This is the effect of Hope being in Rosa's past."

I'm sorry!" I shouted, guiltily, when finally the shaking ceased.

"What the hell did you do?" Eva shouted.

"I'm sorry," I replied. "How is she?"

"Nearly dead! What did you expect? You drank from an old lady, Hope!"

"Esperanza," Baptiste whispered. "You okay?" His voice was firm and laden with genuine older-brother concern.

"I think so."

"How can she be okay when she's crying tears of blood!" Ryan exclaimed.

I touched my cheeks. A trickle of blood stained my skin.

"And her hair," Eva said. "Look!"

"What? What's wrong with my hair?"

"It's changing color!" Ryan cried out.

I grabbed a hand handful of my hair and watched as the pale tips suddenly spread. Streaks moved upward another two inches with the same lightening intensity as before.

"Where's Rosa?" I questioned, panicked.

"There," Baptiste replied, signalling the couch across from me.

I turned to look at her. Henry was hovering over her protectively. Rosa was still lying on her side, incapacitated and speckled in a dusting of her own blood.

"God!"I exclaimed.

"God's the least of your worries," Baptiste insisted.

I bit my lip. I knew he was right. I'd burn in hell...on the stake or even in an oven for what I'd done this time!

"She's trying to speak," Henry suddenly exclaimed. "She's saying something."

I perked up and tried to listen.

"What is it Henry?" My tone was eager. "What did she say?"

He heaved a sigh.

"Henry!" I insisted. "What did Rosa say?"

"I...I'm not sure."

"You're not sure of what she said?"

"No," he replied, shaking his head. "I do know what she said."

"Then tell us."

He shook his head again. "But I don't think I should."

My shoulders sank. I was suddenly speechless.

"What the hell did she say?" Eva exclaimed, worriedly.

"Una vez mas," Henry replied, reluctantly.

"Tell me in English!" I demanded.

"Once again," Baptiste muttered.

"Once again?"

"Yes, Esperanza. Once again."

I couldn't believe my ears! Did Rosa really want me to go into her past again? I straightened my shoulders and wiped the blood stains from my cheeks. I was ready.

"She's completely incoherent!" Eva insisted. "You can't trust anything coming out of her mouth right now!"

"Again!" Rosa shouted.

"No Rosie," Henry retorted. "You don't know what you're saying. You're depleted. You need rest."

"I rest when I dead."

"And you'll be dead if you let her drink from you again!" Eva snarled.

"Again," Rosa shouted. "I is okay."

"Rose," Henry whispered. "Don't do this to yourself...or to Hope."

I stood up and walked toward Rosa's side. I looked down at her and smiled. She was weak, frail and old—nothing like her youthful self in the past. We were onto something then; a partnership—a real apprenticeship. I knew it and I think she knew it too.

Rosa grabbed my hand with her wrinkly fingers and pulled me close. I leaned in. Her breath was spicy and smelled a little like death.

"Hope," she whispered. "I know what you do. I remember it. I feel it is right."

"I feel it too, but it's not worth your life."

She grinned. Her wrinkly skin stretched tightly, giving the faded illusion of her former, youthful self.

"I not die today," she said, confidently.

"How can you be so sure?"

She shrugged and smirked. "I trust you. Now go."

A moment later she pulled me toward her jugular. The steady thump of her heart made me come alive from within. My fangs shot out again. Hunger coursed through my veins. I dug down deep into her flesh and began my descent into her past once more.

16. Back Down The Rabbit Hole

"That old black magic has me in its spell.
That old black magic that you weave so well.
Those icy fingers up and down my spine.
The same old witchcraft when your eyes meet mine."

That Old Black Magic – Frank Sinatra

The familiar pull of something fighting to take over began.
Inhale.

With a deep breath I triggered the shift and began my descent back inside Rosa's past.

Light and color merged together in a seamless unification and sounds began blurring into static. The concave time tunnel opened and I shifted through the wormhole of Rosa's memories again. And while I should have been elated by the very fact that Rosa allowed me to do this, I couldn't help but focus on Eradan instead.

Was he really my son? I touched my stomach. The rock was still there, sitting heavily, deep in the pit of my gut.

"Eradan," I mumbled, foolishly, in my head. *"I know you can read my thoughts, so maybe, if it really is you in there, you can hear me."* I waited for a response. I felt nothing. The rock still felt like a rock.

A flash of Ambrose House suddenly flickered before my eyes. I exhaled. Everything slowed to a stop. The wormhole of Rosa's memories shattered into the familiar millions of fragmented pieces. I was back.

The serape was warm. The bed was hard. I wiped my eyes and let them adjust. The room was dimly lit and sparsely decorated, except for the large crucifix that hung over the doorway. I looked up to the ceiling.

"No!" I exclaimed.

The glowing eyes had returned, staring down at me from above. They were intense, like angry stars in a sky of wickedness. I pulled the serape tighter and higher, up to my nose and continued watching the eyes watching me, when all of a sudden they vanished—this time by their own accord, disappearing like smoke in the wind!

I blinked my lashes a few times and tried refocusing my sight. The eyes were definitely gone. I wondered how they found me—even here, in Rosa's past.

I pulled back my cover and slipped out of bed.

"My god!" I exclaimed. I was nearly naked! My clothes were gone. I was topless and wearing nothing but my black, lace thong!

I grabbed the serape and wrapped it around me. I scanned the room for my clothes. A stack of clothes sat on the nearby dresser. They were folded in a neat pile. I walked toward them and sifted through the pile. They weren't my clothes, but I knew they'd have to do.

The pale yellow sweater-shirt was totally June Cleaver. The black, tapered slacks weren't so bad, but the rest of the stuff was completely nuts! The crème colored granny panties were hilarious and thin lacy bra with really, really pointy cups was definitely old-fashioned.

"Found the clothes?" Rosa snickered, standing in the doorway watching me holding the granny panties.

"Where are *my* clothes?"

"Garbage," she said, smiling, her gorgeous body was poured in a tight, red dress.

"You tossed my clothes in the garbage?"

"Si."

"But—"

"You is here to learn. You need fit in."

"And this is your idea of fitting in?" I held up the granny panties.

She laughed, walking toward me. "Anyway, yours is broken," she said, tugging at the blanket, exposing my butt.

"Hey!" I exclaimed. "Ever heard of privacy!"

"See, broken," she said, pointing at my thong.

"It's not broken. It's called a thong, Rosa. And it happens to be considered very sexy."

"So not broken?"

"No." I grabbed the serape and rewrapped it around myself. "And it's a heck of a lot better than these." I held the panties higher. "Do you actually wear these things?"

"No. I not wear any under—"

"Okay. I get the idea."

"You need fit in, so I go out and buy you these," she said, refolding the clothes back into a neat pile on the dresser.

"For me?"

"Si."

I grinned. I couldn't imagine Rosa actually going to a store and picking out clothes just for me.

"Thanks," I replied, pleased.

"De nada. Besides, you is too—*how you say*—flat chest to fit into any of my clothes."

And there it was; the Rosa tactlessness I'd grown so accustomed to hearing. I shook my head and laughed.

"Okay," she said, reaching behind her ear and lighting up a cigarette. "Get dressed now and meet in kitchen. We have much to do."

"And only a little time to do it," I added, recalling the sad state of poor, elderly Rosa in the present.

She nodded and turned to leave.

"Hey Rosa," I called out.

"Si?"

"Is there anyone else hanging around...like a Mr. Rosa that I need to worry about?"

"No Mr," she smirked.

"But there was one once—right?"

"Si. But he leave me for blonde, all-American girl like you."

I swallowed, uncomfortably.

"It okay. He was no good bum. I is better off now."

I half-smiled. I didn't know much about Rosa's personal history—except for the fact that she had the hots for my grandfather. It was kinda interesting getting to know her a little better.

"Only person ever come here is my Marco."

"Marco?" I said, shocked.

"Marco. Mi hijo. My son."

"You mean grandson."

"Grandson? Dios mio no, no, no! Marco is son. Why...I look like old grandma to you?"

"Well, no..."

She laughed. "But now my Marco is run off to Miami with pretty Cuban girl. He only teenager, but he in love." She rolled her eyes.

I nodded, empathetically.

"I is just silly madre. He not take advice from me no more." She blew circles of smoke from her lips. There was a genuine sadness in her eyes. I began to wonder what happens to her son in the future—whether he died, or left for good, or maybe even disappeared like her grandson Marco in the present.

"Okay!" she said, startling me. "No more chat. You get dressed and come to kitchen. Si?"

"Si," I replied, smiling.

I listened as Rosa clip-clopped her way out of the bedroom and down the hallway toward the kitchen. It was weird seeing such a different side of her and not just physically either, but the sensitive emotional side too. I was almost starting to understand why she became so damn ornery and unpleasant in the future; her husband leaving her for another woman and her son leaving her too. She really was an independent woman in a time when independent women weren't so accepted.

I picked up the bra and eyeballed the pointy cups again. I just couldn't do it. I knew I'd rather go top-commando than express myself like Madonna in one of these pointy contraptions. I grabbed the yellow sweater-shirt and put it on—sans bra. It looked good—not great, but definitely 1950's passable.

Next, I grabbed the granny panties. There was no way in hell I was going to wear them! I tossed them back atop the dresser and reached for the black pants instead. I slid them on, over my thong and up to my waist. They were a good fit. Rosa really pegged my size dead on. I was impressed. I fastened the zipper and slipped into the pair of size 7 black flats she'd left for me at the foot of the dresser.

I looked around the room once more before I left. The eyes were definitely gone. There was no sense in telling 1950's Rosa about my strange visions; clearly I had enough on my plate already. I closed the bedroom door behind me and started for the kitchen.

I'd been in Rosa's house before. I knew where everything was. I'd just never seen it in such pristine condition. The tiled floors were shiny and without cracks. The walls looked as though they'd been freshly painted in bright white and the staggering number of religious relics that lined the walls were totally cobweb-free.

"What is this?" she snapped, the moment I entered the kitchen.

"What?"

"You not put on bra!"

I shrunk back and tried covering myself.

"Thought you want blend?"

"I do. I put on the shirt and these pants and the shoes too."

She cocked her head to the side and eyeballed my lower-half. "You not put on the under—"

"I'm sorry Rosa. I just couldn't do it. In my time we just don't cover up so much."

She rolled her eyes and grunted. I knew that grunt—a little too well.

"What?" I asked, nervously.

"Your hair."

I touched my hair and grimaced. The lightened white tips were kinda weird, especially for this decade.

"Sit," she said, pointing to the wooden chair at the table in the centre of the room.

I nodded and sat down. Rosa moved behind me and ran her fingers through my hair.

"Soft," she muttered, tenderly as she began sorting strands into place for a braid.

I grinned. It felt nice having someone do my hair for me.

"Dios mio!" she suddenly exclaimed.

"What?"

She dropped my long locks and froze. I turned around. The expression on her face was appalling.

"What Rosa? What's the matter?"

She reached out and touched the back of my neck. "You has tattoo." Her voice was panicked.

"It's cute, isn't it," I said, casually.

"Cute?" she grunted. "If you is sailor or prostitute..."

"Oh my god, Rosa! It's just a tattoo. Everybody has them."

"Not now." She kissed her teeth.

I bit my lip. "Can you hide it?"

"Si," she sighed, finishing the braid. A moment later she was done. "All finish."

I smiled as she moved from behind me and took a seat at the table.

"Now, what you want learn?" she asked.

"I don't know."

She laughed. "You come all this way and not know what you want learn?"

"Teach me how to use my power."

"What kind power you got?"

"Witch power," I shrugged.

She laughed.

"What's so funny?"

"You really not know magic, eh?"

I shook my head.

"Okay." She grabbed the glass salt and pepper shakers from the centre of the table and put them in front of me. "Now you move them. With your power."

"How?"

"You feel inside you, si?"

"I feel energy. A lot of it. Sometimes so much that I can hardly contain it."

"That your power. It move through you, through me, through everything around us."

"Yeah, but how do I control it? How do I *use* it?"

"You no *use* it like some tool. You bend it—you borrow it. You let flow through you." She smiled. "Now try."

I eyed the salt and pepper shakers. I felt the waves of energy—the power, flowing through my body. I focused on the feeling and tried borrowing it and bending it to my will. Nothing happened.

"It okay. You try again."

I nodded, stared at the shakers and focused on the power. Nothing happened. "Damn it!" I exclaimed, thrusting my hands in the air when suddenly energy surged from my fingers, bolting straight across the table toward the shakers!

Glass exploded like fireworks! Droplets of ice and glass floated through the air.

"I'm sorry! I told you. I don't know how to control it."

"Shh," Rosa replied. She reached across the table and grabbed hold of the salt shaker remnants. Ice had coated what remained of the shard glass.

"Did I do that?"

"Si," she answered, eyeing the ice.

"And that's normal? I mean for witch powers?"

Rosa shook her head. "No. Not normal." She put the shaker down on the table and glared at me. "Who is you? Tell me," she insisted.

"I told you. My name is Hope and I'm from the future—your future."

She kissed her teeth again.

"What's wrong Rosa? Please," I begged.

She grabbed her head.

"Rosa?"

She reached behind her ear and pulled out a cigarette. I rubbed my fingers together and lit it up for her. She took a long drag on her smoke and leaned back in her chair.

"Talk to me, Rosa. Please."

A big puff of smoke emerged from between her lips, bathing me in fogginess. When the smoke cleared she looked petrified.

"Rosa. Tell me what the hell is going on!"

"You!" she exclaimed.

"Me? What did I do?"

"It not what you do. It what you are!"

"Well what am I?"

"Diablo Blanco! White Devil!"

17. Evil Queen

"Cause I knew you were trouble when you walked in,
So shame on me now."

I Knew You Were Trouble – Taylor Swift

"White devil?" I mumbled, perplexed. My brow furrowed. I remembered Rosa calling Christian that in the present.

"Si."

"It can't be. There must be some mistake. I'm just a witch, a time-shifter with no control over her power. I'm no devil!"

Rosa shook her head. A panicked expression hung on her face. "When I was a girl I hear stories...cuentos de hadas...fairy stories. These stories about the Diablo Blanco—about you!"

"This is ridiculous!" I exclaimed.

"Okay," she said, moving toward a large bookshelf perched against the back-end of the kitchen. "Me show you."

I stood up and walked toward her. Over a hundred books lined the shelves. Some were old and well worn and looked like spell-books, while others were new and seemed more like cookbooks.

"Here," she said, extracting a very well-worn, leather bound book from the shelf.

"Cuentos de encantamiento," I said, reading the cover.

"Mi madre read this book of fairy stories when I was growing. Here," she said, opening the book to the middle and showing me the pages.

"El Diablo Blanco," I read. There was a picture of very beautiful white butterfly against a black background.

"All ninos know this story...like Snow White or Cinderella."

"That's great, but that doesn't mean it's about me."

"It don't mean it not either."

"Oh come on Rosa. This sounds crazy!"

"I think so too, but then you coming to my car and telling me you from future and you want me train you...that is crazy too!"

"I guess."

"Then you have this white hair."

"My hair?" I laughed. "It's not all white."

She snorted. "And you turn things cold. You make ice of my salt and pepper!"

"You asked me to try and—"

"And when I see your tattoo...mariposa. Dios mio! I know you is her—El Diablo Blanco!"

"Rosa! Stop this. You're totally overreacting. I'm not some legend from a fairy tale. I'm just a time-shifter in need of some help. Please."

She scowled at me before moving back to the kitchen table. She sat down and placed the heavy book on the table in front of her.

"Habia un vez," she said, reading from the book.

"I don't understand Spanish."

"Once upon a time," she translated, "there lived beautiful woman."

"Oh my god, are you really going to read me a bedtime story? I didn't come all the way back in time for this!"

"Hope!" she shouted. "Me don't think you come back in time to be apprentice to me."

"You don't?"

"I think you come back to learn about fate."

"My fate?"

"Si. I think if you listen to this story you better understand."

"I really don't have time for this nonsense."

"It not nonsense. Please."

I looked her in the eyes. There was a strange urgency and sorrow I couldn't pinpoint.

"Fine," I said, taking a seat beside her at the table. "But can't you just kinda summarize the main points for me?"

Rosa nodded before turning her attention back to the book again.

"This beautiful woman, Esperanza—"

"Her name is Esperanza?" I asked, intrigued.

"Si," she replied. "Come to learn she magical and she possess all powers of world."

"Well there you go!" I exclaimed. "It's not me. I certainly don't possess—"

"You want me keep telling?" she interrupted.

I nodded.

"Young Esperanza fall in love with *impio*...wicked man."

"Christian is not wicked!"

"I thought you say this not you?"

My eyes narrowed. "Go on."

"Her love for this man so great she beg him to make her like him."

"Wicked?"

"Si. And he does. Esperanza become most dangerous woman in world now! She has all power of the humankind and of wickedness too."

"So what happens?" I asked, eagerly.

"She want more."

"More of what?"

"All...everything. More love, sin, lust. She become with child and the mix of his love and hers makes her even more hungry!"

"Well what happens to her?"

"She go mad...loco. Instead of protect and keep happy world, she start to change it."

"*Change it*?"

"Esperanza make sun turn into storm and lightness into darkness, health to sickness and joy to sadness. Death surround her. Those she love become enemy."

"Just because she wanted to be like the man she loved?" I asked.

"Si."

"That's not fair."

"Perhaps. Can I keep read?"

"Yeah," I said, captivated.

"Esperanza become—how you say, no emotion."

"Emotionless."

"Si. Emotionless. Her heart become frozen and she become El Diablo Blanco. Her skin turn pale, her hair turn white. Everything she touch turn to ice."

"And the man she loved?"

Rosa shakes her head.

"She kills him?"

"She not human anymore. She only power." She leaned back in the chair. "You realize story is *allegorty*."

"You mean *allegory* and I get that. And I also realize that it's about self-indulgence and addiction, I just don't understand why you think it's all about me?"

"You skin white."

"So?"

"You hair white."

"Rosa, we've been over this."

"You come from other time. You change history by come here to me."

"Did I? Or was I meant to come all along?"

She grunted. "You wear the mariposa of El Diablo Blanco on your back."

"My butterfly tattoo? That's ridiculous. Christian gave me this tattoo for fun. And besides, what does a butterfly have to do with this El Diablo creature?"

Rosa snorted. "You love Christian."

"Yes, well—"

"He is vampire. Vampire is *maldad*...wickedness."

"Christian is not wicked!"

"And you make ice of my salt shaker with power!"

"But that doesn't mean I'm El Diablo Blanco!"

"And you is with child." Her voice was hard.

I clenched my teeth, speechless.

"I is witch, Hope. You not have tell me. I know tell these things."

I sank back in my seat.

"Look," she said touching my arm. "This is just story. Maybe I make much of it. Maybe I wrong about you."

I rolled my eyes and hid my face in my palms. "How does it end?" I asked, forlornly.

Rosa turned back to the book again. "On eve of beloved's death it end."

"So he does die?"

"Listen," she insisted. "On eve of beloved's death, Esperanza come to him. Know she caus all his pain and pain in world, her heart break. She cry. As she cry her tears melt beloved's body. He become free from death-state and breathe again."

"So it's happily ever after?"

"As he begin to live, Esperanza begin to die. Her body turn to ice, cracking and breaking into glass that crumble and become mariposa."

"What?" I exclaimed, devastated.

"Mariposa is only—*how you say*—crystalids?"

"Chrysalis?"

"Si, chrysalis. And she begin to live again. El fin. The end."

"That's it?"

"Si." She closed the book.

"So I must die to save my Christian and the world, basically."

"Hope," Rosa said, expressively. "You know this only allegory. If you believe you El Diablo Blanco, then interpret story in own way."

"Own way? God! Even if I do save my beloved, I still die! This sucks."

"I not know what sucks is, but I tell this. El Diablo Blanco does not die. She only change...she become mariposa and live again! It happy ending. Si?"

I nodded, despondently. When all of a sudden there was a knock on the door.

"You expecting someone?" I asked, concerned.

"No. Stay," she instructed, rising from her seat.

She left the kitchen and went to answer the door. I moved from the table to the edge of the hallway and tried to listen.

"Now is not good time," she said, irritably.

I listened a little more intently.

"I say no! It not good time. Come back. Okay!"

A moment later I heard her shouting. Rosa's tone was loud and aggressive. I rushed down the hallway toward her. When I rounded the corner I spotted the doorway. My jaw dropped open. My face paled.

BOOM! My heart thumped inside my chest. It was Christian—my young, beautiful, vampire Christian and he was just the way he looked in my childhood!

"You!" he uttered, eyeing me.

"Go Christian," Rosa shouted, closing the door on him.

"Who are you?" he muttered, in his fading English-accent.

"She no one," Rosa replied.

"Invite me in Rosa." His voice was compelling. "Introduce me to your friend."

"She not friend. Now leave!"

"I will do no such thing! You have company and Henry insisted that I fix your Frigidaire. Invite me in your house."

I melted inside. I couldn't take my eyes off him. This was my Christian—my hero, savior, creator, the one true love of my life standing before me in all his former glory.

"Invite me in Rosa." His tone was both bitter and charming simultaneously.

"Fine. Come," she uttered, grudgingly.

He ran his fingers through his, slicked back hair and grinned stepping over the threshold.

"I show you kitchen. You fix Frigidaire then you leave."

"Okay," he replied, stealing glimpses of me as he moved past. It was love at first sight for him and I felt it instantly.

The moment Christian retreated to the kitchen Rosa stopped me.

"You say he your love, si?"

"Yeah," I gushed, "more than anything."

"Then stay away from him."

"What?"

"Think. You see him in this time and you change things."

"But I can keep my cool. I swear. I won't say anything unusual or suspicious."

"Hey Rose," Christian hollered, from the kitchen. "You got anything to drink around here?"

Rosa shook her head. "El Diablo Blanco," she muttered, threateningly as she walked toward the kitchen.

I followed behind. I was going to stay away from Christian about as much as I was going to wear those damn granny panties of hers!

I rounded the corner and went inside. Christian was leaning over Rosa's baby blue, 50's style refrigerator drinking a bottle of Coke. He was wearing a snug fitting white T-shirt and blue jeans with the cuffs rolled up a little. His high-top converse peeked out from beneath his pants. He looked amazing!

"Well Rosa," he said, captivatingly, "aren't you going to introduce me to your beautiful not-friend?"

"No," she snapped.

I extended my hand to him. "I'm—"

"Aurora," Rosa interrupted. "Her name Aurora and she my niece."

"Funny," he said, puzzled. "She doesn't look like she could be your niece."

My brother married guera...white woman." Rosa rolled her eyes.

"Well she's simply stunning," he said, running his long, pale fingers through his hair like usual.

"Thank you," I replied, flattered. Compliments from my Christian were always a pleasure.

He smiled. His white teeth sparkled as his lips moved. I wanted nothing more than to wrap my arms around him, but I couldn't. I promised Rosa that I wouldn't do anything suspicious and the thought of causing even more residuals—knowing that I was the monster written about in Spanish folklore, made me even more insecure.

"So you fix Frigidaire or you stand here and eyeball niece all day?"

Christian laughed and turned his attention back to the fridge.

"Come Aurora," she insisted grabbing me by the arm. "We have much to do."

I followed her out of the kitchen when suddenly Christian grabbed me by the hand. I froze.

"Meet me outside," he whispered, passionately. "By the pink rosebush tonight at dusk."

"Okay," I answered, recklessly.

I left the kitchen and rushed to catch up to Rosa. I could hardly wait until nightfall.

18. Heigh-Ho Heigh-Ho

"Every little thing she does is magic,
Everything she does just turns me on,
Even though my life before was tragic,
Now I know my love for her goes on."

Every Little Thing She Does Is Magic – The Police

Dusk felt like an eternity away. I had no idea how I was going to preoccupy myself until then. All I wanted to do was be with Christian. I couldn't get him off my mind. I had no idea how I was going to manage until dawn.

Rosa led me outback. She had a nice size yard and a lot of open space.

"To learn *magia*, you learn elementos y sentidos."

My eyes widened with intrigue.

"You want learn?"

"Of course." I hung my head a little. "You still want to teach me... considering I'm the White Devil and all?"

Rosa grumbled. "El Diablo Blanco is only story, Hope. How many times I tell you this?"

I shrugged. "But what about my hair...and my butterfly tattoo?"

"Aye yi yi!" Rosa sighed. She put her hand on my shoulder. "Butterfly is only moth forced to live in daylight." She smiled. "You see?"

"Not really."

"Things change. More you learn—more you change. Si?"

"I guess so."

"So," she said, clapping her hands together. "You want learn or no?"

"I do."

Rosa smiled, and pulled a cigarette out from a small box hidden in a nearby tree. She snapped her fingers and lit it up. "All *magia* work by cuatro elementos," she whispered, exhaling smoke.

"The four elements?"

"Si. Four elementos."

"Fire, water, earth, air."

"Si. Also by cinco sentidos."

"What's that?"

"You know...tacto, el gusto..."

"The five senses?"

"Si. Cinco sentidos."

"Sight, sound, taste, touch, smell?"

"Si," she grinned. "Now, use eyes to see. What you see?"

I looked around and shrugged. "Trees, flowers...I don't know."

"No," she snapped. "You see, but you not look. Try. Look."

I felt a headache coming on. This was suddenly feeling like yet another lecture on *Ma*.

"Feel power in body. Feel power through you as breathe, see, live. Feel as you look. Now what you see?"

I looked around again only this time I looked at the world the same way I looked at those peculiar blank pages in my grandmother's journal.

"My god!" I exclaimed.

As I gazed around, the world this time was interleaved with the most wonderful things. Where initially I'd only noticed trees and flowers, I now noticed beautiful dew-studded cobwebs hiding in crevices, microscopic creepy-crawlies dwelling in nooks, flying insects twinkling like stardust through shafts of sunlight and more! I saw everything around me. The world was alive—every last bit of it.

"Now I think you see," Rosa praised, inhaling on her cigarette.

"I do and it's amazing."

"Si. It amazing. Okay. Now, do same again...take in world through breath."

"I can't."

"Por que?"

"Breathing is tricky for me. Inhales and exhales move me through time."

Rosa's mascara laden eyes widened.

"I don't think I should mess with breathing."

"Okay," she agreed. "Then use power to taste."

"Oh, I don't wanna mess around with tasting stuff either."

"Por que now why?" she said, frustrated.

"Trust me," I said, reminded of the way my-body kicks into gear with the taste of blood. "I'd rather not."

Rosa reacted with displeasure. "Then I teach you touch?"

"Okay."

She nodded, satisfied. She walked toward a nearby bush of yellow gardenias and ruthlessly snapped off a bloom. She held it in her hand and returned to me.

"Take," she said, passing it over.

I took the bloom and eyed it.

"What you feel?"

"A flower," I shrugged.

"Think!" she exclaimed. "Use power to feel. Touch flower to understand...to know it."

I tried focusing on the stupid gardenia in my hand. I concentrated hard on the softness of its petals and their paper-like thinness when suddenly ice began consuming it! The tips of the petals began freezing over! The palm of my hand was like a glacial vortex, robbing the gardenia of its life and color!

"Dios mio!" Rosa exclaimed, moving closer.

The petals were lightening white in colour and studded with beads of ice!

"Diablo Blanco," I muttered, worriedly. "That stupid story...it is me. Isn't it?"

"No!" Rosa grunted, slapping the icy bloom out of my hand and onto the floor. "It only story." A moment later she snapped her fingers together and flicked a flame of fire at the fallen bloom, charring it instantly.

"Maybe you shouldn't teach me," I said, anxiously. "Maybe you—"

"Stop! You is master of own destiny. More you learn more—*how you say*—control, you have."

I bit my lip, fretfully.

"I show you this," she said, tugging at her earlobe.

My brow furrowed, intrigued.

"You no need hand or eye. You only listen."

"The sense of sound?"

"Si," she replied, smiling. "Come."

I followed Rosa to a small bunkie at the back of the yard.

"What is this place?" I asked, following her inside.

"Storage."

I looked around. The small room was full of boxes, mason jars filled with strange things and even more books.

"You know bat?"

"Bat?"

"Si," she said, flapping her arms like a pair of wings.

"Oh, bats. Of course."

"You know how bat find food?"

"Um…" I shrugged.

"Okay. Close eyes," she ordered.

I closed my eyes.

"Listen."

I concentrated on the sounds around me. I heard Rosa shuffling a little, sound of a creaking floorboard, the clinking of mason jars and even the faint squeak of a nearby mouse.

"Still listen," she continued.

A moment later I heard Rosa chanting followed by the sound of rain pouring down outside. Weighty drops pounded the roof of the bunkie. It was a full-on rain shower and it sounded incredibly heavy. The rain continued for several minutes until it stopped altogether. A steady silence resonated.

Then, suddenly, and most unexpectedly, I heard the startling tone of voices echoing. They were distant and nearly inaudible, but they were present. I heard the voice of a man and a young boy too. They were speaking in Spanish. I couldn't understand what they were saying. Then, silence resounded again. I opened my eyes.

"You listen?" Rosa asked, fascinated.

"I heard the rain storm and then I heard voices. A man's voice and I think a boy's voice too."

"Si," she smiled.

"Was someone else in here with us?"

"No. You hear echo."

"Echo?"

"Waves of sound is everywhere. They not die. They always here... moving around us."

"So what I was hearing was a real conversation?"

"Si," she smiled. "You hear conversation between mi husband and mi son in this room from long time ago."

"But how was I even hearing it at all? I mean first I heard the rain—"

"The rain only a spell to conjure sound."

"It wasn't real?"

Rosa shook her head.

"No way," I said, disbelievingly. I pushed opened the bunkie door and went outside. The sky was blue and cloudless and nothing was wet. I walked back inside. "Teach me how to do this," I pleaded, eagerly.

Rosa grinned and turned toward an open book sitting on a nearby shelf. "Every family grimoire write spell a little different."

"Teach me your way."

"Si," she smiled. "Our family do it by tone."

"Tone?"

"Si," she said, her dark eyes widening. "We use vibration and channel quality, source, strength and—*how you say*—potch?"

"Pitch."

"Si," she grinned, "pitch. It is tone that tell us what happen in a place... the past."

"It's like time-shifting without having to travel into the past!"

"Si."

"And no residuals either!"

"Res...idu?"

"Never mind," I said, breathlessly. "This is awesome! You have to let me try. Please."

Rosa grinned. "Wave of sound very powerful energy."

I nodded.

"Ancient Egyptians use waves to make pyramids."

"And bats use sound waves in echolocation! That's why you asked me about bats. I thought you were just mocking me because I'm a vampire!"

She smiled. "In spell, water help make sleeping sound come alive again."

"Sleeping sound?"

"Old sound—*how you say*—doormutt?"

"Oh, dormant!"

"Si, dormant tone. This spell wake them up." She moved her hands to the book and read the page like she was reading a recipe list. She grabbed a nearby mason jar and opened it up.

"Put in bowl," she insisted.

"What is it?"

"Salt."

I nodded, reaching inside the mason jar and extracted a little salt.

"Take candle," she instructed.

I grabbed a small white candle.

"Put candle on table and draw salt circle around."

I put the candle down and sprinkled salt around it as instructed.

"Good. Now make fire to burn it."

I nodded, rubbed my fingertips together until I struck a flame and flicked it at the candle. The contents began to burn.

"Now memorize. Si?"

"I'll try."

Rosa nodded. "*Elementum recolligo huic locus.*"

"*Elementum recolligo huic locus.*"

"*Commodo mihi vestri vox,*" she continued.

"*Commodo mihi vestri vox.*"

"*Elementum unda ego dico vos.*"

"*Elementum unda ego dico vos.*

"*Permissum pluit is est meus nos sic vadum is exsisto.*"

"*Permissum pluit is est meus nos sic vadum is exsisto,*" I repeated.

All of a sudden, rain began to fall against the roof of the bunkie again!

"My god!" I uttered, elatedly. I'd cast a spell!

"Now listen," Rosa instructed.

I closed my eyes and listened intensely, waiting ever so patiently for voices to come into range. Then a voice came in clear. It was Henry—my very own grandfather!

"But Rosie," he said. "I am married. I will not break my vow to her despite how I may feel."

My eyes flew opened.

"Hope!" Rosa said, quickly.

I scowled. I was really starting to like 1957 Rosa, but the fact that she remained a total grandpa stealer was completely repulsive!

"Don't get wrong idea," she pleaded, grasping my hand.

I rolled my eyes.

"Please," she continued. "I not that kind of girl," she maintained.

I pursed my lips and grunted. If only she knew that Henry was my grandfather!

"I not able to help myself. I try. Really I do. I even make spell to stop think of him, but he so wonderful. I not able to get him out of my head!"

I couldn't bear hearing any more. I covered my ears with my hand and hung my head.

"Listen," she pleaded, withdrawing my hands from my ears. "This man different. He kind and sweet and good to me and to my boy Marco when his father leave. You must understand."

"And what about his wife?" I asked, cheekily. "How does she fit into your conscience?"

"I not want to hurt her. She is nice lady too. Please know this. You must believe I not like mi marido...my husband."

"But you're trying to lure a married man into your den of...of *magia*!" I exclaimed, a little too concerned.

"Love is strange thing," she said, putting her arm around me. "It be unkind and tricky. I not choose to love a married man. My heart choose it for me."

I shook my head. "Do you mind if I lay down for a while?"

"Lay down?" she asked, surprised.

"It's been a long day. I've learned so much and I'm exhausted."

"Si," she replied. "And it getting late. It nearly dusk."

Dusk. The sound of the word sent shivers up my spine. I'd nearly forgotten about my secret meeting with Christian by the pink rosebush at dusk!

"I'll just be in my room."

She nodded. I turned to leave.

"Hope," she said, stopping me.

I turned around.

"You understand si?"

"What, about you and this married man?"

She nodded.

"I don't think I'll ever understand."

Her dark eyes sank with sorrow.

"But," I added. "I do believe you."

Her brow furrowed.

"That your heart chose him, not you."

"Gracias," she replied, relieved. "Gracias."

I half-smiled and turned to leave again. Maybe Rosa was right. Love was tricky and totally unpredictable and who the hell was I to judge who her heart decided to choose.

19. Briar Rose

"If you could only see the beast you've made of me,
I held it in but now it seems you've set it running free,
Screaming in the dark, I howl when we're apart,
Drag my teeth across your chest to taste your beating heart."

Howl - Florence And The Machine

There was one thing on my mind when I reached the bedroom: Christian. I had to see him again. I knew it was totally wrong, but I simply had too. Love really was tricky and I knew that better than anyone. I'd seen the man I loved as a human in the late 1700's, as a vampire in my childhood, as a human in my present and now as a strapping, young vampire again in Rosa's past. I loved him no matter *when* I saw him and I needed to see him again straight-away.

Once inside my bedroom, I propped open the window and climbed outside. I scanned the surroundings. Rosa lived in a busy area. It was nothing like Perish. Here, houses were lined up right next door to each other and kids roamed the streets playing. I looked across her yard for the pink rosebush.

"Bingo!" I muttered, to myself, spotting it next to the bunkie.

I looked around for Rosa, making sure that the coast was clear before darting across the lawn.

When I reached the rosebush I looked for Christian. He wasn't there. I walked around to the back of the thorny tangle when suddenly I felt myself being swept off of my feet! Not a moment too soon I felt lips—soft, perfect, full lips, pressing against mine in a kiss!

My body numbed. It was heaven on earth and for this one perfect moment all of my choices seemed worth it.

"I'm sorry," Christian whispered, withdrawing. "I just had to—"

I grinned and pulled him back to my lips again. I wanted more! I wanted to taste his sweet tin-cinnamon and linger in the faultlessness of him as a vampire for just a little longer. I ran my hands up his back, under his T-shirt, like always and dug my nails deep into his flesh.

"Jeeze," he exclaimed, pulling away.

"I'm sorry!" I quickly apologized.

"It's okay," he replied, startled, yet pleased.

"Yeah?"

"Yeah," he mumbled, pulling me close again. His mouth hit mine like an explosion! We fell back into a kiss; an intense and perfect kiss!

His hands roamed my body and I welcomed every touch—despite the fact that it was over my clothes and totally PG. I, on the other hand, simply couldn't seem to get enough of him. I dug my nails into his back again and stroked the breadth of his shoulders, but still I craved for more. I tugged on his shirt. He willingly responded. I withdrew and watched him pull it off, over his head. I ogled his naked chest. It was perfect. *He* was perfect. I pushed him to the ground, amid the rosebush and straddled him. The rose thorns pricked through my flesh, drawing blood, but I didn't care—all I wanted was to feel his lips on me! I kissed him again only this time much slower and deeper.

"*I want you,*" I suddenly heard him saying inside my thoughts.

I lit up like a bonfire! He was back! *We* were back! I missed being inside his thoughts and having him inside mine. Ever since he became human I'd longed for him to be like this again.

"*I want you too,*" I mumbled, using my inner-voice.

His pretty green eyes widened as he withdrew to stare at me.

"You can hear me?" he said, taken aback.

I nodded.

"Who are you?" he asked, astounded.

"The girl of your dreams," I replied. "*Now kiss me again,*" I continued through our secret line of silent communication.

He beamed from ear to ear and pulled me by the back of the neck toward him. We kissed once more and this time it was even more profound. His tongue was gentle and passionate and his hands were more focussed and intense. Before long he'd already slid his hand up my shirt.

"*God!*" he uttered, soundlessly. "*You're not wearing a—*"

"*Sorry.*"

"*You really are the girl of my dreams!*"

I laughed inside. The sound of his feathery, inner-voice was like sweet music to my ears. I ran my hand along his chest; along each muscle and definition. When I reached the top of his jeans, I slid my hand inside.

"*Jesus!*" he exclaimed, noiselessly.

I withdrew my hand and pulled away, but he abruptly guided me back. Before long, I felt him reaching for the zipper on *my* pants. I nearly melted inside. And when he slid them down and caressed my backside, I nearly fainted!

"What are you wearing?" he exclaimed, intrigued.

"I'm...um..." I would have blushed ten shades of red if I could have. "It's called a thong," I replied, awkwardly.

"Thong," he whispered, beaming from ear to ear. "I like it. I like it a lot."

I wanted to be embarrassed, but couldn't. This wasn't some tryst with a hot guy. It was *my* hot guy—the father of the unborn child in my belly. It was Christian! And it was him who had bought me the damn thong in the first place!

"God, you're sexy," he whispered, pulling me close.

A moment later he pressed himself against me. He felt amazing; utterly strong and omnipotent. I wanted him more than I'd ever wanted him before. I tilted my head upward to meet with his and kissed him. He kissed me back.

"*You smell so good,*" he groaned.

"*Like what?*"

"*Not like a girl.*"

"*What does that mean?*" I giggled, soundlessly.

"*Like a...*" he moaned.

"*Like a what?*"

"*Like a vampire,*" he said. "*Oh Aurora!*"

I stopped. Pulled away and looked him in the eye. He was absolutely gorgeous standing there half-naked in front of me, and I wanted him, but there was something morally wrong about what I was doing. He didn't know me yet. Hell—I hadn't even been born yet! I felt as though I was manipulating him into wanting me in the same way that I wanted him. This situation was impossible. And I'd be damned (even more than I already was) if I'd let him screw me while calling me by a name other than my own!

"Hey," he said, tenderly. "Is it something I—"

"No. It isn't you."

He sat on the ground beside me. His fair skin was also covered in a bloody stippling of rose thorn prickles. I slid back into my pants and watched as his cuts healed over almost instantly.

"Just so you know," he said, matter-of-factly. "I'm not one of those fast guys."

"Oh?"

"I don't do this sort of thing often."

"Is that so?"

"In fact, I never do it."

I smiled, relieved. At the very least I knew for certain that he hadn't lied to me about any indiscretions over the years.

"Hey," he whispered, stroking my jaw line. "I'm trying to read your mind, but..."

I grinned. "It's a little trick I learned." I wanted to tell him the truth—that I'd learned how to block certain thoughts from him, but I knew I couldn't.

"Can I tell you a secret?"

"Sure," I said, pulling my sweater back into place.

"I wanted to kiss you from the moment I first saw you today."

"You did."

He nodded. "Hey," he continued, playfully. "Can I tell you another secret?"

I nodded again.

"And don't get upset."

"Believe me I won't."

"I feel like we've met before."

I perked up, intrigued.

"In fact, I think we have met before."

"You do?" I asked, keenly.

"That's why I wanted to kiss you."

"What do you mean?"

"When we met before," he said. "It was you that kissed me."

"I did?"

He nodded, grinning. "And it was the best kiss of my life!" He leaned back. "A man doesn't forget that kind of kiss. To be honest I was convinced that you weren't even real! I contemplated that you were some kind of figment of my imagination, an angel or a siren even!" He laughed.

I smiled, knowing full well that he was recalling the time I kissed him on the HMS Ambrose.

"The Ambrose," I said, wryly.

"Why yes! You know of my ship?"

I nodded.

"So it really was you!"

"It was me," I divulged, guilt suddenly underscoring my tone. "I shouldn't have done it then and I shouldn't be doing this now."

"What are you talking about Aurora?"

"First, my name is not Aurora."

"It's not?"

"And I'm not Rosa's niece."

"Well I kinda figured that."

"I never should have met with you here." I rose to my feet. "Truthfully, I never should have come here at all."

"What are you?" he asked, standing up beside me. "The way that you were able to visit me so long ago on the Ambrose and then here again...I mean I know you're a vampire, I can smell that, but you're clearly something more."

I smiled, leaned in close and kissed him on the cheek. "I am El Diablo Blanco," I uttered, sorrowfully, turning away.

"El Diab...the White Devil? I don't understand."

"It's better this way," I said, leaving. "And Christian," I called out, turning back. "Can I ask you a favor?"

"Anything."

"Stay away from me while I'm here."

"But—"

"Please."

He ran his hands through his hair, like he always did when he was frustrated.

I turned around again and continued walking through the thorns, away from the rosebush and away from Christian.

"I don't even know your real name?" he called out.

I didn't respond. I just continued walking, my heart breaking all over again with every step I took.

20. Off To Work We Go

"On a cloud of sound I drift in the night.
Any place it goes is right.
Goes far, flies near.
To the stars away from here."

Magic Carpet Ride - Steppenwolf

"Hope," a familiar voice whispered.

"What?" I groaned, hiding beneath the serape.

"What are you doing here again?"

I pulled back the blanket. "Not you!" It was Eradan and he was pissed. I covered myself with the serape once more.

"You shouldn't be here."

"You shouldn't be here either!" I hiccupped, an empty bottle of Tequila lying next to me in the bed. "H-hey there mister, how dare you drop this huge bomb on me about being my son and then disappear! Honestly!"

He ran his fingers through his hair, just like his father, and sighed.

"Don't you do that," I shouted. "That's a Christian move—not yours!"

"Running my hands through my hair?"

I nodded.

He eyed the empty bottle of Tequila. "Are you drunk?"

"No," I said, burping.

"You're wasting precious time!"

"Time is of the essence!" I mocked, in his stodgy voice.

"Hope, I need you stop this bullshit right now!"

"That's no way to talk to your mother!"

"Oh please," he groaned, pulling me out of bed.

"Don't!" I protested. "And why do you call me Hope anyway? If I really am your mother you should call me mom...or mum...or mummy..." I started laughing. "Let me look at you," I said, eyeballing his face. I pushed his circular spectacles atop his head and grinned. "You look like your father."

"Gee, you think?" he mocked.

"And you're sarcastic like him too."

"C'mon," he said, putting my shoes on my feet. "You really must get going."

"Where? Why? What's the point? Haven't you heard? I'm El Diablo Blanco!"

"El who?"

"The White Devil! The one that steals all happiness from the universe and kills everyone she ever cared about with her icy magic."

"Don't be ridiculous!"

"Look," I said, angrily. "Don't come to see me for a while. I need some space from you...okay?"

"What?" he said, taken aback.

"I can't handle thinking that you're my son...and you're in my belly right now...and...and just leave me alone for a bit!"

"But—"

"No but! I'm learning to harness my power from Rosa. I'm trying to figure all this out for myself. I don't need you popping in and out all the time helping me or whatever it is you're doing."

"Now listen. I don't think that it's—"

"I don't care!" I exclaimed. "If you really are my son, then you will respect my wishes!" I exclaimed, accidently knocking the empty Tequila bottle out of the bed and onto the floor. It smashed into zillions of pieces!

"Hope!" Rosa shouted, suddenly bursting through the door.

"Hola!" I said, waving.

"What this?" she said, spotting the broken bottle on the floor. "Tequila? You drunk?"

"Si senorita!" I froze and looked around. "Eradan," I whispered. "Where are you?"

"Who you talk to?" Rosa asked, placing the waste paper bin in the centre of the room.

"No one," I lied. I looked around again. "Eradan," I whispered again, but he really was gone.

Rosa waved her index finger in a circular motion around the glass on the floor. "Moveo moti motum," she chanted in Latin and suddenly, the glass began moving!

"W-O-W!" I gushed, impressed.

Like a stream of water cycling down the drain, the glass began travelling toward the waste paper bin in the center of the room.

"How are you doing this?" I asked, amazed.

"Easy."

"Easy for you. Not so easy for the White Devil!"

"Oh Hope," she said, collecting the bin and moving it to the side of the bedroom. "I never should tell you that story."

"Too late now!" I laughed, pathetically.

She sat beside me on the bed. "I not tell it to make you misery. I tell you only as warning."

"Well it scared the shit outta me alright!"

"I think about it after and I think maybe you was right."

"I was?"

"About being apprentice."

"But you said that's not why I came. You said—"

"I know what I say."

"So you changed your mind now?"

She took a deep breath. "Hope, you know how *magia* work?"

I shrugged. "I don't know anything anymore!"

"*Magia* is a gift. It taught down in families from one generation to next."

"Yeah, yeah. You lectured me on this already in the present."

"Okay, then you know some."

"Not really."

"Well, you know that mi madre taught me and I plan to teach me son...but—"

"He ran off with a cute Cuban girl to live in Miami. I get it."

"Si," she replied.

"So what's the problem?"

"Problem is I not suppose to teach you. You're mama suppose to teach you."

"But I no have my mama," I said, mimicking her accent. "Or grandmamma...or daddy or even step-daddy...or—"

"Okay, okay," she interrupted. "I see why you come here."

"But I've got a grimoire! Yes indeedy!"

"Bueno," she said.

"I didn't bring it with me though...guess I forgot to pack it in my time-travellers' carry-on!" I laughed, with myself.

Rosa grinned, confused.

"Henry told me to trust you," I said, hiccupping.

"Henry?" Her eyes widening.

"My sweet Rosie...she's like family," I said, mimicking Henry's voice.

"Henry say this?"

"Si."

Rosa's face flushed with color. She beamed from ear to ear.

"Wait a second here. Don't go gettin' any ideas about my grandpa just 'cause—"

"Henry is you grandpa?"

"Shit! I gotta shut up. I keep making things worse. I keep opening my big mouth and—"

"Oh Hope," she interrupted, abruptly, "I not know this. I am so sorry you have to hear conversation in bunkie. If I know he was your grandpa—"

"Then what? You wouldn't continue pursuing him?" I laughed. "Forget it. You're heart chose him—no you, si?" I smiled. "After all, the heart wants what the heart wants."

"Si, but I feel so bad. I feel you must think I am terrible person."

"I don't know what I think! But I do want to you keep training me."

Rosa nodded. "Of course," she replied. "I keep train you."

"Okay," I replied, taken aback. "But can we continue manana? I've got this killer headache."

"No. We should keep going. You are—how you say—on the roll!"

"On *a* roll, Rosa, not *the* roll."

"Si," she smiled, whipping off the serape. "I make you remedy to fix headache."

"Oh no! I don't trust your remedies."

"What that mean?"

"Oh, never mind," I said, realizing that I was opening my big mouth again.

She grabbed me by the waist and propped my arm around her shoulders.

"Rosa," I said, leaning on her for support. "You sure are nice when you're young."

"Why? I not so nice when old?"

I laughed.

"I see," she said, nodding.

"You're just so pretty...and so tough. I like how tough you are. It's... it's...it's really cool."

"Cool?" she giggled, confused.

"You smell good too and sure do the shit outta magic!"

"Gracias?" she smiled, perplexed.

"I wish I could do magic like you."

"You will Hope."

"Rosa," I said, holding onto her.

"Si?

"I never knew my grandmother and my mom died before I could really remember her."

"I sorry to hear Hope, but maybe you should not tell me anymore—"

"You know something," I said, interrupting her.

"Que?"

"Guess you're kinda like the closest thing to a mom I ever had."

She smiled.

"Rosa."

"Si?"

"Thanks."

"De nada, nina. De nada."

Rosa's version of a remedy for drunkenness, was a horrific drink made from stewed lima beans, essence of sea urchin and mushrooms. I felt sober, but utterly nauseous. I really didn't like Rosa's concoctions—even if they did work.

"Now thrust!" she ordered.

I waved my hand in the air. The wooden baseball bat wiggled back and forth before tearing off across the lawn.

"Bueno!" she shouted. "This time thrust then flick. Now go."

I waved my hand in the air, bringing the baseball bat to life again. It hovered above the ground before tearing toward me. I flicked my finger at it. It froze instantly.

"Excelente!"

A moment later the icy bat fell to the ground. I walked toward it, rubbed my fingers together until I drew a flame and thawed the bat out.

"Good, Hope. You are quick learner."

"You're a good teacher."

She smiled.

"Will you teach me more spells?"

"I think we no have time for that. Besides, real *magia* come from elements—natural world, fancy enchantments come later. Learn this first. Si?"

I nodded.

"You learn how to create fire from within you now. Si?"

I snapped my fingers, drawing a flame again.

"Good. And water, even when frozen, is *you* essence."

"Or my curse."

"Don't say that."

"But if I really am El Diablo Blanco, then—"

"Stop! I not want to hear any more about Diablo Blanco." She grabbed me by the shoulders and stared into my eyes. "You is master of own fate. You make own destiny. Si?"

"Si," I nodded, reluctantly.

"You need learn about earth next."

"You mean the globe with continents on it which orbits around the sun?"

"No. I mean earth—matter, this terrestrial world we live."

"Oh that earth," I replied, grinning.

"Mi madre taught that earth is like mother goddess. You know this?"

"Not so much mother goddess, I know mother earth...not personally of course."

Rosa shook her head. "You like joking."

"I'm sorry Rosa. It's just a lot to take in. I *am* ready."

"Si, she replied. "To channel the power of mother goddess...mother earth...you must feel own strength in creation."

"Okay. And how do I do that?"

"Easy!"

"Can you elaborate?"

Rosa waved her hand above my stomach. "You are mother goddess. You have already begun own strength in creation."

"The baby?"

"Si. Bebe. Your love make baby grow. You channel love and use power of earth."

"How?"

"Shh," she insisted. "Think."

I closed my eyes and tried focusing on the rock as it sat deep inside me. I thought of Eva being pregnant. I remembered how Rosa and I helped her deliver baby Stromboli that day in the forest. I thought of Christian and how much I loved him and how much I wanted to see him be a father. I thought of Eradan. I thought of all he had told me and wondered whether he really was telling me the truth; that he was in fact my son.

"Open your eyes," Rosa said, her voice elated.

I opened my eyes. Large rocks, cement bricks, small pebbles and even shards of dirt peppered the air like snowflakes!

"Beautiful," she gushed.

I grinned. I could feel the power surging through me and although it frightened me a little, it empowered me too.

"You *is* quick learner," Rosa insisted.

"Well a student is only as good as her teacher."

Another smile swept its way across her face.

Slowly, I eased on my power and the rocks gently fell back into place on the ground.

"I think I need a break," I said, exhaustedly.

"Si," Rosa said, lighting up yet another cigarette.

"Mind if I take a walk up the road?"

"I don't know..."

"I promise I'll be careful. I won't talk to anyone."

Rosa bit her scarlet, stained lip.

"Please Rosa...please, please, please,"

"Okay. But you not do any funny-business."

"You're the best!" I exclaimed, kissing her on the cheek.

She smiled. I turned to leave.

I stopped walking. "Um, Rosa?"

"Si?"

"Do you have a few bucks I could borrow?"

"Bucks?"

"Dinero so I can buy a soda at the corner store?"

"Dios mio," she mumbled, under her breath. "You is just like Marco." She reached into her stiletto and pulled out a one dollar bill. "Always needing something." She handed me the dollar. "And bring back change!"

I eyed the dollar bill. "Will there be any change?"

"How much you think soda cost?"

"I don't know, maybe two to four bucks depending on where you're buying it."

She gasped. "Tell me I is rich old lady in future!"

I laughed, suddenly remembering it was 1957. "I'll bring back your change," I said, sweetly. "And thanks."

Rosa grunted, but I could tell that it was happy grunt.

As I walked along the road I kept my head down. I tried blending in and not making any kind of scene whatsoever. The air was fresh—less pollution than I was used to, and the sky was beautifully clear and blue. The sound of little kids running and playing made me smile. A group of rough-looking, teenage boys were hanging out in front of the little corner store. I edged closer.

"Excuse me," I said, trying to enter the shop.

"Where you wanna go lady?" the tall boy asked.

"Inside," I replied.

The boys laughed.

"I'd like to go inside too," the boy with a ducktail hairstyle muttered rudely.

I ignored him and continued trying to push past.

"Hey," the tall boy said. "We can't let you pass. You ain't said the magic word yet."

I stepped back and rolled my eyes. "Please," I exclaimed, mockingly.

The boys snickered and whispered to each other.

"Please what?" he continued.

"Oh c'mon," I said, edgily, forcing my way through them.

"You're a feisty one," the boy, exclaimed, laughing. "I bet you like it rough," he continued, putting his hands on me, when all of a sudden I felt swept off my feet again!

21. Prince Charming

"I'm so en-captured, got me wrapped up in your touch,
Feel so enamored, hold me tight within your clutch,
How do you do it, got me losing every breath,
Why did you kiss me to make my heart beat out my chest?"

Latch – Disclosure featuring Sam Smith

I turned and watched as Christian single-handedly knocked all four of the boys off their feet and onto the ground.

"That was...amazing!" I said, impressed.

The boys rolled around on pavement in pain, whimpering and whining.

"And are you alright?" he asked, gentlemanly.

"I'm fine."

"C'mon," he said, taking my hand and leading me away from the store.

"Thank you for that," I smiled.

"Well those punks deserved it." He tugged on my hand.

"How'd you just so happen to be there to help me?"

He smirked. I smirked back.

"I thought I told you to stay away from me." My voice was teasing.

"Did you?" He grinned.

"Yeah."

He smirked and tightened his hold on my hand.

"Where are you taking me?"

"A little park, just up the way."

"No rosebushes?"

He bit his lip and ran his long fingers through his hair, just like his son.

"About that," he said, evenly.

"Just forget about it."

"I can't. In fact, I don't really want too!"

I half-smiled.

"Don't get the wrong idea."

"What wrong idea?"

"That I'm one of those guys."

"One of what guys?" I pressed, playfully.

"You know."

"No, Christian. Enlighten me."

He stopped walking. He planted his hands on his hips. "Just know that sort of thing doesn't happen to me. I live a rather...conservative life."

"Oh!" I said, pretending to be surprised.

"And yesterday was very out of character for me."

"Really? Because you certainly didn't seem the least bit uncomfortable with any of it!"

He laughed. He was so attractive when he laughed.

"And what about you?" he taunted.

"What about me?"

"Clearly that wasn't your first tumble under the rosebush."

"Excuse me!" I exclaimed.

"Well I mean...um..."

"I know what you mean and I'm terribly insulted," I joked.

"Don't be," he said, self-assuredly. "I've never met anyone quite like you. It's...inspiring. *You're* inspiring."

"I suppose I'll take that as a compliment."

"Please do. It was meant as one." He tugged on my hand and led me through the park toward the shade of an old willow tree. We sat together in the grass.

"I just wanted to apologize for my behavior."

I laughed.

"Is it funny to you?"

"Well, yeah. It's a little funny."

"But why?"

"Why you think you need to apologize to me. We both knew what we were doing."

"That may be so, but I still feel as though I need to apologize for behaving so...so..."

"So carnal?"

He gasped.

"Lustful?"

"That's not quite what I was going to say."

"How about wanton...or sexy or I know...horny—"

"Jesus!" he exclaimed, quickly reaching across to silence me with his hand. "I can't believe you just said that and in public!"

I laughed a muffled laugh from beneath his palm and urged him to release me.

"So inspiring," he teased, withdrawing his hand.

"I'm inspiring because I'm good with adjectives?"

"No. Because you're good with everything." He grabbed me by the waist and pulled me close.

"I can't," I whispered, tearing away.

"Why?"

"It's complicated. I'm complicated."

"I like complicated."

I smiled.

"Why were you walking the streets alone?" he asked, changing the subject.

"I needed to get out."

"It's not the safest part of town, you know."

"Good thing I have you around to follow me!"

He laughed. "I can't get you out of my mind," he whispered, tenderly.

I smiled.

"Truth is I haven't gotten you out of my mind since my sailing days on the old HMS Ambrose!"

My smile faded. Flashes of me once again rewriting history underscored the guilt in my expression.

"Hey," he said, softly, reaching out to touch my face. "Don't be sad."

I looked up at him and half-smiled, desperately working to hold back the tears of blood that had already begun welling in my eyes.

"I'm sorry," he suddenly apologized, "for my beastly behavior at the rosebush. No decent man would have treated you the way that I did. And if you'll forgive me, I promise to prove myself to you in the way that I should have from the beginning."

I smiled, flattered. It was endearing watching him trying so hard to impress me.

"But first," he said, eagerly. "Tell me your real name!"

I grabbed my face and hid within my hands, desperate to protect what little anonymity I had left.

"Please?"

"I can't."

"Why?"

"Believe me, I want to tell you—I want to tell you everything."

"But you can't."

I nodded.

"May I ask you one more question?"

"Sure, but that doesn't mean I can answer it!"

"May I kiss you?"

My eyes widened with surprise. His refined, well-mannered, gentlemanliness impressed me even more than usual. God he was hot! And it was only a kiss. I'd kissed him hundreds of times—maybe even zillions! What was the harm in one more?

"Yes," I whispered, leaning closer and within an instant his lips were upon mine.

His kiss was tender and passionate and exactly what every woman wishes their first kiss to feel like. He was a gentleman, but assertive. I felt wanted without feeling slutty. His hands stayed in his lap as did mine. Today wasn't about making-it in the rosebush; it was something deeper, something a little like falling in love.

"*You are everything,*" he whispered, through our silent internal connection.

I beamed.

"*It's like you were made for me,*" he continued.

I felt butterflies stirring in the pit of my stomach.

"*You make me feel like I could be falling—*"

"No!" I exclaimed, pulling away. "You can't!"

"I can't what?"

"This. You can't get to know me. You can't fall in love with me now!"

"Who said anything about love?"

"You did, in your thoughts."

"What's so bad about love," he continued, stroking my arm.

"Everything!" I stood up and started walking away.

"Stop!" he said, grasping my hand. "Don't leave."

I stared into his mesmerizing green eyes and smiled.

"Please," he continued. "I lost you once before. I couldn't bear to lose you again."

"Truth is," I smiled. "I don't want to go, but I have to."

"At least tell me your name? Leave me with something to know you by."

I swallowed hard. "Hope," I said, recklessly. "My name is Hope."

"Hope," he grinned. My name was sweet on his lips, just as it always had been.

I closed my eyes and turned to leave. I didn't look back and he didn't call out after me either, but I knew he was there; following behind like my own personal guardian angel.

It was dark by the time I returned to Rosa's house. She was standing on the porch, smoking another cigarette. She had her hand on her hip and she looked mad.

"Hi!" I said, approaching.

"Where you been?"

"At the store."

"You lie like child!" She whipped open the front door and rushed inside.

"What do you mean?" I said, chasing after her.

"You not go to store."

"Well I tried, but there were these boys giving me a hard time."

Rosa grunted—and not the good kind. She blew a puff of smoke at me before tearing off toward the kitchen.

"I know you not go to store," she said, sitting at the kitchen table.

"How would you know?"

"I went to store and look for you." She reached for her half-empty cup of coffee and placed it in front of her.

"I'm sorry. I should have come right back."

"Why you lie to me?" she asked, waving her finger through the air, coaxing the sugar bowl to pour itself into her cup.

"I didn't mean to lie. I did go to the store. I just went someplace else too."

"Where you go?" she asked, spinning her finger above her coffee cup, mixing in the sugar with her magic.

"The park," I divulged, sitting beside her.

"By yourself?"

"With Christian."

"No!" she exclaimed. "I thought you not want to take risk or make change?"

"I know. Believe me, I know."

"Then why you do this?"

"I don't know!" I said feeling the red tears welling in my eyes again. "I'm making a mess. It's just like you said. I'm the White Devil and my love for Christian is making me do things—stupid things that I know are changing things in the future!"

"Shh," she consoled, wiping the bloody tears from my eyes. "I not know what things is like in your time, but I know this much. Life for living. You don't take risk—you don't live."

Her voice was curative. I forced myself to stop crying.

"Then," she smiled, "*you* take bigger risk than most peoples." She laughed and pulled me close. I fell into the circle of her warm arms. Rosa's embrace was just the kind of compassion I needed.

"Thanks," I whimpered.

"You not need thank me. You just girl. Girls fall in love. Girls make mistake."

I laughed.

"Love tricky I tell you. Sometime you not get to choose who you love."

"Or even *when*."

"Si," she replied, tightening her hold.

"Oh Rosa, what am I gonna do?"

"You gonna do what you came for," she said, withdrawing. "You gonna keep learning *magia*."

I nodded.

"You stand now."

I rose to my feet.

"You learn how channel air now. Si?"

"Cool."

"Close eyes."

I closed my eyes.

"Wave hand around."

I waved my arms up and down.

"No! Not like silly clown. Wave like you touch the space. Tickle the space. Now try."

Slowly, I moved my fingers through the air.

"Feel air around you. Feel it like it not empty, but like it too is real and take up space. Si?"

I smiled and continued moving my fingers.

"You move air with your power and make window."

"Window?"

"Si. A window... something you want to see or maybe someone else want you to see."

"I don't understand," I said opening my eyes.

"Okay. Think like this. You open yourself to energy in you, energy around you and even energy of others. You understand?"

"I...I'm not sure exactly."

"Think like...foggy window."

"What?"

"You want to see what happen on other side of foggy window. What you do?"

"I wipe the window and clear it."

"Si," she said, grinning. "You wipe window—air...the space, and you see more clearly."

I closed my eyes again and touched the air. I felt the air not as empty this time, but as virtually tangible. I streamed my hands through the air above me as though I was clearing a foggy window and suddenly everything changed! As I fluttered my fingers, the air felt like water and I could feel it moving and flowing against my skin!

"It's amazing!" I exclaimed.

"Bueno."

I continued moving my hands, lingering in the touchable air that surrounded me when out of the blue it happened again!

"No!" I shrieked, horrified.

22. Through The Looking Glass

"There's a crack in the mirror,
And a bloodstain on the bed,
There's a crack in the mirror,
And a bloodstain on the bed."

Bloodletting (The Vampire Song) – Concrete Blonde

The eyes were back! They were staring down at me just like every other time! I continued watching when suddenly they began to change. Eyes turned to small balls of fire and then the fire turned to a searing sheet of whiteness. The sky lit up like a giant, celestial movie screen. I was front row-center in the audience.

I saw a corridor. It was long, white and very sterile looking. I'd seen it before—in Ryan's memories. I continued watching. There was a large set of double doors at the end of corridor. I walked through them and into yet another long, white, sterile corridor. People in white lab coats crowded the halls. There were rooms too, dozens of them, lining the walls. The next thing I knew was being led to a room marked *Specimen #Q1153* on the door.

Inside the room I saw a man in a white lab coat standing over what looked like a patient on an operating table. The doctor moved. I froze! It was Richard—my father, the man who raised me! Then, suddenly, the patient's face came into focus too. It was Christian!

BOOM! My lethargic heart nearly exploded in my chest! Bloody tears streamed down my face. Power surged like wildfire inside my veins when swiftly the vision disappeared.

Blackness enveloped me. I opened my eyes. I was back in Ambrose House again.

"Good god, I thought you'd never return!" Henry's voice was worried.

All of a sudden the room started to shake again!

"Shit!" Eva shouted, "Damn residuals!"

Everyone grabbed hold of something to stabilize themselves until the tremors subsided.

"I'm sorry!" I called out. "I tried to change as little as I could."

"You're crazy!" Eva snarled, in reply. "This earthquake isn't little! You're destroying everything with your time travelling escapades!"

Just then the shaking stopped. I looked around, concerned. "How's Rosa?" I asked, anxiously.

Henry touched her. "Still breathing."

"Did it even work?" Baptiste asked, eagerly. "Did you learn what you needed to do the spell?"

"I don't think I need the spell anymore."

"Why not?" he continued.

"I saw the vision again. Only this time I saw the whole thing!"

"What did you see?" Henry asked, intrigued.

"It was like a message...a glimpse of something. Someone wanted me to see this."

"What did you see, damn it!" Eva's voice was testy.

"I saw Christian!"

"We all saw Christian, Blondie!" she continued. "His TV interview aired last night."

"That's not what I mean. I saw him in New York in a hospital, being...I don't know, examined by Richard."

"Richard your father?" Ryan asked.

"Yeah."

"I didn't know he was working for *them*," Ryan exclaimed.

"Neither did I," I said, getting up from the couch.

"Where are you going?" Henry asked.

"Big Apple. I've gotta get Christian outta there."

"Well I'm coming with you," Baptiste shouted.

"Like hell!" Eva snarled. "You ain't leaving me here with this baby!"

"I'm coming too," Ryan added.

"No. You stay," I insisted. "We need someone to hold down the fort while we're gone."

"I owe Christian a life-debt, Hope. He saved me in Mexico—he saved all of us girls that day."

I nodded.

"Screw this!" Eva snorted. "I wanna go too!"

Suddenly Rosa began to stir.

"Rosa?" I said, eagerly.

"Si," she grumbled. "I is okay. You go. I watch bebe."

Eva's eyes lit up. "Gracias mi amigo! Gracias!"

I rushed to Rosa's side. "You alright?" I asked, concerned.

"Si. Not dead."

"Do you remember..."

"Si. I remember just like it yesterday. And I know you ready. Go!"

"Thanks," I said, kissing her on the forehead.

"What the hell was that?" Eva snarled. "When did you two become all buddy-buddy?"

"1957," I said, grinning. "Now come on Eva, we've got a rescue to plan."

"Where will you go?" Henry asked.

"We'll start with Richard," I explained. "He was my father once. He loved me. You can't just stop that."

"But didn't he disown you at his wedding?" Eva's voice was surly, like usual.

I shrugged.

"Richard used to be one of us," Henry added. "Even you liked him too Eva."

She half-smiled.

"He was a friend to us all at one time." Henry's voice was soft. "If he works for *them*, then he's your way inside."

"But you said he was examining Christian!" Baptiste shouted. "He ain't just gonna let us walk in there and take Christian out—that is if he's even still—"

"Don't say it B!" My tone was harsh. "Christian *is* still alive and we're gonna get him out."

"How?" Eva snapped. "Cause the good old days of pillaging and plundering are over! We're heading into *their* territory. You need a plan, Blondie and something that doesn't involve using your time-bending trickery. You need an iron clad plan that will get us in without getting us killed!"

"I know," I replied.

"So?" she rebutted. "What is it?"

"I don't know."

"Henry?" Baptiste insisted. "This is when you usually give us insight."

Henry nodded. "I'm afraid I just don't know what to say." He heaved a sigh.

"I do," Ryan suddenly interjected.

"You do?" I asked, surprised.

"I worked for them forever. I know a few things."

"Like what?" Eva snorted.

"Like where that medical bay is Hope saw in her vision."

"So?" Eva countered. "That might get us to Christian, but it ain't gonna get us inside...past their security systems."

"You're right," she replied. "But that's when we can be grateful Fate has decided to bless us with her presence!"

"What are you talking about?" I asked with deep interest.

"Pedro worked headquarters' security for over 75 years. He's just the man we need escorting us around."

"Who the hell is Pedro?" Eva snapped.

"He's a friend...and expat and he's been staying in the boathouse with Andy and Sara."

"Who?" Eva continued, confused.

With all that had been going on in my own life I had nearly forgotten about our boathouse visitors. "Forget about Eva," I continued. "Tell me more."

"Andy worked their computer department—hell, he pretty much *ran* the department singlehandedly! He eats, sleeps and thinks in code. He can literally get us authorized into any part of headquarters just by working his magic on the computer. And Sara, well, she worked in-take."

"In-take?" I asked.

"When new recruits were brought to HQ, Sara and her team were the officers that would conduct all the necessary in-take protocol."

"Like slicing a whole in your arm and shoving in a feeding device?" Eva's voice was bitter.

"No. Implants were done by the medics." Ryan turned to look at me. "Highly skilled surgeons, humans even, like Richard were acquired by HQ to perform such tasks."

My heart sank a little deeper in my chest. Was Richard putting an implant in Christian in my vision? My body froze.

"We've got to get going," I pleaded, urgently.

"I'll get my friends," Ryan said, "I'll try talking them into helping. It won't be easy. After all they just defected."

"Eva and I will come too," Baptise said, flexing his muscles. "Just in case they need a little...convincing."

I nodded and watched them leave. I turned to Henry.

"Take care of Rosa," I said, kissing them both on the forehead.

"Take care of you," he replied, touching my hand.

I smiled before zooming up the stairs to my bedroom at super-sonic, vampire speed. I grabbed one of Christian's old army-duffle bags and looked for some clothes. As I rummaged through one of my drawers, I spotted my grandmother's truth mirror at the bottom. I pulled it out.

It was still shattered from being tossed across the room. Surely, had I been a better witch, I could have said something freaky in Latin to fix the crack, but I wasn't there just yet. I grabbed the mirror and dared myself to look into it. When Henry gave me my grandmother's mirror he told me that it had the power to show the truth, not just a reflection.

I stole a glimpse. My jaw dropped open! I was pale, ghostly pale, and my hair was entirely white and covered in patches of ice! I looked dreadful, sickly and irrefutably like the description of Rosa's El Diablo Blanco! I couldn't bare the sight of myself any longer. I tossed the mirror back into the drawer and turned away.

I tried forcing my thoughts away from that stupid legend and started focusing my attention on the quest ahead. I wasn't packing for a holiday—I was packing for a rescue mission. I was definitely gonna need a little more than thongs and tank-tops to save Christian this time.

I opened the large, wooden chest at the side of the room. It was Christian's toy-box, so to speak. It was his arsenal, but not just any arsenal. Christian liked artillery and he'd collected some pretty awesome pieces over the years. There were antique pistols and muskets from his navy days aboard the HMS Ambrose and tons of daggers and swords, some that even dated as far back as Neolithic times!

I pulled out the 1873 Colt. It was one of Christian's prized possessions, maybe because it was Billy the Kid's, legendary, lost revolver. Nevertheless, the Kid's colt wasn't gonna get through modern day airport scanners. I searched deeper. I found Napolean's gold-encrusted sword and one of King Henry VIII's daggers. Hell, even had I found Excalibur in Christian's toy-box, there was no way I'd get it on an airplane! I needed weaponry that wasn't made of metal. I needed something lethal, concealable and undetectable. I dug deeper.

I touched the edge of something slim and sharp. I pulled it from the chest. It was about the size of my hand and rather antiquated. The entire weapon was carved of bone. I couldn't tell whether it was animal or human bone, but it didn't matter. It was compact and sharp and could be easily smuggled through airport scanners.

I grabbed the bone dagger, shoved it in my bag and headed downstairs, hell-bent on kicking the shit outta *them* and bringing my sweet Christian home.

23. The Yellow Brick Road

"You're a rich girl, and you've gone too far,
'Cause you know it don't matter anyway,
You can rely on the old man's money,

Rich Girl — Hall & Oats

Most people knew it as The Big Apple. I knew it as The *Poisoned* Apple. It was the leading gateway for legal immigration into the United States, and also the foremost portal for vampire expats fleeing the Society for the freedom-land in the South.

I couldn't help but weirdly connect the reality of NYC and the Underground Railroad with this bizarre new fight for freedom. Granted the world had changed somewhat since the days of slavery. And this new suppression didn't care whether you were black, white, or whatever, but the similarities were striking.

"This is where you grew up?" Eva exclaimed, as we reached Richard's upstate mansion.

"Yeah," I said, suddenly recalling my formative years; the many missed birthdays and constant abandonment.

As the cab rounded the long driveway I started getting cold feet.

"Esperanza," Baptiste purred. "Why'd you wanna leave a place like this?"

I looked ahead, to the main house. It was just as I remembered: imposing and luxurious. The trees and shrubbery were all finely manicured, and the house itself was like a classic castle in the distance. I remembered likening myself to poor Rapunzel a little; empathizing with the way she'd been trapped to live inside her castle with an evil step-parent too.

"Hope," Ryan said. "It's just nerves. Don't worry. You got this."

I smiled at her before getting out of the cab.

The four of us marched toward the front door. We were quite the motley mix of freaks; Eva in her leatherette cat-suit, Ryan with her geisha-like appearance, Baptiste and his ridiculously huge muscles and menacing head tattoos and me with my weird frosty-tipped hair.

I rang the doorbell.

"Man," Eva gushed, "even the bell sounds expensive!"

The front door opened. A short Latin looking woman in housekeeping attire stood before us. I didn't recognize her.

"Hola," she greeted, nervously.

"Hi," I replied, "we're here to see Richard."

"You have appointment?"

"No."

"Sorry," she said, closing the door.

"Wait!" I exclaimed. "I'm his daughter. My name is Hope."

Her brown eyes widened.

"Do you know if Martha's around?"

"Martha not work here no more."

"Really?" I said, shocked. Martha had worked for Richard for as long as I could remember. She was older, sweet and a really good cook too. In fact she made the best meatloaf I'd ever tasted! I couldn't imagine her not working here anymore.

"The Mrs. is here," the maid asserted.

"No!" I exclaimed. "That's okay. Thanks for your help." I turned around to leave.

"Hope," Eva said, grabbing my arm. "Just veil her. She'll tell us where to find him."

I turned back, only this time instead of facing the maid, I was facing Richard's latest bimbo, Cindy.

"Well I'll be a monkey's uncle!" she giggled, goofily. "Is that you Hope?"

Cindy was young, dumb and a self-described gold digger. As a former Miss. Texas, she fit my father's MO for potential wives perfectly. She agreed to marry him after only two dates and several bottles of Dom Perignon. She had blonde hair that was so big it literally framed her face like a mane. Her Southern accent added to her charm. It was almost too easy to make-fun of Cindy.

"Hello Cindy," I greeted.

"I must be dreamin'!" she squeaked. "I can't believe you're really here. And what have you done to your hair?"

"Nothing," I dismissed. "I'm looking for Richard. Do you know where he is?"

"Um, he's either at the hospital golfing or at the club working. I'm always so confused!" She laughed. "But you know, sugar, I don't think he's gonna be all too happy to see you."

"Oh?"

"Well you just up and left with that cute boy, right there in the middle of our weddin'! Richie was madder than a skunk on a barbeque that night."

I nodded.

"He told me I ain't ever to invite you in if you came callin' again." She giggled. "Ain't that just the silliest thing you ever heard—a father not wantin' to invite his own daughter back inside the house that she grew up in!"

"Yeah, real silly," I replied, dejectedly.

"Want me to tell him you were here?"

"No. Don't bother."

"Sure, honey." She smiled. "Well it was real nice seeing you again." She eyeballed Eva, Baptiste and Ryan. "And your...friends too," she said, nervously.

"Yeah," I said, discouraged. "You too."

We turned to leave. Cindy shut the door behind us.

"So much for starting with Richard," Eva barked.

Just then a long, black limousine pulled up in the circular driveway. My heart thumped in my chest. The back door swung open.

"Richard!" I exclaimed.

He got out of the car. He looked the same as always; tall, slim, salt and peppery hair. He slammed the door shut behind him.

"Hope," he said, beckoning me closer.

His tone wasn't angry and he didn't seem altogether surprised to see me either.

"How are you?" I asked, walking toward him.

"Much better now," he whispered.

My brow furrowed. "Are you pissed off that I'm here?"

"Why would I be? I was the one that summoned you."

"What?"

"It sure took you long enough though." He put his hands on his hips.

"What are you talking about Richard?" My voice was curt.

"I kept projecting...hoping you'd listen. I sent eyes and balls of fire and—"

"That was you?" I said, taken aback.

"Yes. I needed you, but I couldn't call you or text you or come to you so I had a witch summon you."

"My god!" I said, stunned.

"It's not safe here," he said, looking around. "Still remember the house in the Hamptons?"

"Of course," I said, grinning.

"The key is in the planter. Go there. Take your friends too. I'll come when I can."

"Are you sure?" I said, skeptically.

He nodded.

"Go quickly."

I turned to leave. I stopped. "We don't have a car," I said, turning back.

"How did you get here?" he asked, confused.

"Cab."

"Cab?" he laughed.

I shrugged.

"Here," he said, fumbling through his pocket. He tossed me a key.

The winged Bentley logo sat atop the key like a crest. I looked up at Richard and grinned. "There's four of us."

"So?" he replied.

"Can we take the twins?"

Richard laughed and shook his head. "You always did know how to drive a hard bargain."

I cocked my head to the side and grinned.

"I can't believe I'm letting you do this," he said. "The keys are still on the wall in the garage."

"Thanks," I replied, throwing the Bentley's key back.

"Don't hurt them!" he ordered.

"I won't," I grinned. "I promise."

Richard shook his head. "Later then."

"Later," I replied, turning away.

We entered the garage. I quickly found the two sets of Austin Healey keys hanging in a little wooden box on the wall.

"Damn girl! Seems like you got him wrapped around your finger!" Baptiste grinned.

I shrugged. "I don't know why he's being so accommodating." My voice was skeptical.

"Never look a gift horse in the mouth!" Eva said, taking one set of keys out of my hand and skipping off toward the cars.

We all followed behind. Richard's twins: two perfectly restored 1976 Austin Healey 3000s—one in red and one in blue, sat awaiting us.

"Dibs on red!" Eva shrieked, jumping in the car and behind the wheel.

I smiled, and watched as Baptiste struggled to fit his burly body beside her in the passenger seat.

"Richard must make a pretty penny working for *them*," Ryan muttered, eyeing the collection of luxurious, classic and contemporary cars lined up in the garage.

"I can only imagine," I said, sitting behind the wheel of the blue car.

Ryan got in next to me, just as I started the engine. I opened the convertible top and leaned my head out the window.

"Follow me, Eva, okay?" I said, sternly.

"You'll have to catch up to me first!" she replied, suddenly flooring it and speeding off.

"Damn her!" I shouted, pressing my foot on the gas and tearing off to catch up to her.

We raced down the long driveway. The wind soared as we drove. Eva laughed, Ryan smiled and I think I even heard Baptiste muttering a few

Hail Marys in Spanish. It was fun, but short lived. Once we reached the main road things got serious again. Eva finally allowed me lead the way. She even managed to behave as she followed me all the way to Richard's house in the Hamptons.

When we reached the house, I had a sneaking feeling something wasn't right. How did I know I could trust Richard? After all, he was the one working on Christian in my vision?

"Whoa Esperanza," Baptiste muttered, as we approached. "This is some getaway house."

I smiled. The house was exactly as I remembered. It was sprawling, beautiful and sat on over two-hundred feet of beachfront property.

"You was one lucky rich girl," Eva whispered, brusquely. "And you gave it all up for Christian? Jeeze!"

I shook my head and hurried toward the wide, wooden front door. I eyed the planter next to it. I reached my hand inside and sifted through the dirt.

"Got it," I said, pleased. I smiled, extracted the key and slipped it into the lock on the front door.

"Don't we have to be invited inside?" Eva asked, skeptically.

"He said you were all welcomed to come here," I assured.

"Good enough for me," Eva insisted, pushing the door open. She stepped foot across the threshold. "It worked!" she boasted, prancing her way inside the house.

"Mi casa et tu casa!" Baptiste said, walking inside behind her.

Ryan smiled and went inside too.

"This place is bigger than all of Perish Key!" Eva laughed, loudly.

I grinned and stepped inside as well. I looked around. Not much had changed since my last visit years ago. The walls were still white, the décor was modern and tasteful and every room still boasted a spectacular view of the water.

"It's like heaven in here!" Eva shouted, collapsing on the oversized, white sectional sofa in the centre of the great room.

I laughed. It was fun watching them fawn over the extreme decadence and excess I'd grown up with.

"Sara and the boys said they're aiming to meet up with us tomorrow." Ryan's voice was stern.

"How'd you ever get them to agree to help us?" I asked, intrigued. "I mean they just defected!"

Ryan rolled her eyes. "Believe me, I don't think they wanted to help, but Baptiste managed to convince them."

I nodded knowingly.

"Is Richard meeting us here?" Ryan asked.

"Yeah."

"Do you think he's on the level?"

"I don't know. The man lied to me my entire childhood. I have no reason to trust him."

"And yet you do," she said, studying my expression.

I shrugged.

"OMG!" Eva shrieked, searching through Richard's wine closet. "He's got bottles of Dom Perignon, Bollinger and Cristal stocked in here like its Coke and Pepsi!"

"Why don't you open one?" I shouted from across the room.

"Really?"

"Why the hell not!"

Eva laughed and studied the bottles again. A moment later I heard the sound of the front door opening. I grabbed Christian's bone-dagger from my duffle bag and rushed toward the entrance at my super-sonic vampire speed.

"You expecting someone?" Ryan asked, suspiciously.

"Hell no," I replied, tightening my grasp on the dagger.

24. Breadcrumb Trail

"You might be the one who's running things,
Well, you can ring anybody's bell to get what you want,
You see, it's easy to ignore a trouble,
When you're living in a bubble."

Ain't It Fun - Paramore

"Richard?" I said with surprise. "I didn't think you'd be here so soon."

"Apparently," he said, eyeing the dagger in my hand.

"I'm glad you made it," I insisted, withdrawing the dagger and slipping it into the back of my waistband.

"I couldn't take a chance talking to you at the house." He rushed inside.

"What's going on?" Ryan asked, sternly.

"Yeah, what's going on?" Eva asked too, uncorking a bottle of Dom with her teeth.

"Well," he said, impatiently. "I've been summoning Hope with the intention of bringing her here to emancipate an important friend of yours."

"You can say his name Richard," Eva's voice was curt. "You don't have to be all enigmatic. We know *you* and those Stepford vamp freaks *captured* Christian."

Richard cleared his throat. "I had nothing to do with his capture, but yes. Christian is with them."

"Is he okay?" I asked, worriedly.

"For the moment, but Christian is not why I summoned you here."

"He's not?"

"They captured your friend Marco several weeks ago."

"Marco!" I shouted.

"Rosa's grandson?" Eva blurted.

"They've been torturing him for information regarding the cure he concocted," Richard explained.

"Why?" I asked.

"Why else? The cure. And when Christian, the idiot that he is, came to New York on the pretense of some ridiculous TV interview, they took him too." Richard shook his head. "I didn't know he was human."

I nodded. "He and Marco created the stupid cure together. And it worked."

"Clearly," Richard replied.

Ryan asked with distrust, "What's your involvement in all this?"

"They recruited me when Hope was just a girl. I worked as a medic for them all this time."

"Embedding sustenance implants?" Ryan continued.

"Yes, among other things."

"How did you learn of Marco's capture?" Baptiste inquired.

"Coincidence. I wasn't supposed to be working that day, but they called me in at the last minute to cover another medic's shift. I was asked to anesthetize a somewhat volatile patient. The anesthetic wasn't working on him, and they realized that he was *brujo*."

"And how did you know of Marco's connection to us?" Baptiste continued.

"His chart. When I read his last name. I thought of Rosa instantly."

Eva snickered. "No one forgets Rosa!"

"I asked him if he was related to her, and naturally he said yes. He told me that she was his grandmother."

"So you've been drugging and torturing Marco ever since?" Ryan pressed.

"I declared Marco my patient! I've been protecting him! He's damn lucky our paths crossed."

"I don't believe in luck," Ryan insisted, icily.

"Why should we trust you Richard?" My tone was hard.

"I suppose you shouldn't. I may have withheld many important things from you Hope, but I tried my best to protect you all those years. I really did love your mother." He reached out to touch my shoulder. "And you."

I smiled.

"This after-school special, family reunion thing is wonderful," Eva mocked, "but we really do need to get going on saving our friends here. Have you got a way for us to get inside HQ?"

Richard snorted. "I've been going over it with Marco."

"You have?" I asked, stunned.

"Don't seem so surprised. I told you, I've been protecting him."

"And what have you come up with?" Ryan asked.

"Shift changes and break times."

"That's it?" she snarled.

"Look, Marco and I spent all our energy trying to summon Hope here! We've barely begun to scratch the surface of developing an escape plan."

"Leave it to us," Eva said, with poise.

"Some friends are joining us tomorrow," I added. "If we can assure your solidarity on this Richard..."

"Trust me," he pleaded. "You've got it. My shift begins at 0500."

I nodded. "Tonight we sleep. Tomorrow at dawn, we'll begin."

"What do *I* do?" Richard asked, concerned.

"Carry on as usual," I replied.

"And give us those shift changes and break times you mentioned."

Ryan handed him a piece of newspaper and a pen. Richard nodded and scribed a few notes on the paper.

"Truth is," he said. "I've never seen any of my superiors. I don't know who anyone is or even what they do. Please be careful. You'll be coming in virtually blind." He turned to leave.

"Aren't you staying here?" I asked.

"Are you kidding? Cindy will have the police perform a man-hunt if I'm not back by dinner time!"

"God, why'd you marry her?" I asked, revolted.

"Because I don't expect to find love in marriage." He leaned in close and ran his hand aside my cheek. "A long time ago a beautiful woman and her little girl stole my heart." He smiled. "Love is tricky, Hope."

"So I've been told."

He smiled. I smiled too. A moment later he left the house.

It didn't take long for sleep to seduce me. The soft, feather duvet imported from Paris and authentic Egyptian cotton sheets in the master suite felt like lying on a cloud. I had forgotten about the former luxuries of my former life. Some of them, ahem, the luxurious bedding, was pretty awesome.

"Hope," Ryan whispered, tapping at the door.

"Yeah," I replied, opening my eyes.

"They're here."

"Who?" I said, anxiously, springing from the bed and putting on my black boots.

"Pedro, Andy and Sara. They made it back faster than expected."

"And they're here—in the house?"

She nodded.

"Did I oversleep?" I checked my phone. It was only a little after three in the morning.

"I've been awake all night," Ryan divulged. "B and Eva too."

"Really?" I said, surprised.

"We've been talking tactics while you were sleeping."

"You have?"

She nodded.

"Did I miss out on all the good stuff?"

"God no," she exclaimed, putting her hand on my shoulder. "The real good stuff is about to happen. C'mon," she said, leading me down the stairway to the great room.

"Bella Durmiente!" Baptiste smiled, the moment I arrived.

"What's that mean B?" I asked, naive.

"Sleeping Beauty!"

I smiled. It was a hell of a lot better than being called Diablo Blanco!

"While you were slumbering," Eva snarled, "us adults connived the best break-in-break-out plan of all time!"

"Really?" I sat in the big, comfy, leather chair by the window.

"Andy," she continued, "is a total hacker. He's like the lovechild of Bill Gates and that dude from WikiLeaks. He's already showed us a little of what he's capable of on his laptop."

I widened my eyes and smiled. Andy peeked up from his computer to smile back. He was young with that classic anti-social I'm-a-nerd-with-a-chip-on-my-shoulder look.

"Pedro and I," Baptiste added, "are ready to muscle out anyone that gets in our way at HQ."

I looked at Pedro. He saluted me. I smiled back. He was tall and burly, much like Baptiste. His eyes were dark and hard and the menacing expression on his face was unbreakable. It was easy to see why Baptiste liked him.

"This is Sara," Ryan said, introducing her.

"Pleased to finally meet you," she said, extending her hand.

I shook her hand, briefly eyeing the scar left on her wrist from an implant removal.

"You've been so generous letting us stay with you," she continued. "You saved us...really you did."

"You're welcome," I replied.

Sara was homely looking. Her dishwater brown hair and forgettable features made her seem uncomplicated, but the strange scar across her forehead that peeked out from beneath her bangs, made me think otherwise. We'd all faced a few demons at one point or another. The secret to survival, however, whether you were an expat or born in the wild, lay in how you chose to continue living.

"Like I told you," Ryan said. "Sara worked in-take. She's gonna get you into HQ without them even noticing."

"How?" I asked, intrigued.

"She's going to go to work."

"But she's already defected. Don't you think they'll kind of notice that?"

"Not when I'm pretending to be my sister," she added.

"Sara's a twin. Her sister still works for them," Ryan explained.

"And if you go in pretending to be her, where's your sister going to be?"

"Already taken care of that," Baptiste said, grinning.

"I don't even wanna know what that means," I replied, rolling my eyes.

"Look," Ryan assured. "We've worked it out. Every detail has been taken care of. All you have to do is come along for the ride, Hope."

My brow furrowed.

Eva scowled. "Blondie's mad because she didn't get to put her time-shifting stamp on our plan."

"I know it's hard riding shotgun," Ryan consoled, "but you—and Christian, you've been through enough. Let us take the reins this time, okay?"

I half-smiled. I wasn't totally comfortable not knowing every detail of the plan, but it seemed like I had no other choice. It was gonna happen and it was gonna happen soon.

An alarm suddenly beeped. Everyone jumped.

"Shift change," Andy said, silencing the alarm on his laptop.

"It's time," Ryan answered. "Let's move."

We hopped back in Richard's twin Austin Healeys and headed to the city.

Andy stayed behind at the Hampton house to work his magic remotely, while Sara and Pedro took the car they'd arrived in—er stolen and met us in the alley across from the HQ main entrance.

"You two take the service entrance," Ryan ordered, eyeing Pedro and Baptiste. "Stay on task and stay connected at all times. Andy will give you cues as we go...when he disables alarms...when he immobilizes electrical... you get the idea."

"Si," Baptiste replied, before kissing Eva on the check and disappearing around the block with Pedro.

"Eva," Ryan said. "You take the main doors. Do just as we planned last night."

She nodded and grinned.

"Strut your stuff," Ryan continued. "And take these sons-of-bitches by storm!"

"With pleasure!" she replied, suddenly morphing into the visage of a middle-aged Japanese man in a lab coat.

I smiled. I loved watching Eva shape-shift with such ease.

"You're Doctor Hironaka now. You must think, breathe, feel that you belong at HQ."

"Domo," she replied, bowing and nodding.

"Do your thing," Ryan said, nodding back.

Eva smiled and hurried across the road toward the front entrance.

"You and Sara will be working together Hope." Ryan's dark eyes sparkled as she spoke.

"What do I do?" I asked, anxiously.

"Pretend like you've been collected for in-take. You don't have an implant scar, so it's a perfect cover."

I nodded.

"Sit with the others," she continued, "and wait with them as though you're one of them. When you're called in, you'll meet with Sara."

"Well," Sara interjected. "I'll still look like me, but I'll be pretending I'm my sister Abby."

I nodded.

"Sara will get you into HQ, but once you're in there it's up to you to find Richard and get Christian and Marco out. Okay?"

My expression suddenly contorted.

"What's the matter?" Ryan asked.

"Well if I'm the one basically rescuing Christian and Marco singlehandedly, what exactly is everybody else doing?"

Ryan's eyes sparkled, wildly.

"I thought this was a rescue mission! Not a suicide mission!" My voice was heated.

"Everything will be fine," Ryan assured, "if we all stick to the plan."

"The plan," I mumbled, bitterly.

"Take the side door over there," she said, pointing to a small door beneath a sign that read *Deliveries*. "Slip in when the coast is clear. HQ is the building marked with the inverted triangle—the one behind the regular hospital."

"Yeah," I replied.

"You're looking for the large waiting area next to the ER."

"Okay. I got it."

"I'll be securing our getaway car," Ryan added.

"You mean you'll be *stealing* our getaway car."

"Whatever. Either way, I'll be here waiting in this alley, for all of you to return. You've got one hour from now," she said, depressing a timer button on her phone. "If you're not back by then, you're not coming home."

I nodded. Sara nodded too.

"Good-bye," I said, the way Ryan and I always did when we parted. "See ya. Ciao."

"Until we meet again," she said with a smile, before turning to leave.

I looked to the sky. The sun had nearly risen and I knew that Richard would be starting his shift soon.

"I'd better get going too," Sara said, meekly. "See you in there?"

"Yeah. See you in there."

I bit my lip and looked across the street. I stared at the hospital where I'd spent many years coming to visit Richard on duty. I had no idea that he was really working in a secret facility that catered to *them*.

I felt sick inside. Nausea weighed on me like a rock. I started to leave when suddenly I felt a hand on my shoulder. I turned around. "Eradan!" I exclaimed, eagerly.

25. Let Down Your Long Hair

"I'm waking up to ash and dust,
I wipe my brow and I sweat my rust."

Radioactive – Imagine Dragons

"Where have you been?" I asked.

"You told me to stay away. You told me you needed some space."

"I did?"

"You were drunk. And you were mad." He heaved a sigh and pushed his glasses atop his head. I could see his eyes again. They were beautiful and ever so reminiscent of Christian's eyes.

"I was worried," I divulged.

"You were?" He seemed surprised.

I nodded.

"You said that if I really was your son, then I'd respect your wishes."

"So you did."

He nodded.

"Because you really are my..."

He nodded again.

I smiled.

"You're not mad anymore?" he asked.

"No. But I am in the middle of a rescue mission."

"Who are you rescuing?"

"Christian."

"From HQ?" Eradan exclaimed.

I nodded.

"I didn't see this coming," he mumbled, cryptically.

"You usually see everything coming?"

"Well not like I'm a seer or psychic, but to me this is the past. I know your stories. I've seen some of them first-hand. I just don't recall a time when Dad was captured by HQ."

"*Dad?*" I exclaimed, taken aback.

He half-smiled. "This concerns me that I didn't see it."

"Things change, Eradan."

"I suppose you're right. Even the past."

"Especially the past!"

"Well, with the way you wield it..."

"Hey!" I scorned.

The expression on his face eased a little.

"Fate isn't set in stone, you know. Life...love...it's always changing all the time."

"Like now?" he said, edgily.

"Like *right* now," I agreed. "So you think you can help me with this? Saving Christian...*your* father?"

He nodded.

"Will you help get me in there?"

"Yes."

I smiled. "This friend of Ryan's, her name is Sara, she's gonna help us make our way to Richard."

"Grandpa?" he said, surprised.

"*Grand-what?*" I exclaimed, taken aback.

"I'll get you to him," he said, diverting.

"If we take that door over there, the one marked Deliveries—"

"Forget that!" he interrupted. "My way's much faster." He smiled, took my hand and suddenly we vanished. A moment later we were standing in the familiar, sterile corridor lined with rooms.

"I need the one marked *Specimen #Q1153* on the door." We walked a little farther. "Here it is!" I said, finding it. I pushed the door open and went inside. "I...I don't understand." The room was empty. There wasn't even an operating table left inside. "In the vision...when Marco summoned me...I saw Christian in here."

"They obviously must have moved him," Eradan continued. "But how will we find out where?"

"Like this," I said, suddenly recalling my tutelage. There was a box marked *First Aid* on a nearby shelf. I grabbed the box, ripped it open and sifted through the contents. Amid bandages and gauze, I spotted a candle. I grabbed the candle and put it on the shelf.

"What's that for?" Eradan asked.

"You'll see," I said, eyeing the garbage. I rummaged through the contents of an old take-out container. "Bingo!" I exclaimed, extracting an unopened salt packet.

"Now this is more the you I'm used to seeing," he mumbled, pleased.

I smiled. Tore open the salt packet and drew a circle with it around the candle. I rubbed my fingers together and ignited the candle wick. I closed my eyes and began to chant, hopeful that I'd memorized it just as Rosa had instructed.

"Elementum recolligo huic locus. Commodo mihi vestri vox. Elementum unda ego dico vos. Permissum pluit is est meus nos sic vadum is exsisto."

Just then, rain fell within the confines of the small hospital room! There were no windows and if I was to get these walls to talk, I needed to soften them one way or another.

"How are you doing this?" Eradan, awed, as droplets fell against his pretty face.

"Shh," I replied, grinning.

All of a sudden, the rain stopped. Silence resonated. A moment later the voices emerged.

"What have you done with my patient?" It was Richard. I could tell instantly.

"He's become...uncooperative," an edgy voice replied. *"He's been moved to the OR pending a procedure."*

"A procedure! For what exactly?"

"That's classified."

"But I'm his medic! I wasn't informed of this transfer. I didn't authorize it."

"Orders came from above. Your authorization wasn't required."

I opened my eyes. "The OR," I said. "They've taken him to the OR."

"C'mon," Eradan replied, grabbing my hand again.

Instantly we vanished and not a moment too soon we were in the OR holding zone. I withdrew from Eradan and frantically began searching the rooms for Christian.

"Over here," Eradan, called through my thoughts.

I hurried up the hallway toward him. "God!" I muttered, spotting Christian. He was lying on an examination table, nearly comatose. His body was laden with thousands of pinprick sized wounds.

"Christian," I whispered, "we're getting you the hell outta here."

He didn't respond. He fluttered his eyelashes a little, but that was all. Eradan grabbed Christian's hand and locked it with mine and suddenly the three of us vanished together. Almost instantly we were back in the alleyway across from HQ.

"Christian!" I exclaimed, rushing to his side. He was lying on the pavement. "You're alive!" I gushed. "You're here!"

"I don't mean to ruin your reunion," Eradan said, "but Uncle Marco...I mean your friend Marco, he's still inside."

"You're right," I uttered, nodding. "Can you stay with Christian...just until I get back?"

Eradan shook his head. "You stay with him. I'll get Marco."

"Thank you," I replied, familiar bloody tears welling in my eyes.

Eradan disappeared like an inky flash and not a moment too soon, Ryan suddenly pulled up the alley, behind the wheel of a large, black Lincoln.

"Damn it!" she roared, hopping out of the car. "What did they do to him?"

"I don't know, but at least he's alive."

Ryan nodded and looked at the timer on her phone. "Eleven minutes."

"What are they doing in there?" I asked with rage.

"Vengeance...revenge...justice."

"Then I'm surprised you aren't in there with them!"

Ryan nodded. "You know, I spent most of my freedom wishing for a chance at revenge, but somehow, I don't know." She sighed. "Being with all of you...and my girls...and Alex." She smiled. "Perish has softened me, Hope. It's like the home I never had. I want to see to it that I get back there."

I smiled, pulled Christian over my shoulder and gently placed him in the back of the SUV.

"I don't want to waste my freedom fighting," Ryan divulged

"Me either," I said, touching her arm.

All of a sudden Eva returned. Sara was at her side. They were breathless and gasping for air as though they were being chased.

"Someone after you?" Ryan asked, anxiously.

Eva shook her head. "Just wanted the hell outta there is all."

"You never came," Sara mumbled, winded.

"I know," I replied. "I found another way."

"Did you accomplish it?" Ryan asked, matter-of-factly.

"Hell yeah," Eva said, grinning. She was back to looking like herself again.

"Where's Baptiste and Pedro?" Ryan asked with distress.

Sara shook her head.

"Shit," Eva barked. "How much time have we got left until the security systems are armed again?"

Ryan looked at her phone. "Four minutes and counting."

"I never shoulda let him go off without me!" she continued. "Damn it!"

Just then Eradan appeared. Masked behind a large dumpster, he was helping Marco make his way toward us. I nodded at him and grinned.

"*Thank you Eradan*, I said, through my thoughts. "*For always being there...for everything.*"

He smiled and disappeared again. I rushed toward the dumpster and took hold of Marco. He was woozy and falling in and out of consciousness.

"Took you long enough," he mumbled, groggily.

"Thanks for summoning me," I replied, escorting him to the SUV. "I'm still new at this witchcraft thing."

He smiled in reply and struggled to make his way inside the car.

"Hope," Ryan called out.

"Yeah," I said, shutting the door.

"Was that Marco?"

I nodded.

"But I didn't see him with you before. I saw Christian, but not him. He wasn't here all along, was he?"

I widened my eyes and smiled. Just then we were distracted by the sound of Baptiste growling as he thumped his way up the alley.

"Damn you!" Eva shouted, relieved. "With only one minute to spare."

"I'm here baby," he said, kissing her on the cheek.

"Wait!" a voice suddenly called out.

I looked ahead. It was Pedro. He was holding someone, helping them walk toward us.

"Pedro!" Ryan shouted, "Who you got there?"

"It's Marco," he replied. "You nearly left him in there!"

I looked closely. The man under Pedro's arm was tall and slim, middle-aged, with dark features. Granted, he looked a lot like Marco, but it definitely wasn't him.

"That's not Marco," Eva insisted, coolly.

"It's not?" Pedro replied, confused. "But his chart said, MARCO RAMIREZ GONZALES. It has to be him."

I moved even closer. I studied him carefully. His clothes were tattered and out of style. His hair was long and there was a bushy beard covering his face. He looked dirty, disheveled and fatigued, as though he'd been kept as a prisoner for quite a long time. His eyes were weary, but they were open.

"Marco," I said. "Are you related to Rosa?"

"Yes," he replied, softly. "She was my mother."

My heart thumped in my chest. This was Marco Senior—Rosa's son and Marco's father!

"C'mon," I uttered, eagerly. "We'll get you home."

"You're a miracle," he replied, weakly. "A real miracle."

I smiled and helped get him inside the SUV, when suddenly the beeper rang on Ryan's phone.

"Time's up," she uttered, jumping inside the Lincoln and behind the wheel.

Eva and B hopped in the back. Sara and Pedro got in too. I climbed in the passenger seat next to Ryan and rode shotgun. She started the engine and pressed on the gas. We tore off along the alleyway to the main road when suddenly, KABOOM! The harrowing crash of a huge explosion resonated! Ryan slammed on the breaks. We all turned toward the source of the sound.

"HQ!" I shouted.

Society headquarters suddenly collapsed! The ground shook. Dust and rubble speckled air like a sandstorm! Car alarms blared. Everything was in utter turmoil!

Ryan hit the gas and we sped off into the sunrise, hell bent on getting as far away from the ruins of HQ as possible.

26. Off With Their Heads!

"I've been walkin', I've been freezin',
Freezin' from a love, I left behind."

Long Cold Winter - Cinderella

"**W**hat the hell did you do?" I raged, the moment we fled the scene of the crime.

"Annihilated them!" Eva cackled, proudly.

"And you also probably annihilated a ton of innocent vampires and humans too. Did any of you stop to consider that in your *plan*?"

"Hope," Ryan asserted. "They were doing what they felt was just."

"Just?" I barked. "There is nothing just about killing innocents!" I groaned aloud with frustration. Power surged beneath my skin like wildfire.

"Then go back in time and fix it, why don't you." Eva's voice was surly.

"I can't," I replied, scathingly. "You killed those people. They're dead now. It can't be fixed." I groaned again. "I can't believe all of you! I thought this was a rescue mission." I shook my head. "You might have won this battle, but the reality is you've started a war!"

"What do mean Esperanza?" Baptiste's voice was hard. "They're all dead."

176

"Retaliation somehow supersedes death when you're omnipotent!" My tone was harsh. "You wait. It's coming." I turned to look out the window. "Did anyone happen to see Richard at HQ?"

"No," Sara expressed, solemnly.

"Shit," I muttered, enraged. My eyes welling with tears again. Poor Richard, just when he had a change of heart, this had to happen. He never made it out of HQ. And I knew that his shift coincided with their plan. It was inevitable; Richard was dead.

"I'm sorry," Baptiste whispered, touching my shoulder.

"So am I," Eva added, tenderly.

I closed my eyes and tried emptying my thoughts. I knew it was going to be a very long and unpleasant trip back to Perish.

The moment we returned the end began. Ambrose House was dark. An icy wind swept through her opened windows carrying with it the undeniable smell of danger.

"Where are the girls?" Ryan asked, concerned.

"Where's my baby?" Eva panicked.

"Rosa!" I called out, but there was no answer.

"I'll check upstairs," Baptiste declared, zooming up the stairs at super-sonic speed.

"Pedro," Ryan ordered. "You and Sara help me get Christian, Marco and his father to safety."

Pedro and Sara nodded.

"Where will you take them?" I asked.

"The boathouse."

"Be careful. Please."

"You too," she said, turning to leave.

Eva and B wasted no time in exploring the rest of the house. I rushed ahead, to the kitchen, to be with them.

"I just want my baby!" Eva shouted.

"I know," Baptiste consoled. "And we'll find him."

"Where is everyone?" I asked, entering the kitchen.

"Don't know," Baptiste replied.

"What the hell is going on?" Eva shouted.

"I hate to say it, but I told you so."

"Shut it, Hope!"

"You think this is retaliation?" Baptiste asked, frantically.

"Of course!"

"But so soon?" he continued. "We've barely even arrived home ourselves!"

I rushed to the centre of the room, closed my eyes and began waving my hands through the air.

"What the hell are you doing?" Eva barked. "We don't have time for games."

"This isn't a game," I replied, opening my eyes. "I'm looking to get a glimpse."

"A glimpse?"

"If they did come here, then I'll see it. Now shh, and let me concentrate."

Eva nodded. I closed my eyes again and began concentrating. I waved my hand through the air in front of me as though I was tickling the space between my fingers. Slowly, I continued dragging my fingers until the air didn't feel like air anymore. It became tangible, like water. I trailed my fingers again, through the space in front of me, just like I was wiping away the fog on a window, when suddenly the glimpse appeared!

I saw four shadowed figures standing in the living room at Ambrose House. And then I saw them—Ryan's friends, Alex, Henry and even Rosa grasping baby Stromboli in her arms! I continued watching, when abruptly the glimpse changed. Now, I was looking at Richard. He was tied to a tree in the forest adjacent to Ambrose House. He'd been cut and beaten and was bleeding profusely, but he was alive!

My eyes flew open.

"What did you see?" Eva asked, eagerly.

"They were here, in the house, all together. Strombo is with Rosa."

"Well, where are they now?" Baptiste shouted.

"I don't know!" I replied, rushing toward the back door. "But I saw Richard too. He was tied to a tree in the forest outback."

I opened the door and hurried outside. Eva and Baptiste followed behind. It was dark and it was night. The moon was barely bright enough to light our way, but it didn't matter. We flew across the yard toward the forest. I scanned the trees, when suddenly, it came to me. The smell of Richard's blood was like a trail of breadcrumbs leading our way.

"Richard!" I exclaimed as I approached. I moved closer and tore the binding from his mouth.

"Be careful," he uttered in panic. "They're...they're..." and then suddenly he passed out.

"Damn it!" Eva shouted, disappointed.

"Hope!" a familiar voice called out.

I pivoted around. "Christian? Is that you?"

I looked ahead. It *was* him! He wobbled as he walked and was still dressed in the same clothes I'd found him in.

"I've been looking for you everywhere," he said.

I rushed toward him and wrapped my arms around him. "Thank god you're okay! Thank god you're..." and then I stopped speaking. I withdrew from him straight away.

"Hope?" Eva said, skeptically. "What's going on?"

Something wasn't right. I continued retreating from him. He didn't smell like him. He didn't even feel like him either.

"Blondie," Eva pressed. "What's on your mind?"

I gingerly inhaled again and let the tang of Christian's smell play on my senses. BOOM! My heart thumped in my chest. This Christian wasn't human—he was a vampire!

"It's not him!" I shouted. "It's not Christian!"

Swiftly, the Christian imposter sprung into action. His sharp fangs shot through his gums! He flashed them at us and growled!

"Shit!" Eva exclaimed. "He's vicious!"

Subsequently, an Eva doppelganger suddenly jumped out from behind the trees! *Her* hair was fiery and *her* fangs were razor-sharp. She lunged at the real Eva with a savage intensity. The real Eva hit the ground. The sound of her bones breaking on impact sent shivers up my spine.

"Eva!" Baptiste hollered, leaping forward to take his ladylove away from her evil-twin, when unexpectedly he was sideswiped by his own duplicate!

"No!" I hollered, moving in to pull Baptiste's double off of him, when suddenly I was struck in the arm. I turned around. The Christian imitator was standing behind me. With a swift yank on my braid, he extracted me from Baptiste's double and tossed me through the air! I crash-landed near a fallen tree trunk.

"C'mon!" he taunted, wickedly.

I hurried to my feet.

"What you waiting for, bitch?" His tone was icy and hard and incredibly difficult for me to hear. This man—this evil shape-shifter from the Society, looked and sounded exactly like my Christian! How was I supposed to fight him?

I dashed through the trees at top speed, but he followed behind.

"Think you're gonna get away from me that easily?" he whispered, nearing from behind.

My body surged with waves of power. I could feel him close behind and I was ready to attack, when all of a sudden he grabbed hold of the chain around my neck—the one that Christian had given to me, and pulled on it so hard that it sliced the underside of my jaw!

I howled with pain.

"You like that baby?" he purred, in my ear, continuing to tug even harder and harder on the chain.

I closed my eyes and touched his hands, prying him off the chain. He screeched like a banshee and quickly released his grasp. I withdrew from him immediately and watched as his hands turned to ice!

"What have you done?" he shouted. "What are you?"

I didn't reply, but simply chose to watch as his entire body eventually became consumed by ice. When he was frozen entirely, I snapped my fingers together and flicked fire at him. Flames engulfed his icy corpse with ease, and soon he was nothing more than a pile of charred ash on the ground.

I zoomed through the air back to Eva and Baptiste. They were still entangled in fierce hand-to-hand combat with their second-selves.

I wanted to eradicate their doubles, just as I'd done with Christian's, but I needed to know which ones were the real Eva and B first!

"Eva!" I shouted.

"Not a good time, Blondie!" she struggled to reply.

"I wanna help you."

"Then help!"

"But I need to know which one of you is really you."

They stopped fighting. Both Evas turned to face me.

"I'm the real Eva," one said.

"No you're not, bitch! I'm the real Eva."

"Oh, yeah," the first Eva replied. "Then can do you this?" She shifted into the likeness of Doctor Hironaka and I knew instantly that she was my Eva!

I thrust my hands in the air toward the fake Eva. Bolts of unbridled energy surged from my fingertips towards her. A moment later she exploded like fireworks, shattering into pieces! Chunks of ice and flesh fell through the sky.

"Shit, Blondie," Eva said. "That was freakin' gross!"

I laughed. She laughed too. I helped her to her feet and we started toward Baptiste.

"How'd you do that?" she asked, impressed.

"Rosa taught me, although it definitely wasn't that gross when I did it with her salt and pepper shakers!"

Eva smiled, but before long her smile faded. The guttural growl of Baptiste fighting for his life echoed with a thunderous roar.

"Can't you do something?" she asked, impatiently.

I eyed the two burly Baptistes rolling around on the ground. "Yeah," I insisted. "But stand back."

Eva nodded and moved away. I, on the other hand, moved in closer. The element of earth came to mind. I remembered the way I so adroitly levitated the large rocks in Rosa's yard. Baptiste and his doppelganger were big like rocks. I had this!

I focused my energy on the power of creation and particularly my connection to mother earth and suddenly the two men rose from the ground!

"Well I'll be damned!" Eva awed.

I moved my fingers ever so slightly until the two men were distanced from one another.

"B," I shouted. "This might hurt a little."

"Can't hurt bruja," the real Baptiste replied. "You know I ain't got no pain receptors!"

"I know that," I replied, grinning. "But he does!"

I flicked my fingers and suddenly the two men plummeted to the ground, both simultaneously smashing into the jagged rocks, sharp coral shards and splintery tree trunks beneath them.

"Thanks for the warning, Esperanza," the real Baptiste muttered. He rose to his feet while removing the hefty wooden slivers and sharp rocks that had become embedded in his torso.

I nodded at him before turning my attention to the impostor Baptiste. He was laying on the ground, rock, coral and wood severely penetrating his entire body. He was wincing with pain, immovable and near death.

"Who sent you here?" I asked.

"Screw you!" he replied.

"Wrong answer," I shook my head at him and turned away. He deserved to suffer a little before he died. Mother earth heeded my call and swiftly consumed him; crushing his bones and swallowing him whole.

"Hope," Baptiste said, rushing toward me. "I had no idea you were so..."

"Powerful?"

"Yeah."

"Me neither," Eva added.

"You kicked their asses like it was child's play, Esperanza!" Batiste was excited.

I flashed him a smile. "C'mon," I said, eagerly. "We should get Richard and take him to the boathouse with the others."

Eva, Baptiste and I zoomed through the woods back to where we'd left Richard. He was still there; tied to a tree and completely incapacitated.

"I'll cut him down," Baptiste said, willingly.

"I'll catch him," I replied.

"Uh, guys," Eva interjected.

"Not now, Eva," Baptiste's voice was hard.

"No. Seriously," she said, frantically. "I think you'd better take a look at this."

Baptiste and I stopped fussing over Richard. I drew my eyes upward. BOOM! My heart thumped again. My eyes bulged, I was speechless.

Baptiste's eyes bulged too. "Holy fu—"

"Hope," Eva interrupted. "How powerful are you, honey?"

"Not this freakin powerful," I said eyeballing the army of our clones that were trudging through the woods towards us!

27. Attack Of The Card Soldiers

*"I'm friends with the monster that's under my bed,
Get along with the voices inside of my head."*

The Monster – EMINEM featuring Rihanna

"Shit!" Eva shouted. "That was not the answer I wanted from you, Blondie!"

As the army of our clones neared, I could tell they looked hungry for blood. With fangs sharper than razorblades and eyes angrier than lightening, these damn things wanted revenge. Clearly, this shape-shifting army was sent by the Society to retaliate against what we'd done to their headquarters. We had to find a way of fighting back.

"Why do they all look like us?" Baptiste asked.

"Maybe they thought this was ironic," I asserted. "Sending hundreds of us to kill ourselves?"

"We gotta get outta here!" Eva panicked, trying to run. "We gotta find Strombo!"

"Slow down," I said, apprehending her. "If you make a move you're dead."

"We're dead anyhow!" she barked.

"Not yet we aren't."

"Esperanza," Baptiste insisted. "There is only three of us and...my god...hundreds of them. We can't defeat all of them!"

"We can if we have our own army!"

"And where we gonna get an army to fight with us on such short notice?" Eva's voice was curt.

"Underwater."

I looked ahead, to the coastline through the trees in the distance. "Think about it," I said. "Hundreds of ghosts of dead sailors from fallen vessels are down there just itching for a chance to join in battle again!"

"And how would you do this?" Baptiste asked. "I mean bring these ghosts to fight with us?"

"A spell."

"Do it then!" Eva snapped.

"I can't do it here. I need to get back to Ambrose House. I need my grandmother's grimoire."

"Fine," Baptiste replied. "Then let's go. I'll grab Richard."

We flew through the trees faster than speed itself while the creepy, clone army was still making its way through the woods.

"It will only take me a second to get it," I said, tearing up the stairs towards my bedroom.

"Hurry," Eva insisted.

"We don't have long," Baptiste added, placing Richard on the red couch in living room.

I pushed open the bedroom door and stepped inside.

"Not again!" I exclaimed, spotting yet another imposter Christian standing at the backend of the room!

His fangs cut through his gums and he lunged toward me. I recoiled, thrust my hand at him and froze him in mid-lunge. A moment later his body iced over completely. He fell to the ground with a hard thud, before exploding into millions of icy, fleshy particles upon my bedroom floor.

"Now," I said, turning away. "Where'd I leave that grimoire."

I moved to the bed and ran my fingertips beneath it until I touched the edges of the journals, but this time I didn't feel any journals—I felt a hand instead! I pulled away quickly, but I was still attached to whatever had been hiding beneath my bed! I tugged harder and managed to pull it out.

"Oh my god!" I gasped, horrified. It was *me* this time! I stared at the eerie mirror reflection of me and wondered whether I had the strength to do it; kill myself.

"C'mere, bitch!" my double barked, tugging me closer.

I grimaced and could feel my power coming alive again beneath my skin. I closed my eyes and concentrated on the energy within me and all around me. I focused on her touch—the way her hand felt grasping mine and suddenly I could feel the icy sharpness of her flesh freezing over. I opened my eyes, withdrew my hand from hers and stared as she turned into an icy corpse.

This time, I looked away instead of watching the fireworks. There was something altogether irreverent about seeing yourself (even in clone form) scattered into bits of flesh and ice around your bedroom.

"Here it is!" I said, extracting the grimoire from the stack of other journals beneath the bed. I held it in my hands and zoomed to the front of the house.

"Did you get it?" Eva asked.

"Yeah," I replied, showing it to her. "But they're in here you know."

"Who?"

"Who do you think? *Them*."

Eva's pretty eyes bulged. She looked around the room in panic when suddenly, yet another Baptiste jumped out at us from the kitchen!

"Shit!" Eva said, lunging at him.

"Stop!" he insisted. "It's me baby. The *real* me."

Eva stopped hitting him and withdrew. She looked into his dark eyes and smiled. "What are you doing jumping out at us like that?"

"It was only a joke."

"It wasn't funny!"

"I'm sorry," he apologized, kissing her on the forehead. "So you got the grimoire?"

"Yeah," I said, scanning the pages. "And I think this spell just might work." I pointed to the page that read, SPIRIT SUMMONING AND SUBJUGATION.

Eva glanced at it and smiled. "Honey, if you think that will resurrect ghostly sailors to fight for us, I'm on board."

"What do you need?" Baptiste inquired.

I reread the spell. Most of it was written in Latin and the parts that weren't were utterly cryptic. "I think I need Marco."

"Marco Senior or Marco Junior?" Eva asked, mockingly.

"Either. Can you get him from the boathouse and bring him here?"

"But the boathouse is in the forest, Hope. I don't think B or I should be waltzing through the woods with those things out there."

"Suppose you're right," I agreed. "I could go."

"Don't be foolish, Esperanza." Baptiste's voice was firm. "You are in just as much danger as we are."

"Then how in the hell are we going to get Marco here?" I said, deflated.

"I'll get him," Eradan offered, suddenly manifesting before us.

Eva and Baptiste gasped.

"Eradan!" I exclaimed, happily. "You angel! You hero! Thank god you're always stalking me!"

"Who is this?" Eva snarled.

I looked at Eradan and he looked back at me.

"I'm just a friend...a friend that Hope met somewhere in time," he said, extending his gloved hand to Eva. "Pleasure to make your acquaintance."

"And yours," she awed.

"Sir," he said, extending his hand to Baptiste.

"Hey," Baptiste replied, perplexed.

Eradan withdrew his hand from Baptiste and turned to me again. "Back in a flash," he said, vanishing with an inky bolt.

"Who was that?" Eva's voice was elated. "Have you been cheating on Christian? I mean he's gorgeous obviously...but Hope—"

"He's my son."

"Come again?" she insisted, dramatically.

"He's my son," I confessed, touching my stomach. "And he's a time-shifter like me, but he's from the future and—"

"It's cool," Baptiste purred, patting me on the shoulder. "You don't need to explain."

"Just don't tell him I told you, okay? I don't think he wants anyone to know."

"Okay," Eva agreed, taking a bottle of Absinthe from the living room liquor cabinet and uncorking it as usual with her teeth.

"My lips are sealed too, Esperanza," Baptiste promised.

Just then Eradan reappeared. He was holding Marco Junior and Marco Senior at his sides.

"You brought them both!" I exclaimed.

"One can never have too many witches in the kitchen...or something like that." He rested them on the red, velvet couch facing the window.

"I'll try young Marco first." I approached him and tapped him on the shoulder. I briefly eyed the huge tattoo of the Dia De Los Muertos skull and flanking raiz de la vida—root of life on his bicep that Christian had done. Had it not been for that day when the pair first met in La Fuente, there never would have been any cure. Marco and Christian never would have created it and likely the Society never would have captured them.

"Hope?" he said, groggily.

"I need you to help me Marco."

"I-I feel sick. I've been... drugged," he said, struggling to a sitting position.

"Lemme use one of Rosa's hangover remedies. What's the one with lima beans and sea urchin?"

"Mal de la Cabeza," he muttered "Cure for being sick in the head."

"Yeah, that's one!"

"You have essence of sea urchin lying around?"

"No."

"Use sobrio incantation," he grumbled. "It's a sobering spell."

"How? I don't know that one."

"My hair. Grab some."

My eyes narrowed. I leaned in close and pulled out a few tiny strands from his facial hair.

"My blood," he groaned. "Take it and put it all in a bowl."

I grabbed a glass ashtray from the side table and put the hair in it. I picked up Marco's hand and extended his index finger. I let my fangs extract from within my gums and gently slid the tip of his finger across the razor-sharp edge of my tooth. His flesh severed with ease and blood pooled instantly. I leaned his finger over the ashtray and allowed several drops to drip inside.

"You need alcohol," he said. "Poor it over and light it."

Eva passed me the bottle of Absinthe that she'd been sipping. I nodded at her and poured a little of the potent, green liquid into the ashtray too. I snapped my fingers and tossed a flame at the concoction.

"Say this," Marco whispered. "*Tui Gratia Jovis Gratia Sit Cura.*"

I nodded, waved my fingers over the fire and repeated, "*Tui Gratia Jovis Gratia Sit Cura.*"

The fire died out completely. Marco collapsed on the couch.

"Marco!" I exclaimed, turning toward him.

A moment later, he suddenly straightened his posture.

"I feel better," he said.

"Good, 'cause I need you to help me with a big-ass spell."

His dark eyes widened. "First," he said. "Thank you for coming for me. Second. Where's Richard. Third—"

"Richard is right there," I said, pointing toward the other couch. "And you're welcome for the rescue, it was all him," I continued, pointing up at Eradan.

"Who's he?"

"A friend," Eradan replied, vaguely.

"I need you to help me cast this spell." I opened my grandmother's grimoire and showed him the page.

"SPIRIT SUMMONING AND SUBJUGATION." Marco heaved a sigh. "What do you need it for?"

"I need to resurrect the spirits of the sailors that reside at the bottom of the ocean, just off our shores."

"Ghost sailors?"

"Yeah. I need an army of them, a big one, and I need them now!"

"An army? For what?"

"To fight those freakin' vamp-clones of us out there!" I pointed to the window.

Marco's brow furrowed. He walked toward the window that overlooked the yard. He looked outside. Masses of *them* had already started back toward Ambrose House—toward us!

"What the hell!" he shouted."

"We don't have long and we can't fight them off ourselves."

Marco nodded.

"I need you to help me conjure the sailors. Will you do it?"

Marco sighed.

"Marco!" I barked. "There is no time for indecision."

"I don't know," he hesitated. "It's no small thing...summoning an army of dead sailors."

"Shit Marco! We just risked our lives saving your ass from HQ! You owe it to us!"

"Alright. Fine," he replied.

I nodded, pleased. Marco's dark eyes turned even darker. I could tell that he wasn't happy about helping, but that he felt obligated to do it anyway.

"What exactly do you want from me?" he asked, grudgingly.

I grabbed my grandmother's grimoire again. I opened the book to page with the spirit summoning spell and handed it to Marco.

"Your ability to read Latin," I insisted. "Can you translate it?"

He scanned the page. "Yeah."

"Then what the hell are we waiting for!"

28. When The Clock Strikes Twelve

"No more dreaming of the dead as if death itself was undone,
No more calling like a crow for a boy, for a body in the garden,"

"Snow White's stitching up your circuit-boards,
Someone's slipping through the hidden door,"

Blinding - Florence and the Machine

Optimism coursed through my veins as I watched Marco reading the spell. I felt empowered and eager to get started.

"This won't work," Marco said, suddenly.

I froze, my veins icing over with disappointment.

"This spell ain't gonna work," he continued. "It's for spirit summoning. You can't fight with an army of ghosts."

"What? I don't understand?"

"Think about it," he said, peering up at me from behind the book. "You need bodies to fight, not ghosts."

I bit my lip and grabbed the book from his hands I thumbed through the pages in a desperate effort to find something else.

"What are you doing?" he asked.

"Looking for another spell."

He shook his head. "You won't find one."

"How can you be so sure?"

"Because," he insisted. "Our family grimoires are filled with admirable spells...spells that protect and shield and maintain. Not spells that teach you how to resurrect the dead!"

"Resurrect the dead!" I exclaimed. "I'm not trying to bring them back to life. I just need them to fight for a while!"

Marco laughed. I stopped thumbing through the book and looked up at him.

"You are one determined girl," he uttered.

"I'll take that as a compliment," I replied, turning back to the grimoire again.

"Stop!" he insisted "Like I told you, you ain't gonna find what you need in that book!"

"Well what about in *your* family grimoire? Doesn't Rosa keep it—"

"No," he interrupted. "There are no spells that you need in those books."

"Is that it? Are we just supposed to give up?"

"I'm not saying that."

"Well what are you saying? 'Cause none of it is helping and we've got some pretty hungry vamp soldiers just outside that window waiting to eat us all alive!"

Marco heaved a sigh. "What I'm saying is that you're never gonna find a spell to do what you need in *that* book."

My brow furrowed. "But I might in another book?" I was confused, but intrigued.

"Exactly!" He grinned. "Ain't no white magic gonna be able to conjure an army of ghost soldiers the way you need."

"White magic won't work," I uttered, cagily.

He nodded.

"But black magic might."

He nodded again. This time the corners of his mouth rose up at the ends.

"Oh I don't know Marco. I've barely begun learning how to use white magic. I don't think I want to—"

"You don't have another choice," he asserted.

I looked him in the eyes and nodded.

"Hope," Eva suddenly interjected. "Don't do something you might regret."

"I know," I replied. "But what other choice do we have?"

"We can try to fight them ourselves!" Baptiste insisted, honorably.

"And we'll die doing it," I replied. "It's suicide if we go out there. We won't even last five minutes against them."

"Unless you have an army to back you up," Marco maintained.

I nodded.

"But I must remind you there's always consequences when working in *magia negra*. You know that right?"

"Well I saw what happened to you." My voice was hard.

"You think I was captured by the Society because I worked *magia negra*?"

"Of course!"

He laughed.

"After you and Christian created that stupid cure, Rosa told me that you'd have to pay the price for what'd you done."

"She told you that?"

"Yeah."

He shook his head.

"Don't you believe it's true?" I asked, confused.

"Working in black magic isn't about karma. Just because I channeled a little dark energy doesn't mean that I'm walking around with a target on my back waiting for something bad to happen to me!"

"But you got caught! How do you explain that?"

"I don't know," he shrugged "Coincidence."

"I don't believe in coincidence."

"Well, I do," he asserted. "Christian and I being captured had more to do with the fact that they wanted to make a replica of our cure and absolutely nothing to do with me channeling dark energy!"

"Okay Professor Snape," Eva barked, with her eyes to the window. "Hogwarts is about to crumble if you and Hermione can't find a way to save our asses in the next five minutes."

"Fine!" I said. "Let's do it then."

"Good," Marco replied, "but there's no *let's* in any of this. It's all on you."

"What?"

"Since being stuck in HQ I've been...silenced."

"Silenced?"

He nodded. "I can't channel dark energy."

"It's karma!" I insisted.

"Well whatever it is, I can't do it and believe me I've tried. When those bastards were torturing me I'd given my right arm to have thrown a little *magia negra* their way!"

"So you can't summon the sailors with me?" I was confused.

"No."

"Then I'll just have to do it myself."

"Hope," Eva shouted. "Are you sure?"

"We've got nothing else." I turned to face Marco. "How do I do it?"

He took a deep breath. "It's not that difficult."

"Good."

"Black Magic is like white magic in most ways."

"I'm listening."

"Get in touch with your energy. Feel it within you."

"Okay." I could feel my body coming alive from within.

"Make like you're going to channel your energy for goodness."

"But I'm not this time, am I?"

"No."

I felt the power surging through the veins beneath my skin.

"We'll do it like a simple curse."

"A curse?" I said, alarmed.

Marco nodded. "It's no big deal. It's just a curse."

I shrugged.

"We'll resurrect the ghosts of these fallen sailors with a resurrection, born of hate, anger and revenge."

"That sounds lethal."

"It will be. And they'll fight for us, soul for soul."

"Soul for soul," I said. "What does that mean?"

"For every soul of our enemy that dies, one of our army will return to their grave again. Cool?"

"Cool."

He looked out the window. "What time is it?" he asked, anxiously.

Baptiste checked his phone. "Nearly midnight."

"Tell me exactly," he ordered.

"Eleven fifty-seven."

Marco nodded.

"Why do you need to know the time?" I asked. "Got a date or something?"

"No, but your curse relies on the time."

"It does?"

"You will only have a half hour to use your army. Do you understand?"

"No!" I panicked.

"White magic and black magic work in different ways Hope." His dark eyes were enlivened.

"Okay."

"This is hoodoo you're about to channel. It's serious business."

"I know."

"Do you about dead time?"

"No," I said, shaking my head.

"It surrounds the midnight hour."

"Okay."

"All magic is most potent at this time."

"And when the hands of the clock strike twelve, I lose my shoe and my car turns back into a pumpkin?" My tone was cheeky.

Marco grabbed my arm. "This is not a joke."

"Okay," I said, shaking him off.

He withdrew his hand from me and sighed. "Maybe you're not ready for this."

"I'm ready," I insisted. My tone was like ice.

"The half hour leading up to midnight is for working *magia blanca*. The half hour after midnight is for *magia negra*. Do you understand?"

"Yeah."

"What time is it?" Marco asked, again.

Baptiste checked his phone. "Midnight exactly."

Marco nodded. "Now it begins."

I nodded in reply.

"After you channel them you will only have half an hour to use them to fight. Got it?"

"Got it," I replied, eagerly.

"Someone, get Hope a glass of water," Marco insisted.

"I'll get it," Eva replied, rushing to the kitchen. A moment later she returned holding a wine glass filled with tap water.

"Thanks," I said, taking the glass.

"Drink," Marco instructed.

I drank down the entire contents of the cup.

"Now," he said. "Repeat after me. Moarte,va,vine,in,viata."

I cleared my throat. "Moarte,va,vine,in,viata."

"Say it again," he insisted.

"Moarte,va,vine,in,viata."

"And again!"

"Moarte,va,vine,in,viata!" My voice was hard and my tone was resolute. All of a sudden I began to choke!

"Hope?" Eva inquired rushing toward me.

The choking continued. I couldn't speak. I could barely breathe!

"Hope!" Eva asked. "Are you okay?"

I shook my head and continued choking. I reached from my throat with my hands as though I was gasping for air until suddenly I couldn't breathe at all!

"Shit!" Eva yelled. "What did you do to her Marco?"

Water spewed from deep within my lungs and out through my lips! It pooled along the wooden floor of the living room.

"I'm not doing this," Marco defended. "She's doing it to herself. She's summoning them."

"Well it looks like she's drowning to me!" Eva rebutted.

"She's not drowning damn it!"

"Help her!" Eva shouted.

"Don't!" Marco barked. "If you touch her it will stop the conjuring. She needs to complete the curse for the army to manifest."

Just then I fell to the floor, water still spewing from my mouth.

"And if we don't stop her, she's gonna drown to death!" Eva reached out and grabbed my arm.

"Eva," Marco shouted. "Don't you dare touch her! I'm warning you!"

"Don't you talk to my Eva that way!" Baptiste roared.

"Fine," Marco replied. "But I insist that you all step back. A witch in action is more volatile than a tornado in full swing. If you touch her—if you distract her, even a little, while she's still working she could easily turn on you. Do you want that to happen?"

Eva shook her head.

"And you?" Marco snarled, eyeing Baptiste. "Do you want that on you?"

"No," he replied, grudgingly.

"Then let her do her thing," Marco insisted. "Just shut up for a second and let her finish this!"

29. Mad As A Hatter

"Meat-eating orchids forgive no one just yet,
Cut myself on angel's hair and baby's breath,
Broken hymen of your highness I'm left back,
Throw down your umbilical noose so I can climb right back."

Heart-Shaped Box - Nirvana

I doubled over on the floor. Water continued rushing from my lips. I really did feel as though I was drowning. I'd always had a fear of drowning—and this was it; the feeling of being crushed from the inside out.

"Stay strong," Marco coaxed. "Keep channeling your power. Think of the sailors—think of them rising from the bottom of the sea!"

With eyes closed I tried refocusing on the energy within me. And then I saw them; the sailors at the bottom of the ocean, laying dormant within the wreckage of the fallen vessels that brought them to Perish Key. I watched, like a voyeur, as they emerged from deep within their watery graves. Like black smoke, their spirits ascended to the surface. I continued watching as an immense tidal wave of souls suddenly burst through!

And when the ocean settled, moonlight cast its gloomy sheen upon my newly resurrected army of sailors. As they emerged from water their bodies took form. Some were flesh covered and still dressed in bits and pieces of their tattered uniforms, while others looked like skeletons rising up from the sand. They marched in unison toward Ambrose House, like a ghostly resurrected garrison, intent on destroying anything that got in their way!

"Hope!" Eva shouted. "Are you okay?"

The last of the water had finally fallen from my lips. I didn't feel like I was drowning anymore and the choking had stopped too. I opened my eyes. "It's done," I said, rising to my feet.

Marco nodded.

I rushed to the window and looked outside. The army of our doubles was waiting on the lawn, taunting us out with vulgar heckling and fierce demonstrations of their aggression.

"What do we do?" Eva asked, anxiously.

"What else—fight them," Batiste replied, smashing his fists together.

"You'll never win," Marco Senior said as he finally struggled to consciousness.

"You're awake!" I exclaimed.

"Even if you manage to destroy this batch, they'll likely send more," he continued.

"Who are you?" Eva asked, confused.

"I'm Marco, Rosa's son."

The young Marco widened his eyes and turned to stare at Marco Senior. The resemblance between the two of them was uncanny. It was easy to see that they were indeed related.

"Who did you say you were?" the young Marco asked.

"Marco Ramirez Gonzales. The son of Beliarosa Ramirez Gonzales."

"No!" he replied, shocked. "You can't be. The man you speak of ran away on my Abuela many years ago."

"Abuela?" Marco senior, exclaimed, taken aback.

The young Marco nodded. "The man you speak of abandoned my mother—*god rest her soul*—and when she got sick, she begged my grandmother to raise me."

"You are Marco Gonzales?" Marco Senior asked, moving toward him.

Young Marco nodded.

"Dio Mio!" Marco Senior exclaimed, embracing him. "When your mother found out she was pregnant, I was captured by the Society. I've been imprisoned for many years—all of your life in fact!" He embraced him tighter. "I dreamed of the day I would lay my eyes upon my son for the first time," he beamed, "and today is that day!"

"You're my father?"

"Yes!" he exclaimed.

The young Marco's eyes widened. He was awestruck.

"You look like me," his father said. "Your eyes...and your chin...you look like your mother too."

Just then the sound of a colossal crash resonated! I rushed to the window and looked outside. Tall trees were falling like sticks in the distance.

"What is it?" Eva asked.

"Our troops," I replied. "They must be arriving."

I continued watching, with my face pressed to the window, when all of a sudden the front door smashed opened! It crashed to the ground with an in-human thrust.

"NO!" Eva shouted, as a crowd of our clones pushed their way inside the house.

"Someone protect Richard!" I yelled, before charging in to take on two Eva imitators.

I waved my hands through the air in an effort to freeze them with my power, but they were quick. Bolts of electric energy shot from my fingertips, through the house, bouncing against the walls and leaving trails of ice in their path.

"Careful there, Blondie!" the real Eva snarled, from across the room.

I looked over at her. The edge of her pants had been impaled to the wall behind her by an icy stalactite created by the energy emitted from my fingers! In fact, I'd created dozens of icy stalactites along the ceiling and walls.

"Got you now, bitch!" one of Eva's doubles shouted. She sprung through the air and landed on my back!

I groaned aloud and struggled to shake her off, but she wouldn't budge. Then, suddenly, I felt her fangs digging into my neck.

"Screw this!" I shouted, leaping up into the air as high as I could, impaling her on the nearest stalactite.

The fake Eva screamed with pain. Blood drenched me like a rainstorm from above! And as I fell back down to the ground, she stayed behind, attached to the ceiling, impaled and dead.

I wiped the blood from my face and looked around. Ambrose House had become a battlefield. Everyone was engaged in some kind of fight. Marco Junior was aggressively fighting a version of me, while his father was engaged in some kind of old-fashioned street boxing with a Baptiste impersonator. Even Eradan was there. But I didn't see Richard. He wasn't lying on the couch and he wasn't fighting either.

"*Eradan,*" I said, through my thoughts. "*Where's Richard?*"

Eradan was in the midst of kicking a fake Eva's ass. I watched for a moment, impressed by his masterly skill in fighting. He was tough, strong and entirely experienced. He made hand-to-hand combat seem easy.

"*I hid him in the linen closet,*" he said with his inner voice, suddenly sneaking up behind imposter Eva and snapping her neck. "*Don't think your clones will find him there, unless they get the sudden urge to fold laundry.*"

I grinned and watched as bogus Eva's body fell to the floor dead. "What are you still doing here?" I asked, approaching.

"Helping," he said, punching yet another Eva to the ground.

"You shouldn't be here. This isn't your fight."

"I know," he replied, grinning. "But it seemed like you needed a hand."

I smiled, when suddenly I felt a blow to the spine! I fell forward, crashing to the ground!

Eradan growled with rage and savagely sought to destroy my attacker! I watched from the floor as my son boldly defended my honor, when I felt a strange pain radiating from within my abdomen. I struggled to sit up, but fell back down again.

"Shit!" I cried out.

Blood rushed from my lips. I brought my hand to my mouth and tried stopping it.

"Hope!" Eva said, noticing me. She finished vanquishing the last two of her attackers and rushed to my side.

"What's wrong with Esperanza?" Baptiste asked, finishing off the last imposter left in the house.

The rush of blood had finally stopped. I wiped my lips with the back of my hand and winced with pain again. My stomach felt like fire. My body felt like it was burning. And I felt like I was dying!

"What's wrong?" Eva panicked.

I struggled to speak. "I-I...was hit in the spine."

"God!" she replied, "Did they stab you or—"

"HOPE!" Eradan suddenly shouted.

I grabbed hold of my stomach and forced myself to sit. I looked toward him and froze! His body began flickering like a weak signal on a television set. The only time I'd ever seen something similar was when Eva was near-death after a race at The Devil's Tongue.

"What's happening to me?" Eradan panicked.

I closed my eyes. I fought against the pain that was radiating from within me. All of a sudden I felt a pool of blood welling between my legs! I howled at the top of my lungs!

"Oh shit!" Eva exclaimed. "You need a doctor! Quick, she needs a doctor!"

"Richard," Baptiste asserted. "He's a doctor."

"Well wake him up damn it!" Eva's voice was shrill. "Wake him now!"

"Where is he?" Baptiste asked, looking around.

"Linen closet," Eradan mumbled, still flickering. "I hid him there."

Baptiste sped up the stairs toward the linen closet and not a moment too soon Richard was already at my side. His wounds were healed and it was clear that he'd been revived with a little of B's blood.

"Hope," Richard soothed. "I'm here. Everything is going to be okay."

"What's wrong with her?" Eva's voice was hard.

He shook his head and eyed the blood.

"She said she was hit in the spine."

"Hum," Richard muttered. "Does she suffer from clots?"

"No."

"Pelvic infection."

"I don't think so." Eva groaned. "What the hell Doc, help her!"

"I don't know...it could be a ruptured *abdominal* aortic aneurysm or even—"

I screamed again, this time nearly shattering all of the windows in the living room!

"H-O-P-E!" Eradan, continued. His voice was weak and barely audible now.

I fought to see him. I struggled to raise my eyes!

"I'm disappearing!" he continued. "Why? What's happening to me?"

"You do know she's pregnant right?" Eva's voice was terse.

"Pregnant?" Richard's eyes bulged. "That changes everything," he uttered, distraught. "The blow to her spine must have forced the fetus to..."

"To what?" Eva panicked. "What's happening to her?"

"The pregnancy is spontaneously terminating as we speak." He eyed the blood again. "She's loosing the baby, Eva."

"NO!" Eva wailed. "You have to do something! Your her father, damn it! Do something!" she continued.

Baptiste neared Eva and wrapped his strong arms around her.

I closed my eyes. I'd heard everything that Richard had said. I knew *I* wasn't dying—but that Eradan was. Time really was of the essence now. I pushed through the pain and concentrated on the last of my connection to mother earth. Tears of blood pooled in my tightly shut eyes.

"*P-please,*" Eradan said, faintly through my thoughts for the last time. "*Don't let go...don't...*" And then his voice silenced. He was gone.

30. Queen Of Hearts

"Help me I broke apart my insides, help me I've got no soul to sell,
Help me the only thing that works for me, help me get away from myself."

Closer — Nine Inch Nails

Darkness enveloped me. My body was frozen in an icy numbness. My heart was hard and glacial. When I woke there was only one thing on my mind; Eradan.

He didn't deserve to die and it was my fault that he had. I was a terrible mother—if even only briefly. I was a horrible person for asking him to fight my battle in the first place. And I was revolted with myself for not working harder to protect him even as a fetus.

I used my power for ill-will. I conjured an army of dead sailors with black magic. Was Eradan's death my punishment? Was this the karma I warranted for my actions?

Guilt scathed me with impetuous harassment. I was plagued by what I had done and revolted by my ability to physically recover so quickly, as though nothing had even happened.

I pursed my lips until they didn't feel like lips anymore, only flesh cutting through fangs. Blood dripped down my chin and I reveled in it.

"Hope!" Eva exclaimed. "What are you doing?"

I tightened the laces on my boots and straightened my shirt. I rose to my feet and eyeballed the door.

"Esperanza," Baptiste called out. "Where are you going?"

I didn't reply. I walked to the rack by the remains of the front door and reached for my black, leather jacket.

"Hope," Richard expressed. "You've just been through a rather serious medical situation. You need to rest!"

I was a vampire. I didn't need to rest. My wounds were already healed. I stayed silent, zipped up my jacket and walked outside into the darkness. I was hell-bent on one thing and one thing alone; retribution.

I walked along the porch, down the steps and into the backyard. I was weaponless, but fearless nonetheless. My son's untimely death deserved to be vindicated, and this was my chance to do so.

I rounded the corner of the house. I eyed the backyard. Combat marked every corner of the property. Hundreds of our doubles were exchanging blows with the grisly army of dead sailors that I had conjured.

I closed my eyes and called forth my *power*. An icy chill suddenly swept through the air. I opened my eyes and watched as an eerie fog abruptly rolled in from the forest. It blanketed Ambrose's battlefield like rolling smoke. The sky was blacker than coal and the moon had decided to vanish too. Only darkness prevailed.

I stepped foot on the field. Two Christian clones lunged at me from either side! I shot bolts of ice from my fingertips, freezing them like cadaverous icebergs. An instant later they exploded. I continued walking.

Just then, a mammoth Baptiste imitator jumped on my back! I fell to the ground. As he thrashed, growling and salivating upon me like an animal, I channeled a ball of electric, icy energy within the palm of my hand. He flipped me over; I stuffed the ice ball deep inside his mouth. And when he reached to remove it, I hurried away. A moment later his head exploded from the inside out, into zillions of icy-fleshy pieces. I continued walking.

I eyeballed the battlefield, watching as my ghost soldiers valiantly fought for our cause. I let my eyes glaze over. I began to chant. "*Elementum recolligo huic locus. Commodo mihi vestri vox. Elementum unda ego dico vos. Permissum pluit is est meus nos sic vadum is exsisto.*"

Raindrops descended from the sky. I extend my fingertips towards them, turning them too to ice. In a single sweep, I coaxed the frozen droplets to fall. Like glacial arrows they violently speared through the flesh of the clones, leaving them dead. I continued walking.

All of a sudden three Eva replicas moved in on me! I extended my fingertips and compelled my power to turn my nails into razor-sharp icicles. Frozen blades extend from my nail beds. And when the first Eva charged, I was ready.

I dug my icy nails deep into her chest and flicked her away dead. When the second Eva attacked, I stuck her with my icy index finger and threw her off too. The third Eva was much feistier. She was cunning and more calculating in her assault. She flew through the air and jumped on my back! She sat on my shoulders and wrapped her long legs around my neck. I tried throwing her off, but she was resilient and just wouldn't let go. I extended my right hand, parted my index and middle fingers and thrust them upward, shoving my icy nails deep inside her eye sockets. She screamed with pain. I withdrew my fingers as she fell from my shoulders. I watched as her entire body turned to ice before exploding.

I wiped the bits of her carnage from my face and continued walking. As I moved through the rolling fog, more and more of these disturbing doubles continued attacking me. Soon, it didn't matter whether they wore the face of Eva, Baptiste, Christian or even myself; all that mattered to me was that they died.

I dug my blade-like nails into their chests and extracted their hearts. Their cries only served to empower my rage! Bodies of my enemies exploded like frozen fireworks around me. I felt supreme fighting alongside my battalion of dead souls!

Doubles sprung in front of me, charged me from the sides, leapt on my back and even attacked me from above, but I didn't panic. I used my nails to slice their throats. I used my energy to freeze them whole and shatter them apart. And with every kill, I grew stronger and steadfast and hungrier for more death.

As the fog thickened, I could barely see how many of my enemies remained. A row of five of them stood before me. They were angrier than hell and fixed on my destruction. I looked them in the eyes. They growled and flashed their fangs. I kneeled down before them. They watched intently, ecstatic with my seeming submission. I closed my eyes and channeled my power again. I thought of the bone-dagger I'd had in New York. I recalled the way it felt in my hand and the sharpness of its blade, when suddenly I felt my power at work. I opened my eyes and looked to the ground. A long, medieval style sword made of ice sat before me. Its blade was sharper than a katana and its hilt was icy, elegant and shaped like a butterfly. Chills surged through my body as I reached for it. It was weighty and lethal. I held the ice-sword in my hand, rose to my feet and swung it hard. Heads of the five enemies fell instantly, severed from their torsos, falling to the ground. I retracted my sword and continued walking.

Through the fog I marched, dragging my blood-stained sword of ice behind me. I cut enemies down with ease as I trudged, slicing and severing them to pieces. I projected even more stalactites from my fingertips. Only this time they were massive and towered over my enemies. I skewered dozens of them together, straight through their hearts, with effortlessness. I was a perilous force to reckon with. I was on a vengeance rampage and I was unstoppable!

But as the fog began to clear, I realized that the battlefield was nearly empty. The more enemies I'd killed, the more dead sailors I'd returned back to their watery graves. And before long only one duplicate remained. It was a Christian clone. I grabbed him by the jaw and thrust him against a tree.

"Who sent you?" I demanded, enraged.

"Go to hell!"

"Where are the others?" I snarled. "Rosa, Henry...the baby?"

He spit in my face. My eyes widened. I brought the tip of my icy sword to his chest and pressed it into him a little.

"Who do you work for?" I continued.

He winced. I pressed it a little deeper crimson staining his clothes.

"I-I don't know!"

"You don't know?" I dug my nails into the thin skin on his throat. Blood pooled at the wounds.

"I don't know his name!" he exclaimed.

"Where is he keeping my family?"

"I-I..."

"Tell me damn it!" I raged, digging the sword into him even more.

His eyes suddenly lessened and slowly they began to close.

"Speak!" I insisted.

"They're in a boat," he said, wearily. "Off shore..."

Just then the site where I'd lacerated him with my nails began freezing over. It didn't take long for his entire body to ice up too. I withdrew my sword from his torso and backed away. I watched as he exploded into the familiar glacial mess of ice and flesh. The last of my soldiers had already begun to vanish too.

I looked around. There were no bodies left on the battlefield, but the war was definitely over.

I dropped my sword to the ground. I snapped my fingers and tossed a flame at it. Fire consumed my icy weapon within an instant. I turned around, marched across the grass and made my way back inside the house.

I was covered in blood, dirt and even cartilage when I reached Ambrose House. I walked straight through the front door and into the living room.

"God!" Eva shrieked, alarmed.

"That's the thanks I get for saving your asses?" I snarled, wiping blood off my face.

"That wasn't just saving," Baptiste interjected. "That was annihilation, Esperanza!" His voice was animated. "You were like some ice-queen Xena or something out there!"

I half-smiled in reply, a little unsure whether to feel pride or disgust with what I'd done.

"Your hair!" Eva exclaimed. "It's changed color again."

I reached for my hair. It was pure white now—all of it. I pushed it back behind my ears and looked around the room. Marco and his father were sitting together on the couch. They looked bloodied, beaten and exhausted.

"We watched you from in here," Richard exclaimed. "It was..."

"Spectacular?" I said, sardonically.

"Atrocious!" he replied.

My eyes narrowed.

"Are they dead?" Eva asked.

"All of them," I said. "And the last of them divulged where they're keeping Strombo, Henry, Rosa and the others."

"My god!" she exclaimed with elation.

"They're close. They're on a boat, off shore." I turned toward the door again.

"Let's go," Eva said, readily. Her and Baptiste moved across the room and started toward the door.

"Aren't any of you coming?" I said, suddenly realizing that the others weren't following behind us.

"No," young Marco asserted. "The three of us have been through enough. We're still weak."

I nodded.

"Please bring my Abuela home," he pleaded.

I nodded again. I turned around and led the way outside.

"What about Christian?" Eva asked, the moment we neared the forest.

"What about him?"

"He should be with us. We've got to get him."

Baptiste nodded in agreement.

"But he's only human," I insisted. "He's a liability."

"A liability?" Eva snarled. "What's happened to you, Hope? I thought you loved him? I thought you'd want him to be with us in this?"

I shrugged. I didn't have time for love. My heart had been overshadowed by hate. I stormed through the forest towards the ocean. When we reached the beach I spotted a luxurious yacht floating just off shore in the moonlight.

"There!" I said, marching across the sand.

"What's your plan?" Eva asked, grabbing my arm.

"I'm done with plans," I replied, sharply. "Your last plan brought this hell to our shores." I pulled away and continued walking towards the water.

"What are you gonna do?" she asked. "Jump on board and start kicking their asses?"

"Why not?" I replied. "You got a better idea?"

"We could wait until dawn," Baptiste added. "When they—"

"NO!" I interrupted. "It's now or never."

Baptiste agreed. A moment later Eva nodded too. The three of us entered the dark ocean together and sped beneath the water toward the yacht. When we reached the stern, we came to the surface.

"There are guards everywhere," Eva whispered, eyeing them above.

I looked up. Men dressed in black uniforms, grasping heavy artillery, stood at nearly every entry point along the length of the yacht.

"There must be at least five on each side," she continued. "We really need a plan of attack."

"I can take these three," Baptiste said, pointing aloft.

"Yeah, but that leaves two more on this side," Eva insisted.

As I listened to them talking, I continued watching the guard right above us fiddle with his lighter. A cigarette dangled from his mouth and he struggled to ignite it.

"While you two continue talking," I whispered, "I'm gonna go up there and finish this!" A moment later I jumped aboard. "Need a light?" I said, facing the guard and snapping my fingers to make fire.

His eyes bulged. He dropped the cigarette and reached for his gun. I summoned my power again and swiftly slit his throat with my icy nails. He was dead instantaneously and without a sound. I kicked him overboard and continued on.

"Hope!" Eva called out, climbing aboard. "Behind you!"

I turned around. Another guard was approaching. He aimed his gun at me and started to depress the trigger. I shot a bolt of icy energy at his weapon and froze it solid. He tossed the useless machine to the floor and lunged forward to attack me, when suddenly, Batiste intercepted! He threw the guard to the ground and wrestled him hard. Baptiste whaled on him like an animal, eventually twisting his neck and killing him.

As we tossed the body overboard, two more guards jumped on us! Eva took the smallest of the pair. She kicked his gun out of his hands, knocking him in the face simultaneously. He growled at her, but she was determined. As he moved in close, she thrust the sharp heel of her boot deep inside his chest! She withdrew her foot, carrying the guard's heart on the tip of her heel! He wobbled for a moment, dead, before finally falling over the edge of the yacht and into the water.

At the same time, two more guards had arrived to join in the fight. Neither of us held back. Baptiste didn't hesitate to pulverize any of them and I didn't refrain from using my power. And within a few short moments all three of them were dead. We kicked their corpses overboard too.

"Damn," Eva groaned, exhausted. "How many more of them are there?"

"Four," I replied, closing my eyes and suddenly channeling my power to manifest the ice sword again. I opened my eyes and smiled. I picked the ice-sword up from the ground and continued moving through the yacht.

"Esperanza!" Baptiste suddenly called out. "Two...on your left!"

I turned to my left and spotted the guards approaching. I swept my weighty sword of ice toward them and swiftly cut them down like trees the forest. Their torsos separated from their abdomens and their severed bodies slid in differing directions as they hit the water.

A moment later, the last two guards emerged. Dressed in heavy tactical gear and equipped with enough artillery to fill a bunker, their attack was serious. They growled at us before firing their weapons. An abundant spray of bullets stippled the air. Eva and Baptiste hit the deck and took cover. I, on the other hand, stayed standing and faced the ammunition bravely. I channeled my energy and froze the bullets in-mid air. I urged them around and pushed them back to their source of origin. Ammo tore through the air into the bodies of the two guards. In seconds they were dead and on the floor of the yacht. I walked toward them and kicked them overboard and into the water like the others.

Just then, I was distracted by the sound of someone clapping. It was sharp and distinct and coming closer.

"Bravo!" a voice said, applauding. "Bravo, my dear Hope!"

My hard heart thumped in my chest. That voice—it was familiar. Slowly, I turned around.

31 – Behind The Curtain

"Saw Cinderella in a party dress, she was looking for a nightgown.
I saw the devil wrapping up his hands, he's getting ready for the showdown.
I saw the ending when they turned the page, I
threw my money and I ran away."

A Dustland Fairytale – The Killers

"You?" I exclaimed, shocked.

"Expecting someone else?" the voice teased.

My eyes bulged. I couldn't believe who I was looking at. It was Gabe. Squirrely, art-nerd, had-a-crush-on-me-since-forever, Gabe! But he was different. His clothes were fancy and his demeanour was uber confident. He was wearing an expensive looking dress shirt with the top few buttons undone. His pants were dark and neatly pressed. His hair was slicked back and GQ in style and he'd shaved off all of his facial hair. Even his body language was different. He was secure and debonair.

"I'd grown so tired of looking like vermin." He grinned, stroking his freshly shaven face. "I really don't understand the youth of today...so vulgar and dishevelled." His tone was hard. "They have no taste and no class either. It's appalling really."

"But you," I said, bemused. "You helped me. I thought you were my friend."

"I am your friend," he said, taking me by the hand. "Come," he whispered, escorting me inside the yacht.

The interior was undeniably beautiful; decadent and elegant. He led me toward a exquisitely set table inside the main cabin. There were blown glass finger bowls filled with blood, porcelain ramekins of it too, silver tureens and stoneware pitchers, antique wine glasses and tumblers all filled with blood.

"Who are you?" I asked, anxiously.

"Gabriel," he replied in a charming manner. "And you've known that for years Hope!"

My brow furrowed. "Are you vampire?"

"Yes," he smiled.

"Why didn't I smell it in you? Why didn't I—"

"We'll get to that my darling. What's the hurry?" He said, pulling out my chair. "Let's enjoy a little lunch first, shall we?"

I sat down, reluctantly and continued looking at him.

"Didn't your mother ever teach you that it's rude to stare, Hope?"

My eyes hardened.

"Oh my bad!" he laughed. "I forgot. You didn't really have a mother now did you?"

BOOM! There was that familiar tone again inside me. My heart thumped in my chest. I lunged through the air towards him when suddenly he waved his hand at me, stopping me and pushing me back down into my seat again!

"Tsk. Tsk. Tsk," he snarled. "You really need to work on those manners of yours young lady."

I sank in my seat and eyeballed the surroundings. Who the hell was this guy? Was he just a shape-shifter like the others? Or was he really Gabe?

"Really me!" he exclaimed, with open arms. "Doesn't that just blow your mind?"

"Can you read my thoughts?" I asked, fretful.

"Yes."

"So what are you?"

"I'm just like you," he replied, casually. "Only the much better version."

"Vampire *and* Witch?" I queried.

"Something like that, only I'm a much more developed creature than either."

"You mean a *manufactured* creature...like those scientific feeding implants you shove into your drones' arms."

"Don't mock science," he grinned. "It has taken our kind to the next level. We've evolved beyond anything imaginable!"

"I'm not your kind." My tone was cold. I continued eyeballing him.

"Please stop that incessant staring!" he demanded.

I grinned.

"Now what?" he asked.

"I just can't believe it's you."

"What's so hard to believe?" he asked, sipping blood from a fancy green goblet.

I shrugged. "You were so squirrely, and nerdy and—"

"Just the sort of man that could exist undetected!" He laughed. "You really didn't know?"

I shook my head.

"Accept it Hope. I *am* him." His voice was invincible. "I am the bogeyman of your nightmares, the big bad wolf embodying your grandmother, the giant at the top of the beanstalk." His eyes darkened. "I am the one you find when you pull back the curtain!"

"You're Oz."

He smirked. "After the fall of Rome, there was no way in hell we could trust those idiot humans to run the world any longer."

"The fall of Rome?"

"Oh yes." He took another sip of his drink. "I've been around since nearly the beginning my dear."

I sank back in my seat.

"I tried being a good boy," he lamented, "as messenger of the birth of the messiah and all those wonderful things."

My expression widened.

"But being good is just no damn fun!" He laughed. "Who wants to be the teller of the coming of the savior when they they're presented with an opportunity to *become* the savior themselves!"

"The savior?" I said, perplexed.

"Yes! The savior, the leader, the big cheese, the brains behind the machine, whatever you want to call it, it's all me!"

"You're the head of the Society," I said, matter-of-factly.

"Such a clever girl," he purred. "I only had to hand it to you on a silver platter for you to finally see it!"

My eyes narrowed.

"I thought you were smarter than the others Hope. I thought of anyone you would have figured out the truth."

I licked my lips. I suddenly remembered that sordid dream I'd had about a hostile, arrogant version of Gabe. My stomach sank. I felt nauseous as my thoughts inadvertently recalled the feeling of his hands on my skin.

He grinned. I could tell he was reading my thoughts. I could feel him inside my head!

"You've thought of me!" he exclaimed, excitedly.

"I...um..."

He laughed. "I put you up so high on that damn pedestal." He shook his head. "I just needed my feelings to be reciprocated...just a little!"

My brow furrowed. I had no idea what he was a talking about.

"What is it my darling? You look bewildered."

"I am," I admitted.

"Do tell," he implored, excitedly.

"I just can't understand it."

"What? And don't make me read your mind...I so much more enjoy hearing it from those pretty lips of yours instead!"

"I just don't understand why someone as powerful as you would choose to be stuck with *us* all these years?"

"Pardon?" he patronized.

"Why did you stick around all this time?"

"Whatever do you mean?"

"Why did you work at La Fuente?"

"Well..."

"Why did you pretend you were a tattooer!"

He responded, "I've always enjoyed art and—"

"Why did you let us treat you like you were a peon!"

"A peon?" he gasped.

I smirked. "I don't get it Gabe. You're so powerful! You could be anywhere in the world, with anyone in the world—why in the hell did you choose to be with us?"

"I didn't choose it!" he raged. "My heart chose it for me. The heart wants what the heart wants." His voice was hostile and laced with bitterness. The tension between us was awkward. Then suddenly he heaved a sigh and relaxed in his chair again. "Tell me," he said, changing the subject, "how did you come to overthrow ten of my best guards?"

"What?"

"My guards. They were highly skilled, special agents."

I shrugged.

"Okay," he said, "I asked you nicely and you didn't respond. Now I will demand it of you." His face toughened. "How did you overthrow my guards!" he shouted, enraged.

"Where are you keeping my family and friends?" I rebutted.

He grinned, ominously.

"Gabe!"

He rose to his feet and zoomed toward me at vampire speed. I sprang from my chair and started recoiling, but he stopped me. He stood behind me and wrapped his arm around me. The feeling of him touching me was virtually familiar. He pulled me against him and leaned in close to my neck. With his fangs exposed, he dragged their sharp tips across my skin. He licked the tips.

"You taste like an angel," he muttered menacingly.

I fought to release myself. It was all too déjà vu—and things were unfolding as they did in my dream.

"I don't want to hurt you," he continued. "I only want..." he heaved a sigh. "I only want to love you damn it!"

My body froze. *Love me?* Was *I* the reason he'd been hiding here all along?

He inhaled the scent of my skin and sighed. "Oh l'amour," he lamented, "so fickle and unfair." His tone hardened. "But now that I have you," he said, stroking my leg with his hand. "I don't have to ensnare you with REM sleep invasion any longer!"

My expression twisted. Sleep invasion? Had Gabe somehow managed to invade my dreams? Is that why I had that atrocious dream of him?

He smirked. "We'll make your dream a reality! We can rule the world together Hope!"

My body came alive and I could feel the power swelling beneath my veins!

All of a sudden he withdrew his hands from me and moved back to his side of the table. He sat and took another sip from the goblet.

"The moment you arrived it all began for me," he confessed.

"What are you talking about?"

"Our star-crossed romance, of course!"

"Romance? We never had any romance."

"I knew you when you were a child Hope." His voice was dark and grim.

I stiffened my spine and edged away from him.

"Your father used to bring you to HQ when he got called to work late."

My eyes narrowed.

"Don't you remember me?" he smiled.

"No," I insisted coolly.

"Well I knew you were different even then. I knew you were special." His eyes widened. "Your blood was different. I wanted it. I wanted it more than I'd ever wanted anyone's blood before!" He chuckled. "I think I fell in love with you from the very first moment I laid eyes on you."

My expression contorted. I felt sick inside. I wanted to pummel him with my fist. I wanted to shut him up so bad that he'd never speak again!

"And when you went off to college," he continued, "I was there too, always watching and waiting...waiting for just the right opportunity make my move." He stood up again and sped towards me. "I watched you get your heart broken over and over, but I kept my distance."

I pulled back further.

"When you returned to Perish I needed to be close to you."

I felt the energy pulsating beneath my fingertips.

"La Fuente was a perfect way for me to be close to you again. But then *he* got in the way!"

"Christian?"

"Imbecile!" Gabe shouted, shaking his head.

I bit my lip. He moved in close. His face was only an inch from mine.

"I've waited the length of your entire life to do this." He leaned forward and kissed me on the lips! And when his tongue entered my mouth I bit down on it, severing it from his body! I opened my lips and spat out what was left of his tongue. Gabe shrieked in pain and recoiled! Blood poured from his mouth.

All of a sudden the cabin door swung open. I drew my eyes towards it.

"Christian!" I exclaimed in amazement.

He was healed and cognizant and here, standing before me in the flesh! My glacial heart began to thaw at the very sight of him. I rushed towards him and wrapped my arms around him. I gingerly inhaled the sweet scent of his inimitable humanness and melted inside. It was him—the real him and not some shape-shifting clone.

"You...a..re...dea...d!" Gabe struggled to say, charging across the cabin towards us.

"Take cover!" I told Christian, jumping in front of him.

Gabe thrust into me, pushing me to the floor and pinning me there. He leaned forward to bite down into me with his fangs when suddenly, Christian tore him off! Gabe flew through the air, smashing into the elegantly set blood-buffet!

Glass and porcelain, china and silver exploded in a blood-spattered mess, while Gabe landed in midst of it. He was soaked from head to toe in a scarlet staining and struggled to spring to his feet.

"Noooo!" he fought to holler, suddenly reaching for a gun from within a concealed pistol holder on his ankle.

I rose to my feet, leapt across the room towards him and kicked him in the face with my boot. He fell to the floor, unconscious.

"C'mon," Christian said, extending his hand. "Let's go!"

"No," I replied. "We don't deserve to live in world that's run by him!"

"Hope," he uttered, "Don't!"

"I have to Christian. If I can go back, to before he created it, if I can destroy it...the Society—"

"Please," he pleaded. "It's far too dangerous and you've already been through enough!"

"I need to!"

"Don't," he maintained. "Think of yourself...think of our baby!"

BOOM! My heart thumped like iron in my chest. *Our son.* How could I tell him what I'd done? How could I face the truth? Fury swelled beneath my skin and I knew I needed to finish this once and for all.

"I'm going Christian and that's final."

"Why?" he pleaded, desperately.

"Because," I replied. "Then we'll be free!"

He finally nodded.

I smiled one last smile and turned away. I looked at Gabe laying on the floor and let my fangs cut through my gums. I licked my lips and lunged, aiming straight for his jugular.

32. Oz

"Help, I have done it again,
I have been here many times before,
Hurt myself again today,
And the worst part is there's no one else to blame."

Breathe Me - Sia

I ripped a hole the size of Texas right through Gabe's flesh as I bit down into him. His blood was tepid and tasted like shadows as it streamed between my lips. It was nauseating and difficult to swallow, but I forced myself to endure it. I needed to get inside his memories. I needed to find that pivotal moment when he conceived the Society so I could destroy him before he had a chance to create it!

And then it began. I felt the pull of something fighting to take over. *Inhale.*

With a deep breath I triggered the shift and began my descent into Gabriel's past.

Light and color merged together in a seamless unification, while sounds began to blur into a numbing static. The concave time tunnel opened up and suddenly I was traveling inside the wormhole of Gabe's memories.

The tunnel was long and shrouded in darkness, evil and death. I grew angrier and heated the longer I travelled. Pieces of his past flashed before my eyes. Seeing excerpts of the pain and anguish that he'd caused to so many innocents over the years revolted me. He was a monster and there was no doubt in my mind that he deserved to die, but not before the time was right. I need to go farther—deeper, maybe even to the fall of the Roman Empire!

I remembered him saying something about not trusting the humans to run the world after the fall of the Roman Empire. I widened my eyes and continued shifting. After what felt like an eternity, I'd finally reached my destination.

Exhale.

I released a breath of air from my lungs. Everything slowed to a stop. The wormhole of Gabriel's memories shattered into millions of fragmented pieces right before me and when the air cleared, I was there.

Like a history book coming alive, I saw it with my own two eyes! Rome. It was in ruins and still burning to the ground! The pungent scent of charred buildings overwhelmed me instantly. I covered my nose and tried finding a place to hide.

It was dark outside. And the moonlight was barely bright enough to lead my way. I heard voices. I rushed to conceal myself within a nearby structure. I hid inside. The voices neared. They were speaking in a foreign language—Latin. At first, I couldn't understand what they were saying, but then, suddenly their voices became clear and I knew each and every world! Because I was travelling through Gabe's blood, I was reliving his past the way he'd lived it. It didn't matter that I didn't know Latin—he did.

"It's all irrelevant now Romulus," Gabe said. "You've had your chance to rule the world. You failed."

"What are you saying?"

"It's our turn now."

"That's impossible! You people aren't even alive! You can't come out into the sunshine. You live on the lifeblood of rats and vermin. How do you expect to rule the world?"

"We'll learn. We'll build tolerances and fortify ourselves."

"This is outrageous!"

"But it will be a reality. And you must abdicate!"

"I am the Emperor of Rome! I will not!"

"You will."

"Don't do this Gabriel. You'll regret it."

"Perhaps, but that will be my burden to bear."

"Why now, after we've lived together with your kind in peace for so many years?"

"Rome is falling Romulus. It will never be the same again. The world needs order. And I will give them that."

Gabe looked into Romulus' eyes. He chanted something quietly under his breath and suddenly Romulus seemed veiled; passive and meagre, like a true minion under his spell. The two men turned away from one another and disappeared into the darkness.

I kept my eyes on Gabe. He was obviously already a vampire, but from the sound of his conversation he likely hadn't created his new world order yet!

I rushed from where I'd been hiding and followed him. As he walked along the dark path he stopped ever so often to look over his shoulder. He was perceptive and obviously knew that he was being followed, but he continued walking.

The path got darker and more obscured with foliage. There was no one to be seen anywhere. Gabriel stopped walking altogether. He turned around.

"I know you're there," he called out, into the darkness.

I didn't respond.

"Show yourself!" he demanded.

I still didn't respond.

"Don't make me come for you," he taunted.

I felt my power surging beneath my skin. I stepped out onto the path.

"Well!" he said, surprised. "What fair creature might you be?"

"Death," I replied. "I'm the White Devil. And I'm here for your soul."

His eyes widened. He zoomed through the air towards me. His face was only inches away from mine. He looked me up and down and grinned.

"I never imagined death to look so lovely!" His tone was mocking.

I lunged at him, knocking him to the ground, but Gabe was strong and pushed me off with ease.

"How I do enjoy a good fight!" he sneered, rising to his feet.

I fisted my hands and conjured two balls of icy energy in each. I jumped to my feet and threw the balls at him. They flew through the air, when suddenly, he stopped them! He somehow managed to turn them around and fire them back at me! I darted out of the way and hit the ground as they exploded in mid-air.

A moment later he was up in my face again. He inhaled the scent of my skin and smiled.

"You smell heavenly," he sighed.

"Yeah," I teased, "like an angel?"

I channeled my power, forcing my icy nails to emerge. I extended my hands and pierced them through his sides. He wailed with pain as I withdrew and stumbled to the ground, but not a moment too soon he was already standing again.

"Damn!" I snarled, enraged.

"You'll have to do better than that if you want *my* soul!" He laughed.

My eyes narrowed and I could taste fury on my tongue. I sped towards him and jabbed my nails into his chest, just missing his heart.

He grinned.

I extracted my nails. He sped away. I turned around. I couldn't see him anywhere. I looked ahead, into the darkness, but he was gone.

"Shit!" I groaned. I had to find him! I had to kill him here and now!

All of a sudden he appeared again! I whipped around to face him.

"Come now," he said, patronizingly. "Do your worst!"

I scowled and propelled several razor-sharp stalactites at him. He deftly dodged out of the way, missing them entirely.

"That's your worst?" he taunted.

I closed my eyes and summoned my power again. I concentrated on the feeling of the glacial ice sword in the palm of my hand. When I opened my eyes, I was already grasping it.

"What is that?" he uttered, afraid.

I waved it through the air and thrust it at him, missing his torso by a hair! I heaved it forward at him, but he once more managed to evade my strike!

"Your worst needs to be greater than this!" he ridiculed.

I groaned aloud and hauled my glacial sword toward him with all of my might! It flew through the air with poise, like an arrow made of glass! It entered his torso, straight though his heart, expelling the last bit of life from within his lungs.

"That's my worst, bitch," I snarled, before triggering the reversal.

Exhale.

I pushed a breath of air from within me. Everything started moving again. The wormhole of Gabriel's memories restored itself and I began travelling inside of it. The concave, time tunnel opened up to me and I soared speedily through it. When I reached the present, I pushed a little air from my lungs again. The tunnel collapse, the boom tone resounded and I was back.

Gabe was lingering idly on the cabin floor where I'd left him. Blood rushed rampantly from the site at which I'd impaled him in the past. His body oscillated in and out of translucence. There was no doubt about it—he was dead.

"Hope!" Christian exclaimed, rushing towards me.

I rose to my feet and wrapped my arms around him.

"You did it," he smiled. "You destroyed the Society as though it never existed!"

"I did."

I leaned in close to kiss him, when all of a sudden, the ship began heaving! Like a wild ride, it tossed us from port to starboard and back again! Christian and I clung to each other.

"Residuals," I shouted.

He nodded in reply.

This was the butterfly effect of killing Gabriel in the past. When the turbulence subsided, I heard a bang! Christian suddenly waned in my arms.

"Christian?" I said, withdrawing.

I pulled away and watched as blood pooled in a large circle over his heart, staining his white T-shirt.

I looked around. Gabriel was dead, but his finger must have depressed the trigger on his pistol after all, before he vanished.

"My god!" I exclaimed, watching as wisps of smoke still lingered in air from the gunshot.

He fell to the floor.

"No! No! No!" I shouted, touching his face. "Don't die on me! Don't you dare die! Not now! Not after all this!"

"I-I'm s-sorry," he mumbled, blood emerging from between his lips.

"NO!" I exclaimed, crimson tears welling in my own eyes. "You promised me forever!"

His eyes diminished and soon closed shut. I grabbed hold of his weak, failing, human body and brought him to a sitting position.

"Damn you Christian!" I cried. "You lied to me!" Tears of blood streamed down my face. I pulled him even closer and pressed my lips to his in a kiss, but he was turning cold, like ice. "No!" I wailed.

I cried and cried, tears falling against his lips and inside his mouth. Suddenly he began to stir!

My eyes widened. "Christian?"

His blue toned lips began to move, taking in my fallen tears of blood.

"My god!" I exclaimed, abruptly biting into my wrist, drawing blood and holding an even steadier stream above his mouth.

Before long, his entire body began moving again! He extended his arm and grasped my wrist in his hand. He latched his lips against me and drank insatiably of my very essence. Soon, he opened his eyes. They were green and glowing with iridescence one more! He was back. My Christian was back!

A moment later he withdrew.

"How do you feel?" I asked, elatedly.

He filled his gaze with my face and grinned.

"How do you feel, Christian?"

"I feel...I feel like a man reborn to keep his promise."

"Forever," I exclaimed, embracing him.

"Forever."

We came together in a kiss. Not a moment too soon, Eva and Baptiste suddenly entered the cabin.

"What happened here?" Eva asked. She was holding baby Stromboli in her arms and smiling.

I rushed towards her. "You found him!" I gushed. "Thank god. And the others?"

"All accounted for." Baptiste grinned. "Marco and his father have already begun taking them back to house."

I nodded, pleased.

"Christian! You look good, bro," Baptiste's grinned.

Christian smiled.

"B and I saw you go inside the cabin," Eva said. "We thought we'd search the rest of the yacht for the others."

"You saw him?" My tone was hard.

Eva nodded. "I still can't believe it was Gabe all along."

"Neither can I."

Just then the yacht started disappearing beneath our feet!

"What the hell?" Baptiste hollered, as it flickered in and out of visibility.

"Residuals," I replied. "I killed Gabe before he conceived the Society. Everything associated with the Society should have never existed!"

"This boat too?" Eva panicked.

I nodded.

"Let's go," Baptiste hollered.

I nodded too. "Let's get outta here."

33. Mirror Mirror

"'Cause I don't wanna lose you now,
I'm lookin' right at the other half of me,
The vacancy that sat in my heart,
Is a space that now you hold."

Mirrors —Justin Timberlake

When we got back to Ambrose House I couldn't understand why we still had our memories of *them*. Killing Gabe in ancient Rome before he created the Society, should have obliterated everything associated with it.

I walked into the living room to be with the others. I sat down on the couch next to Christian and leaned against a soft pillow.

"Well," Eva muttered, "I remember the way he used to stare at me from behind those creepy wire-framed glasses of his. I always knew he was strange."

"Oh Eva," Baptiste laughed. "You're so full of it."

"Am not! Gabe was odd. I always knew there was something weird about him."

"Oh please," he continued.

"I'm serious. No normal person would ever wear facial hair that thick!" Everyone laughed.

"Hey Hope," Baptiste muttered.

"Yeah?"

"Was Gabe wearing one of those togas when you killed him?"

I cracked a smiled and tossed the pillow at him.

Everyone laughed again.

"What I want to know is why we still remember," Richard's voice was firm. "The memories aren't particularly clear, but I still recall the feeling of working at HQ."

"I've been thinking a lot about that too," I added. "I killed Gabe before he ever created the Society. Everything from that moment on never should have existed—because of the fact that *he* never existed."

"So we shouldn't remember Gabe at all?" Eva asked, confused.

"All of our memories of Gabe and the Society should have vanished from our consciousness the instant I obliterated him."

"But they didn't," Eva insisted.

"Exactly."

"Hope's right," Christian agreed. "I too would have assumed that our memories would have died with Gabriel."

"True," Henry added, "but remember some of the effects of Hope's efforts did indeed manifest."

"Like what?" Eva snorted.

"Well," Henry replied. "Gabriel is dead and Ryan and her friends aren't here anymore."

I nodded. It was going to be difficult moving on without Ryan. She'd become such an integral part of my life. I hoped that she was out there somewhere with her family, probably confused, but free to live the life she always wanted.

"I is gonna miss that lass," Alex added, cheerlessly.

"You and Ryan sure did hit it off," Eva added.

Alex grinned. "Maybe one day I'll go abroad and find her."

I beamed. "I think that's a great idea. And I'll come with you."

"Then we shall find her together," Alex grinned.

Eva rolled her eyes. "Awesome idea ladies. The poor woman finally gets her normal life in order, and then one day gets a knock on door from the likes of you two freaks!"

"So you're coming with us?" I insisted, knowingly.

"Damn straight, Blondie! I'm never one to say no to a road trip."

I smiled.

"Hope," Henry interjected, "the point at which you finally killed Gabriel—had he conceived of the Society?"

I thought about it for a moment. "Well, I remember overhearing him talking to that Romulus guy about taking back the world from the humans...something about a new world order."

"A new world order," Henry muttered.

"Could that be the beginning of the Society?" I inquired.

Henry nodded. "I think it just might be."

"I still don't understand," Eva whined. "Why do we remember him?"

"Perhaps because he'd already conceived of the plan before Hope killed him." Henry's voice was factual.

"Even though he didn't actually begin recruiting for the Society yet?" I asked.

"Yes," Henry replied. "The fact that he had already foreseen its potential may have been enough to prompt the retention of memories."

"And," Rosa added. "You power is strong now, Hope. Energy you use in past to effect world...who knows what—*how you say*—riddle, you cause?"

"Do you mean residual, Rosa?" I smiled.

"Si," she replied, grinning. "Residual."

"Well," Christian asserted, "whatever the reason, I'm just glad we're all here together again."

"Me too," I said, leaning in and kissing him on the cheek.

"And we're very glad to be here too," Marco Senior expressed. He was grasping hands with Rosa and his son.

"And me as well," Richard added, smiling. "It's been far too long."

"Hey Richard," Eva exclaimed. "Remember the time you and Henry took that old rowboat out and got lost?"

Baptiste and Christian laughed.

"It wasn't my fault," Richard defended. "I didn't know the area."

"And I couldn't see where the hell we were going!" Henry added.

Everyone laughed.

"And remember the time Rosa and I pretended we were Baptiste and Richard?" Eva continued.

"Dios mio!" Rosa laughed.

"She cast some cloaking spell and came out all transformed into Richard, then I shape-shifted into B and we headed down to La Fuente to surprise Christian!"

Christian rolled his eyes.

"If you'd seen the look on Christian's face," Eva said. "When we both leaned in and kissed him in front of the clients! It was priceless!"

"And thoroughly embarrassing!" Christian added.

"I didn't know you did this," Baptiste suddenly interjected.

"And neither did I," Richard added, irritated.

"Oh let it go boys!" Eva insisted. "That was ages ago. We've all grown up since then. Haven't we Rosie?"

"Si," she replied, forlornly. "Some of us even managed to grow old."

Everyone laughed and continued swapping stories. As I looked around the living room I was moved by the overwhelming feeling of family around me. Rosa had reunited with her son after many years, Marco had come back to his Abuela, Eva and Baptiste had little Strombo, Richard was seemingly in my life again and Christian had returned to me! Despite the anger I still held in my heart, I couldn't help but feel touched by all the love in the room.

"Rosa," I said, calling out to her. "You gotta second?"

"Si," she replied, intrigued.

I signalled for her to meet me in the hallway. When she arrived I grasped her hand and began pulling her up the stairs toward the bedroom.

"Slow down!" she shouted. "I is old lady remember!"

"Oh you're not that old Rosie."

"Where is you taking me child?"

"Just a little farther."

"Dios mio," she mumbled, under her breath. "Why you just no talk to me downstairs?"

"Because I want to show you something."

"And you no bring it downstairs?" Her voice was playful.

"No Rosie, I can't bring it downstairs!" I smiled. "Besides, it's a secret and I didn't want anyone else hearing our conversation."

"Oh. Secret. Now I is very interested."

"C'mon," I said, helping her up. "You're nearly there."

I pulled her through my bedroom door. She sat with me on the edge of the bed.

"I've been doing a lot of reading lately," I expressed.

"What you read?"

"This," I said, pulling my grandmother's journal out from beneath the bed.

"Good," she sighed. "You learn your family from this. You better understand your grandma through writing. Si?"

"Naw, it's not really her journal."

"It not?"

I shook my head. "Watch!" I focused all my attention on my power and began channeling it. I felt it swelling beneath my fingertips and extending beyond. When it reached the pages of my grandmother's journal I grinned.

"My goodness," Rosa awed.

All of a sudden the blank pages began filling with words. The journal itself thickened and darkened with age spots and wear as I held onto it.

"Your grimoire?" she asked.

"Si," I replied, smirking.

"Let me look." She took the book from my hands and began sifting through the pages. Her old eyes narrowed as she read.

"I've been reading and trying to translate some of the spells in here."

"Good," she mumbled. "You learn much from this book."

"I know," I replied. "It's totally fascinating and I can't wait to try some of the spells."

Rosa smiled.

I stood up and walked toward the dresser across from my bed. I opened the top drawer and pulled out my grandmother's truth mirror.

"What you got now?" Rosa asked, curiously.

"This was my grandmother's too."

"Very beautiful."

"It's a truth mirror," I divulged, extending the mirror towards her. She took it in her hand and eyed the ornate handle.

"If you look into it, you'll see—"

"Verdad," she interrupted. "Truth."

"Have you ever seen one of these?"

"No. I not even know your grandmother had one!"

"When I looked, I saw *her*—the White Devil. I don't ever want to look into this damn thing again!"

"Hope!" she snapped. "I told you stop torturing self with demon story!"

"I know, but I can't help it." I bit my lip. "Anyhow, I think you should look into it."

"Me?" she said, surprised. "Why I look?"

"Because," I explained, sitting beside her on the bed. "I know the real you. I met her in 1957."

"Oh child," Rosa replied "She long gone."

"No she's not," I insisted. "She's still you."

"But I is old now and wrinkly like raisin!"

I laughed.

"It no use for me to see truth."

"The truth is that you're beautiful whether you're young or old Rosa." I smiled. "I just wish you believed that too."

She heaved an audible sigh and turned the mirror around. She stared at her reflection in the cracked glass and gasped.

"Dios mio!" she exclaimed.

I moved beside her and looked at her reflection with her.

"I is so young, so vivacious and so beautiful!"

Her face was olive toned, her lips were stained red, her eyes were big and brown, her hair was shiny and her skin was smooth. She was the spitting-image of herself in the past!

"I no remember looking like this," she cried, tears streaming down her wrinkly cheeks. "If only I stay so young."

"What if you could," I said.

She laughed.

"Seriously. What if you could look like this again?"

"Impossible."

"I'm not so sure."

"Hope," she groaned. "You know better than tease me!"

"I think I may have found something."

Rosa put down the mirror and looked up at me.

"Like I said, I've been doing some reading." I took the grimoire from her lap and began skipping through the pages. "Here," I said, pointing to a page with tons of handwriting scrawled across it.

"What you find?" she uttered, taking a look.

"It's not...*magia negra*...black magic is it?" I asked, nervously.

She continued reading. "No. This not *magia negra*, but also not like usual *magia blanca* either."

"What is it then?"

Rosa shrugged. "I not know. I never seen." She was captivated, utterly and completely engaged in reading.

"I tried translating it myself. I'm pretty sure it has something to do with ageing."

"Si," she said, ardently.

"But it isn't finished. It looks like my grandmother was still working it when she died."

"Si," she replied. "It so unusual. I never seen nothing like this. She combine elemento and...power...and blood of immortal." She looked up at me amazed "Maybe it work." Her eyes sparkled!

"So you think you can finish writing it...the spell?"

She bit her lip.

"Rosa," I repeated. "Do you think you can finish it?"

She looked me in the eyes and grinned. "Si," she replied. "But only if you help me."

"Of course," I replied.

She grasped my hands and pulled me close. Her breath was spicy and warm, as her lips pressed against my cheek.

"Gracias," she muttered. "Gracias, my child."

"You're welcome," I said, withdrawing.

"Can I keep?" she asked, closing the grimoire and tucking it under her arm. "Maybe we start work manana?"

"Si," I replied, smiling and suddenly it was just like old times again.

Rosa stood up and walked towards the door. She stopped and turned back around.

"I can never thanks for all you done," she said, teary-eyed.

"Don't be silly," I replied. "You have done more than your fair share for me as well."

"You bring back grandson and son. You like daughter to me Hope." Her old eyes smiled.

I beamed from ear to ear and watched her leave. It felt good knowing how happy I'd made her—so good that I'd nearly forgotten all the hate in my heart.

I closed my eyes and reclined on the bed. I remembered the last few times Eradan had snuck his way past Ryan and her friends into my room. God I missed him.

34. The White Witch

*"Got me hoping you page me right now your kiss's
Got me hoping you save me right now,
Lookin so crazy your love's got me lookin,
Got me lookin so crazy your love."*

Crazy In Love – Beyonce Knowles

Sleep was like a gift. My body was utterly exhausted and my mind had been working on overdrive. Truth was I hadn't even realized that I'd fallen asleep until Christian slid into bed next to me!

"There you are," he whispered. "I thought you'd disappeared."

I smiled and stretched.

"What were you doing?"

"I was sleeping."

"Well, I guess battling an army of doppelgangers will do that to a girl." He grinned and kissed me on the forehead.

I smiled and thought of how happy he made me feel.

"And you make me happy too," he suddenly whispered, through my thoughts.

My eyes widened. He could hear me and I could hear him too! I was ecstatic having him inside my head again! I sprung from the sheets and jumped on him!

"*I love you! I love you! I love you!*" I exclaimed, thorough our internal connection as I kissed him over and over. His sweet tin-cinnamon taste made me giddy. I withdrew and grinned.

"I missed you," he confessed.

"But I thought you loved being human."

"I love *you* more."

I smiled even wider.

"So you did it Hope," he said, withdrawing. "You've finally got everything you've ever wanted."

My eyes narrowed. Christian was right. I did have it all. I had absolutely everything I'd always talked about wanting. I had a home, a family, friends, paradise and even forever again with him too, but still my heart was frozen inside.

"What is it?" he asked, concerned.

I shrugged and got out of bed.

"Hope?" he continued.

I slid on my boots. As I toyed with the laces I tried masking my thoughts from him. How could I tell him about what I'd done to Eradan? How could I confess that I'd been secretly speaking with the future version of our son and then inadvertently allowed myself to destroy him!

"What's going on?" he said, tearing through my thoughts.

"Don't," I pleaded, bolting from the bedroom. I hurried down the stairs and outside onto the grass.

"Hey," he said, following after me. "Why are you running away?"

"I-I did something," I divulged with shame.

"What?"

"It was bad Christian. Real bad."

"What kind of bad?"

"I knew better, but I did it anyway." I grabbed my face with my hands and shook my head. "There were just too many of them for us to fight!"

"Fight? What are you talking about Hope?"

"*Them*! The shape-shifters sent by the Society. We could never defeat them on our own."

"I understand that."

"So I summoned an army—an army of dead sailors from those ships at the bottom of the ocean."

"Baptiste told me about it. He said it was brilliant. He said you were brilliant!"

"It wasn't brilliant. It was rash and stupid and I was an abomination."

"I don't understand."

"Did B tell you how I summoned them?"

"No."

"I had Marco help me."

"So? Marco's a good witch."

"He might be a good witch, but he practices black magic." My tone hardened.

Christian's brow furrowed.

"I couldn't summon the sailors the way I needed them. I couldn't use white magic and there was nothing in my grandmother's grimoire. We were running out of time."

His eyes were distressed.

"I had no other choice Christian!"

"So you used black magic?"

I nodded.

He groaned aloud and ran his hands through his hair.

"I didn't want to, believe me, but it was the only way."

He heaved a sigh. "You realize there are consequences right?"

"Believe me, I realize it!"

"And is that why your hair turned white?"

"No. Yes. I don't know!"

"Baptiste told me about you on the battlefield. He glorified you like some supreme warrior!"

"I-I wasn't supreme. I was beastly, like some deranged ice-queen version of Vlad the Impaler!"

"I hardly think you were like Vlad—"

"It was scary Christian. I was strong...more powerful than you can imagine."

He heaved another sigh.

"Rosa told me this story," I uttered. "This stupid damn story!"

"What story?" he asked, confused.

"I don't know," I shrugged. "But it's been haunting me ever since."

"And you think you did all this because of something that Rosa said?"

"It wasn't just something she said. It was more than that. She told me of this Spanish fairy tale—this legend about El Diablo Blanco."

"The White Devil? What does this have to do with you?"

"It has everything to do with me!"

He frowned.

"Will you just listen?"

"Of course," he said, willingly.

"The story is about a beautiful woman and how she falls in love with a wicked man."

"Me?" he said, bemused. "Am I the wicked man?"

"This is serious."

"Okay. Go on."

"So she begs this man to make her like him."

"Wicked?"

"Yes. And of course he does. So now she possesses all the power of humanity and all the power of evil too. Basically she becomes the most dangerous woman in the world!"

"And you're saying this is you?" he laughed.

"Christian!"

"I'm listening."

"Her hair turns white."

"Well, I do see that similarity."

"And everything she touches turns to ice."

"Well that's not like you at all."

I sped toward the rosebush across from us at super-sonic speed and snapped off a scarlet red bloom. I sped back to Christian holding the rose bloom in the palm of my hand. I focused my power and suddenly the rose began freezing over.

"How'd you—"

"See," I said, eyeing the beads of ice that adorned the petals. "I'm her."

"The White Devil? I don't think so, Hope."

I dropped the frozen bloom to the ground, snapped my fingers together and tossed a flame at it. The rose charred instantly.

"Just because your hair suddenly turned white and you have this new ability to freeze things, it doesn't make you an evil legend from Spanish folklore!"

My eyes narrowed. "Well, she becomes pregnant by the wicked man and she goes crazy."

"Are you implying that I've made you crazy?"

"Damn it Christian! I'm not implying anything. I just want you to listen to this story, okay? She wants to control everything. She's not human anymore—she's only power."

"I still can't seem to understand what this has to do with you."

"She becomes totally emotionless. And on the eve of her beloved's death, her heart breaks."

"Her beloved dies?"

I nodded.

"How does he die?"

"Everything she touches turns to ice."

"Even him?"

I nodded. "So on the eve of his death she comes to his side. She starts to cry. And her tears melt his body. He becomes free from his death-like state and breathes again! Don't you see?"

"No."

"I'm El Diablo Blanco!"

"Come on Hope. Don't be ridiculous."

"I'm not being ridiculous. Think about it. The white hair, being changed into something wicked by the man I love, having the power to freeze things, it all makes sense!"

"But it's just a story!"

"A bullet went into your chest Christian—Gabriel shot you through the heart. I felt you dying in my arms!"

"Yes," he snapped. "I know all this."

"I cried and my tears—my wicked tears of blood, they streamed from my eyes and fell between your lips! I saved you. I made you vampire again without even realizing that I'd done it!"

"Oh Hope," he groaned.

"I'm her, Christian! I'm the White Devil and my tears saved you from death!"

"So?" he uttered, frustrated. "Even if you really are this legendary myth—why does any of it matter? I'm here. You're here. We're together again! This is our happily ever after, Hope!"

I shook my head.

"What?" he gravely.

"As he begins to live, she begins to die."

His eyes widened.

"In the story her body freezes and shatters into icy shards and then she turns into a butterfly or something."

"What?" he exploded, laughing. "And to think I was actually starting to believe you!"

I grabbed his hand. "It's not a joke. I wear the mark of it here." I swept back my white hair and pointed to the black butterfly tattoo on the back of my neck.

"Oh Hope," he whispered, pulling me close. "I love how you let your imagination run wild."

"It's not my imagination!" I raged, recoiling.

"So what happens now? We wait for you to explode into ice and become a butterfly?" His tone was mocking.

I scowled and turned away. He grabbed my hand and stopped me.

"Look," he said, seriously. "You're the most amazing woman in the world, Hope Havergale. And I love you. I have always loved you. From the first moment I laid eyes on you aboard the HMS Ambrose when you kissed me!" he grinned.

I grinned back.

"And when we had that passionate rendezvous in the rosebushes," he smirked, boyishly.

I laughed.

"And when you returned to Perish and when you wouldn't listen and you let me change you into a vampire." He sighed. "I think I started loving you even more."

I pursed my lips and tried to stop myself from grinning.

"God," he sighed. "Remember Mexico...in that cemetery?"

I nodded and smiled.

"And I loved you even when you were a little girl Hope," he said, holding both my hands. "I've loved you for all of your life. And I don't care if your hair is white, or green or purple. And I don't care if you want to call yourself El Diablo Blanco or a witch or a vampire or whatever." He swallowed nervously. "All that I care about is you and spending the rest of our lives together." His green eyes began glowing with a shimmery iridescence. He ran his fingers through his hair before suddenly getting down on one knee before me. "Hope," he said, softly. "There's something that I've wanted to ask you." He grinned and looked me in the eyes. "Will you marry me?"

35. A Royal Engagement

"I don't wanna brag, but I'll be,
The best you ever had."

Tonight (Best You Ever Had) – John Legend featuring Ludacris

"Yes! Yes! Yes!" I shrieked, tackling him to the ground!

My body tingled with icy currents of power! I pressed my lips to his in a thousand kisses! I never imagined that he'd ask me to marry him! I never thought that he'd want to take that step. Sure I knew he loved me, but I always figured him for more of an anti-establishment type when it came to nuptials.

"*I'm over two-hundred years old,*" he suddenly, whispered through my thoughts. "*I still have old-fashioned values, Hope.*"

I withdrew from him and grinned. I was over the moon! I was in love and more than eager to become Christian's wife. The sound of his sweet voice uttering those words—*will you marry me*, echoed over and over again inside my thoughts. And I knew—although much to his dismay, that I would return to watch him say them again shifting through time!

"Oh, I nearly forgot," he said, moving to a sitting position. He reached into the front pocket of his jeans.

My expression contorted as I watched on tenterhooks. A moment later he extracted the most beautiful ring!

"Oh my god! I gushed. It was an antique-looking, platinum band bordered with diamonds.

He took my left hand and slid the ring into place on my ring finger.

"It was your grandmother's," he divulged.

I tackled him to the ground again and plastered his sweet face in more kisses!

"Hope!" he laughed, struggling to come up for air. "Did you even read the inscription?"

"No! I was too busy letting you put it on my finger to read any inscription!"

"Here," he said, taking it off to show me the interior of the ring.

Several words in a fine script were etched inside the band. "For my siren from her sailor," I read, smiling.

"Do you like it?" he asked, anxiously.

"No," I replied, shaking my head. "I *love* it!"

He grinned, pleased with my reply.

I turned my attention back to the ring again. I couldn't take my eyes off of it!

"I asked your father for your hand a few hours ago," he divulged.

"You did?" I was shocked. I looked up from the ring to stare at him.

He nodded.

"You honestly asked Richard if you could marry me?"

He nodded again.

"And he said yes?"

Christian grinned.

"I'm...I'm totally surprised!"

"Yeah. I was surprised too."

"So he doesn't hate you anymore?"

"Oh he probably still hates me, but at least he finally knows that I'm really serious about how much I love you." He laughed and reached for my hand. He eyed my grandmother's ring as it encircled my finger and smiled.

"I think it was sweet of you to ask him. You really didn't have to do that."

"I know, but like I said, I'm old fashioned. You know how I feel about you, Hope. I believe in love and a little tradition. And if we're to start our family," he said, touching my stomach, "then—"

"Oh shit," I groaned. Reality suddenly hit me like a brick!

"What?" he said, perplexed.

"Are you only doing all this because of the baby?"

"What do you mean?"

"Did you propose just because of the baby, Christian?"

"No. I proposed to you because I love you."

I looked him in the eyes. I scanned through his thoughts.

"Granted," he confessed, "I might not have thought of doing it had you not been—"

"Jesus!" I exclaimed, my eyes suddenly welling with tears again.

"What's going on?"

I reached for the ring and took it off my finger. I handed it back to him. "Take it," I said, irritably.

"No!"

"Take it!"

"I don't want to take. I gave it to you. I proposed to you!"

I groaned.

"Why are you doing this Hope?"

"Just take the damn ring Christian!"

"No! I want you to have it. I want you to marry me!"

"But you didn't before you knew I was pregnant." My face hardened as the words fells form my lips.

"I don't understand."

I groaned again.

"Hope," he pleaded, "Talk to me."

"What do you want me to say?" I snarled.

"Tell me why you don't want to wear this ring!"

"Because!" I snapped.

"Why?"

"Because you didn't want to marry me until you found out I was pregnant!"

"That's not true," he rebutted.

"Bullshit!" I exclaimed, tossing the ring to the ground. It fell to the grass, among the thick emerald blades.

"What are you doing?" he asked, worriedly.

"Leaving," I uttered, hurrying away. I zoomed across the lawn toward the forest.

"Wait!" he shouted, following after me.

I continued ahead and sped off into the trees. A moment later he caught up to me. He reached for my hand and grabbed it. He fluttered his eyelashes and brought the world to a standstill around us.

"Christian!" I shouted, enraged. "Why did you follow me?"

"Because I love you!"

"Just leave me alone!"

"No," he insisted. "Tell me what the hell is wrong?"

"I can't," I said, pulling away.

"Don't you want to be with me? Don't you want to be my wife?"

"I do, but not if the only reason you want me to marry you is because I'm carrying your son!"

"My son?" he said, perplexed.

"Forget it!" I replied, pulling away from him.

"How do you know it's a boy?"

"I don't. And it's not. Forget it."

"Don't lie to me! I can feel you're hiding something from me."

I groaned again with frustration. The sound of my voice was loud and echoed through the trees with tenacity.

"Stop this," he pleaded, touching my arms.

"I can't."

"Why?"

"Because it's gone, Christian."

"What's gone?" he said, confused.

"The baby. It's gone."

"What?"

"I got hit in the spine when I was fighting those things. The blow must have...I don't know...Richard was there too. There was lots of blood...and he said I was losing it."

"Oh my god," he muttered, shocked. "Why didn't you tell me?"

"Because I knew how pissed you'd be."

"I'm not pissed, I'm heartbroken...I-I feel sick about it."

"Yeah well so do I," I snarled, my familiar tears of blood streaming down my cheeks. "And imagine I had to see it with my own two eyes."

"See it?"

"There he was fighting one of them right beside me when all of a sudden he started to disappear."

"What?" Christian asked, perplexed.

"Do you know what it's like to watch your own son die and know that it's entirely your fault?"

He reached for my arm and pulled me close. I fell against him and cried harder. All I could hear was the sound my sniveling and the cracking of our hearts breaking together.

"Shh," he consoled. "It's not your fault."

"It doesn't matter now."

"And you think it's because you're this demon...this Diablo from the Spanish fairy tale?"

"Or because I used black magic to summon the ghost army. Either way, fate has it out for me. I did this. I destroyed our son!"

"Fuck fate!" he exclaimed, withdrawing. "We make our own fate!"

I bit my lip.

"We've crossed oceans of time to be together, Hope. We've made our own choices, *not* fate." He stroked my hand. "This isn't because of you. None of it. And I don't care what it says in some fairy tale!"

His words and his fervor were encouraging. I almost smiled.

He pulled me close again. "Please say you'll marry me," he whispered, tenderly.

"I don't have the baby anymore. You don't have to—"

"I want to," he insisted. "I've always wanted to. I was just too stupid to realize it." He grinned.

I grinned a little too.

"We don't need a baby to be a family Hope." His eyes brightened. He fluttered his long lashes and the world reanimated around us again. "Say you'll marry me."

I wiped the bloody tears from my porcelain white skin and tried to smile.

"Forget the past. Let's look to the future—our future together." He smiled. "Make me the happiest man in the world and become my wife." He reached out and stroked my chin with the tip of his index finger. "Please," he persisted.

I nodded.

He grinned in reply and wrapped his strong arms around me. A moment later I felt him pressing his sweet lips to mine in a kiss. My body tingled with delight again and before long I was lost in the feeling of his kiss and the sheer warmth of his absolute undying love for me.

36. Never Grow Old

"Come out upon my seas,
Cursed missed opportunities,
Am I a part of the cure?
Or am I part of the disease?"

Clocks - Coldplay

When we returned back to Ambrose House Eva was standing on the porch with a bottle of Baptiste's special blend in her hand.

I eyed the bottle. I was incredibly thirsty. "What 'cha drinking?"

"Minotaur," she replied.

"Mino-what?!"

"Baptiste really pulled out all the stops for this one." She took a sip and sighed. "Head of a bull and body of a man! A retired, Chicago Bulls forward was in the shop last week and Baptiste thought it would be fun to mix him with a little juiced up muscle-head!" She took another sip. "It does have a kick!" She licked her lips. "So," she taunted, playfully. "Do we have something to celebrate or what?"

Christian and I turned to each other and giggled.

"Yippee!" she shrieked, "finally some god-damn good new around here!" A moment later she rushed inside the house to tell the others.

"Hey," I said, stopping Christian before we reached the porch. "I'm sorry I tossed the ring away."

"It's okay," he replied, suddenly producing it in the palm of his hand.

My eyes danced. "How'd you—"

"I picked it up before I chased you into the woods."

"You did?" I replied, taking it from him and slipping it back into place on my finger.

"Think you can try and keep it there from now on?" he asked, charmingly.

"Yeah," I replied, smirking. "I'll try."

"C'mon lovebirds," Eva said, suddenly appearing in the broken doorframe again. "Get your asses in here. We've got a post battle-slash-engagement party to start!"

I cracked a smiled and rushed up the stairs to be with her. She threw her thin, pale arms around me and squeezed.

"Let me see the ring!" she asked.

I held out my hand and showed it to her. The diamonds on the band sparkled with a rainbow of colors!

"It's beautiful," she gushed. Her tone was sincere and her manner was genuine. It was the side of Eva I rarely got to see.

"Thanks," I replied.

"Welcome to the family, bitch!" she insisted, more like her usual self.

"Thanks!" I laughed and we walked inside the house together.

"Esperanza," Rosa uttered, the moment I arrived. She was standing in the hallway by the stairs. Her body language was intense and I could tell that she was upset about something.

I moved away from Eva and towards her.

"What is it?" I asked, concerned.

"Richard tell me you lose baby." Her voice was tender and sympathetic.

I nodded.

"When this happen?"

"When I was fighting. I made some bad choices. I should have known better."

Her wrinkly brow furrowed.

"But it's done now and there's nothing I can do about it. Death is death. I can't even go back in time and try to change it."

Rosa's dark, old eyes narrowed. She grabbed my hand just as she'd done on the dock in Mallory Square that first time I met her. She began frantically eyeballing my palm.

"What are you doing?" I asked, perplexed.

"Looking."

"Looking for what Rosa? You've read my palm before."

"Si," she replied. "But I not see this death in your hand." She looked up at me. The expression on her face was severe. "And I not see this death on you either."

"What are saying?" I asked, confused.

She shook her head and grunted, before continuing to inspect my palm. "Here," she said, showing me the tangle of lines on the inside of my palm.

"What?"

"This," she said, pointing to the place at which my life line divided into two distinctly different sections.

"I've got two life lines," I groaned. "I know that already. It's because of a scar—an old scar from a stupid blood pact Christian and I made when I was a kid."

Rosa grunted again. "Don't you see Esperanza?"

I shrugged.

"This is deviating point. Here." She dragged her sharp, talon-like nail across my life line to the point at which it diverted into the two separate lines. "I think this you now," she explained, fervently.

"Now?"

"Si. I think this end of one life and beginning of new life."

I was totally confused, but utterly intrigued by what she was saying.

"This supposed to be fate line," she said, showing me the beginning of a line down the exact centre of my palm.

I looked at it. The line was hardly visible.

"Most people fate line dark and solid. You not have this line." Her old eyes twinkled. "You make own destiny," she grinned. "Fate no control *you*, Esperanza."

I smiled.

She smiled in reply. "You write own destiny. Si? You begin new life here and now."

"Like a second chance?" I asked, captivated.

"Like new beginning," she insisted.

My eyes widened.

"Like mariposa with new wings," she said, grinning, her wrinkly, old face energizing with vigor.

Was this my new beginning—as a married woman? Did I not have to explode into a thousand shards of ice and flesh and return as a butterfly for my new beginning?

"You see child," Rosa continued. "I tell you that story only allegorty."

"Allegory," I corrected.

"Allegory," she replied, smiling. "Come," she said, happily. "You have new life to begin!"

I walked with her into the living room. Christian was standing near the window with a bottle of Baptiste's special blend in his hand. He was gorgeous; immaculate and almighty as a vampire. I gingerly inhaled a little of his sweet scent as it filled the air. I smiled inside. My Tin Man was back!

"Let's have a toast!" he said, the moment I neared.

"Here," Eva said, handing me a glass filled with blood. I cautiously inhaled the contents. It smelled divine, like nothing I'd ever inhaled before.

"Amish," she whispered, with a wink.

I laughed. A moment later I turned my attention back to Christian again as he began his toast.

"To the woman of my dreams, the child in my heart, my best friend and my soon to be wife." Everyone raised their glasses and bottles. "To Hope," he said. "You have made my life worth living and I love you with all of my heart." He took a drink.

"To Hope!" everyone toasted, in unison.

I smiled from ear to ear, a little embarrassed.

"Let's talk dresses," Eva suddenly gushed, changing the subject. "We could try you in a trumpet or maybe mermaid...hum," she said, haughtily. "A modified A-line won't look as flattering as a ball gown but—"

"Eva," I interrupted. "We've not even set a date yet!"

"I know, but that doesn't mean I can't get excited about it. I always dreamed of a wedding at Ambrose House. You will do it here right?"

I smiled. I hadn't thought about where I'd like to get married to my Tin Man.

"It would be perfect you know," she continued, persuasively.

I grinned, when suddenly I heard my name being called from across the room. I looked up.

"Hope!" Henry called.

I started walking towards him when suddenly Eva stopped me.

"Think about it, Blondie," she whispered.

"I will," I said, before making my way towards Henry on the couch.

"May I kiss the bride-to-be?" he asked, gentlemanly as I approached.

"Of course!" I leaned in close and let him plant one on my cheek.

"If only your grandmother could have been here for this."

"I'm sure she is," I insisted, "in spirit."

Henry smiled. I smiled back and patted him on the shoulder.

"Well I'm proud of you," he said, grandfatherly.

"Oh stop!"

"No, I mean it. You've done so much for all of us in this last little while. You've really turned this house into a home again. Thank you."

I kissed him on the forehead.

"Have you and Christian set a date?" he asked.

"No, but that doesn't mean *you* shouldn't start thinking about who you're going to bring as a date Henry."

"A date?" he said, apprehensively.

"Yeah, a date!"

"Oh I don't know," he muttered.

I leaned in close. "She's waited a long time for you," I whispered. "Go for it." I kissed him on the forehead again before moving across the room back to Christian.

"Hope," Richard said, stopping me.

"Hey," I replied, smiling.

"I'm still so sorry about the bab—"

"Let's not talk about it anymore," I said. "Okay?"

He nodded. "But I still would like to examine you. I just want to make sure that you're okay."

"Thanks."

"It's the least I can do."

"I heard Christian asked you for my hand in marriage," I said, changing the subject.

His face lit up. "To be honest it rather surprised me!"

"It surprised me too!" I grinned. "I thought you hated him."

"I do," he said.

I laughed.

"I think all fathers' hate the men that take their daughters away from them."

I grinned.

"But I know he loves you. And I know he'll give you the life you want... fairy tale ending and all."

I beamed.

"Well, congratulations," he said, awkwardly, kissing me on the cheek. He turned around to leave.

"Where are you going?" I asked.

He stopped mid-step and turned around. "I'm not sure. After everything that's happened, I'm not even sure whether my house or even my wife will still be waiting for me when I get back!"

"What will you do for work...now that your previous employer has seemingly disappeared from existence?" I smiled.

He shrugged. "Maybe it's time to do something noble for a change."

"Well we could always use a doctor around here."

He smiled and started to leave again.

"Richard," I said, eagerly.

He turned around.

"Will you do me a favor?"

"Anything."

"Will you walk me down the aisle?"

His face flushed with color. "It would be my honor, Hope."

I smiled. He smiled too. I could tell he was touched—genuinely moved, and I was glad that I could do that for him.

"Before you go," I said, suddenly. "I want to show you something."

His brow furrowed with intrigue.

"Come with me," I whispered, reaching for his hand. I snuck him thorough the living room toward the back door.

"Where are we going" he asked.

"Someplace I think you need to see."

I smiled and held him tightly. I pushed open the back door and zoomed across the lawn and through the forest at my super-sonic speed. Richard was scared stiff holding onto me as we soared through the trees.

"Are we there yet?" he asked, eagerly.

"Almost," I replied, setting him down.

It was beautiful. Moss carpeted the ground with supple softness. Songbirds hummed in harmony, while tall trees loomed overhead like storybook giants.

"Where are we?" he asked.

"Deep in the woods," I answered. "C'mon."

There was a small clearing in the distance. A set of jagged rocks jutting up from the ground marked the spot.

"What is this place?" he asked, moving towards the rocks.

"Memorial grounds."

His face paled. He was whiter than a ghost.

"Richard," I said, concerned. "Are you okay with this?"

He nodded and continued moving forward.

"Just up here," I uttered, leading the way.

I took him towards rock outcropping. We eyed the elegant scripted initials that had been intricately carved into each of them. I watched as he neared the rock bearing the letter A on its surface. He moved in close and knelt down before it. He stroked the jagged edges of its surface and hung his head.

"You knew she was here, didn't you?" My tone was firm.

He nodded and looked up at me. His old eyes were swollen with tears.

"Why did you lead me to believe that my mother was buried in that big fancy cemetery in the city?"

He rose to his feet and wiped his eyes. "You were just a child Hope. It was complex." He turned back to the stone again. "I should have come here before now."

"Why didn't you?"

He shrugged. "I didn't think I'd be welcomed. And...I was scared."

"Of what?"

"Of feeling, I guess." He exhaled a deep breath. "I never should have waited all these years to finally come and visit her...your mother Audrey." He turned towards me and reached for my hand. "Thank you," he said. "Thank you for bringing me here."

I smiled. He smiled too and we stood before my mother's headstone, hand in hand, just being together.

37. Fit For A Princess

"It's a nice day to start again.
It's a nice day for a white wedding.
It's a nice day to start again."

White Wedding – Billy Idol

Time had passed with ease. The seasons changed. Months turned into weeks and weeks into days. Days turned into hours and suddenly the day of our wedding had arrived!

Perish really was our little slice of paradise and we never took a moment of it for granted anymore. Life was resolute and somehow managed to smooth out all of its ruffles just for us.

Every day was better than the day before it and truly made me eager for the years ahead. I knew Christian and I had forever again, but somehow spending time with him never felt like enough. And that was love—not the kind that felt like a falling star, that sparked then faded; the kind that ripened with age and made me long for more of it.

Since obliterating the Society, there hadn't been any sudden or unexpected arrivals on our shores. No strangers, peculiar happenings or even danger had managed to ruin the renewed perfection of our very own Eden. Everything was perfect. And for the first time in my entire life I felt as though I deserved every second of it!

"There you are," Christian said, grabbing me by the waist.

"Christian!" I exclaimed. "Don't you know that it's bad luck to see the bride before the wedding?"

"I don't care," he said, kissing me on the lips.

I laughed and kissed him back.

"You're not dressed," he said, concerned.

I shrugged. I was still wearing my black jeans, white tank-top and flip flops.

"Are you getting cold feet?" he joked.

I swatted him in the arm and smiled. He looked amazing, in his tailor made black suit pants and white dress shirt.

"I can't believe you're going to be mine!" he whispered, excitedly.

"I'm already yours," I replied.

"I know, but this is different. It's official."

I shook my head at him and grinned. He really was adorable in an old-fashioned kind of way.

"I must admit," he said. "I'm really excited about this."

"You are?"

"Of course! I can't wait to marry you!" he uttered, picking me up by the waist and twirling me around in a circle.

"Christian!" I shouted. I beamed from ear to ear, "Put me down!"

"I feel like a big kid today!" he snickered. "I don't know what's wrong with me!"

"I love seeing you happy," I admitted.

His brow furrowed. "I thought you loved me smoldering and mysterious." He ran his hand through his hair and smirked.

"I love that too!"

"When are you going to start getting dressed?" he asked, eagerly.

"I don't know. When's the wedding officiant gonna be here?"

"Why was it that you didn't want to use a minister?" His tone was mocking.

"Uh...maybe because we're the anti-christ!"

"He'll be here in a little over an hour," he replied. "Think you'll be ready?"

"I think I'll manage."

He smiled.

"Where'd you find this guy anyway?"

"Marco hooked us up."

"Oh no," I said, nervously.

"What?"

"Every time you and Marco are together things get outta hand. Remember the cure?" My tone was icy.

"Naw," he assured. "This time it's fine. He promised me that this guy knows his stuff."

I rolled my eyes. "Are you sure he's a real officiant?"

"He's a high priest," Christian insisted.

"Priest?" I exclaimed.

"A hoodoo Priest!"

"What?" I raged.

"I'm just teasing," he laughed.

I bit my lip and scowled.

"C'mon," he said. "Everything is going to be wonderful! I promise." He kissed me on the lips before turning to leave. "Oh," he said, turning back. "The reason I came up in the first place was because there's someone here to see you."

"Me?"

He nodded.

"Who is it?"

He shrugged. "Said they knew you and that they wanted a chance to say hello before the wedding."

My expression twisted, concern suddenly weighing heavily in the pit of my stomach.

"I said I'd check with you first."

"Well did you get their name?" I asked, uneasily.

"I don't think she said, but she asked me to give you this." He reached inside his pocket and pulled out a small box. He handed it over.

"What is it?"

"I don't know. Open it."

I eyed the shiny, black wrapping paper and blood-red, satin ribbon that adorned it.

"Go on, Hope," Christian said, excitedly. "Just tear it open!"

I ripped off the ribbon and tore through the paper. I opened the box.

"What did you get?" he asked, enthusiastically.

"I don't know," I said, eyeing the soft, white batting that lined the interior. I rummaged through it and spotted something at the bottom. "Oh my!" I exclaimed.

"What?"

I reached inside and extracted three, petite, living earthworms that had been twisted into the most impeccable braid!

"What the hell is that?" Christian shouted.

My heart swelled with elation. "It's her," I said. "Maddy!"

"Who?"

"Maddy," I said. "Remember the child vampire that came to our shores?"

"The one with the human parents in the row boat?"

"Yeah," I replied. "The ones we managed to save."

"I remember her," he said. "But this was no child down there, Hope. A woman gave me that."

My eyes narrowed.

"Do you want me to send her up?" he asked, cagily. "It's your wedding day. You don't have to do anything you don't want to do."

"I know," I replied. "But I think I'd like to see her."

"Yeah?"

"Would you mind sending her up?"

"Sure. But I'm staying close," Christian assured.

I smiled. A moment later he left the bedroom and headed downstairs. Before I knew it he was back again and there was a knock on the door. I opened it up. A pretty woman, with shiny, curly, dark hair stood before me.

"Hello," I said, warily.

"Hope," she replied. "Did you get my gift?"

I nodded. "Come inside," I said, bringing her into my bedroom. I shut the door. "Who are you?" I asked, sharply.

"It's me. Maddy!" Her voice was airy and excited.

I studied her face. She vaguely resembled the little wayward vampire-girl we'd had here.

"You look beautiful!" she exclaimed.

"Who are you?" I insisted. "You're not her. You can't be. She was only a child when she left us and that wasn't even long ago."

"I know that," she defended.

I took a cautious whiff of her scent. "And she wasn't a vampire anymore when she left us either."

"You're right," the pretty, olive-skinned woman agreed.

"Then who the hell are you?" I exploded.

"Hope," she soothed. "I'm not here to upset you. But you must believe it really is me!"

My expression contorted. I scrutinized her a little more thoroughly when suddenly I realized that she was wearing an identical ring to mine on her wedding finger!

"My ring!" I exclaimed. "Why are you also wearing my ring?"

She stroked her finger and smiled. "Because *you* gave it to me."

"I did?" I said, confused.

She slipped her ring off her finger and showed me the inscription on the inside of the band.

I took it in my hand and started reading. *"For my siren from her sailor,"* I read. I looked beside it, to the additional words that had been newly inscribed. *"For Maddy love Eradan."* My eyes bulged! I looked at up her in astonishment.

"He's alive, Hope!" Her tone was smooth. "He's my husband and we have three very beautiful children together."

"But I don't under—"

"He didn't know how to tell you." She took her ring back from me and put it into place on her finger again.

I touched my abdomen and shook my head.

"You're still pregnant," she said, smiling.

"But I got hit and there was so much blood and Richard said—"

"I know," she interjected. "But he's tough. Like you. He's a survivor." She reached for my hand. "You're still with child."

My eyes welled with tears and began streaming down my face. Maddy began crying too.

"But how did you meet him," I asked, impatiently. "And how did you become a vampire again and—"

"I know this is overwhelming," she admitted. "And in time all of these answers will make themselves known to you, but for now just be happy with the knowledge that you are still going to be a mother, Hope."

I nodded, grinning. "Thank you," I said still teary-eyed. "Thank you for coming!"

Just then Christian knocked on the door. "Everything okay in there?" he asked, opening it.

"Yes!" I exclaimed. "Everything is wonderful!"

"It is?" he inquired, eyeballing the tears staining our faces.

"I must go," Maddy said, turning to leave.

"Will you stay for the ceremony?" I begged.

"I'll try."

"Thank you!" I said again. "Thank you so much for coming!"

She smiled one last smile before leaving.

"Who was that?" Christian asked, as she vanished from sight.

"Someone very special," I replied. I wrapped my arms around him and grinned.

"Well," he whispered, "no one's quite as special as you Mrs. Livingston."

"Mrs. Livingston," I muttered. "Hum. I thought I was keeping my maiden name." My tone was mocking.

"You're such a strong woman," he purred, praising me.

"And don't you ever forget it!"

"I won't," he grinned. "You won't let me!"

I laughed. Christian laughed too when suddenly there was another knock on the door.

"Hope!" Eva shouted. "I've got the dress and its magnifique!"

"I'm outta here," Christian said, kissing me on the forehead. He opened the door and smiled at Eva.

"What the hell is he doing in here?" she snarled.

"Leaving," he replied, pushing past her and the giant bag full of dress that she was carrying.

"Don't you know that it's bad luck to let the groom see you before the wedding?"

"I know. I know."

"God, Hope! What on earth were you doing with him in here only minutes before the ceremony?"

"We were just chatting."

"Chatting eh," she said, trailing the bag of dress through the air. "Are you ready to see it?"

I watched excitedly as the enormous white bag floated through the air like a parachute before falling gently upon the bed.

"I'm ready!" I replied.

Eva smiled and moved towards it. She unzipped the front of the bag with her long red fingernails and grinned.

I walked towards her, reached inside the bag and touched the dress. My body tingled as my fingers stoked the delicate crinoline and satin.

"Let's take it out," she insisted.

I nodded excitedly and helped her remove it from the bag. My eyes widened. It was beautiful. It was romantic and elegant, strapless and embroidered with lace and rhinestones. With a fitted bodice at the top and all the fullness of a ball-gown at the bottom the dress was perfect! I could see the fairy tale wedding of my dreams definitely coming true in it!

"Don't even ask how many lowly designers and tailors I had to veil to get you this freakin' masterpiece!"

"I love it Eva. I absolutely am in love with it!"

"Well you should be...it cost a damn fortune!"

"How can I ever thank you."

"Ah," she sighed, "try and convince Baptiste to finally marry me one day, will you?" She grinned.

I nodded and wrapped my arms around her in an embrace.

"Wanna try it on?" she asked, impatiently.

"You're damn right I do!" I replied, grinning like a little girl.

38. Whomsoever This Glass Slipper Fits

"Hey little princess, hey little pea,
Come down from your tower and dance with me.
Yah you're the fairest one in the land.
Try on this glass slipper and give me your hand."

Fairytale – Cowboy Junkies

I was a heavenly vision in white as I stood before the mirror in my bedroom! My ivory colored hair was tied up neatly in a twist at the back of my head and adorned with soft, white gardenia blooms. My snowy hued skin was covered in a fine dusting of shimmer powder and my lips had been stained crimson in color. My nails were painted white too and sparkled with a dazzling diamond like quality. But the dress took the cake! It fit me like a glove and made me feel like a princess. I was beautiful and ready to marry the dark prince of my dreams!

"Esperanza," a voice called, from behind my bedroom door.

"Rosa?" I asked. "Is that you?"

"Si. You have second?"

"Of course," I said, shuffling across the room in my gown. I opened the door.

"Esperanza!" she gushed. "You is so beautiful!"

I smiled and watched as tears began welling in Rosa's mascara laden eyes. Her face was smooth and youthful.

"You look beautiful too!" I said, embracing her. Her body was curvy and taut. She looked amazing in the tight fitting, red dress she was wearing. She was gorgeous—1957 gorgeous! "Aren't you glad we finally got that spell to work?" I laughed.

She grinned. "I is glad to be here today," she replied.

"Well of course, Rosa. You've been like a mother to me."

"Ah, child," she smiled, flattered.

"I mean it. You've taught me so much and helped me so much. I don't know what I would have done without you!"

"Gracias," she replied.

"How's Henry?" I asked.

"He so happy for you! He gonna change into bird or something to watch ceremony," she smiled.

"I mean how is Henry with *you?*"

"Oh!" she blushed. "Worth wait," she said, smiling.

I smiled back.

"I came to give you something," she said, handing me a rectangular shaped box.

"You shouldn't have."

"I want to."

I eyed the box. It was wrapped in pale blue paper and tied with a white, silk ribbon.

"Open it child," she encouraged.

I smiled and unfastened the ribbon. It fell to the floor like a leaf in the wind. I tugged on the paper and tore it apart. I pried up the lid and looked inside.

"Oh my god, Rosa!"

The most beautiful pair of shoes sat inside the box. They were radiant and sparkling and adorned in thousands upon thousands of tiny, diamond-like jewels!

"When I marry Marco's father," she said.

"The bum?"

"Si. The bum. I wear these shoes. I feel like princess that day!"

I took the shoes out of the box and held them in my hands. They were literally the most beautiful shoes I had ever laid my eyes upon!

"Try," she insisted.

I smiled and sat down on the edge of my bed in my big gown. I reached for the first shoe and slipped it on my foot.

"It fits like a glove," I grinned.

Rosa nodded, pleased with herself.

I put the other shoe on and rose to my feet.

"Beautiful," she gushed, tears abruptly welling in her eyes again.

I walked across the room towards the mirror. I looked at my reflection. The shoes fit perfectly!

"You have something old?" she asked, concerned.

I thought about it for a moment. "My ring!" I exclaimed. "It belonged to my grandmother."

"You have something new?"

"This dress! Eva had it made for me."

"And now you borrow shoes," she continued, "but you not have something blue." Her voice was worried.

"It's okay," I shrugged.

"Not okay," she said, extracting one of the white gardenias from my hair. She waved her hand over the flower and chanted something softly under her breath. A moment later the petals began changing color! The pure white petals deepened to a beautiful teal hue.

"That's amazing!" I said, as she took the pretty blue flower and secured it back into my hair again. "I don't think I'll ever get tired of watching you do magic, Rosa."

She grinned. "You ready?" she asked, eagerly.

"Yeah," I replied. "I am."

She linked arms with me and we left the bedroom together.

"Rosa," I whispered, as we descended the stairs.

"Si?"

"I think I'm still pregnant."

She nodded.

"You don't seem surprised."

"I not," she said.

"Is this because of my palm...when you read it?"

"Some," she shrugged. "But mostly, I just know."

"You did?" I said, shocked.

"Si. I is witch, Hope. I channel energy and feel it around always. I look you and I feel it."

"It?"

"Baby," she said.

"You do?"

"Si," she replied, tightening her hold on my arm. "And if you focus energy inside you, you feel it too." She smiled.

I smiled back and for the briefest moment I felt the rock again—sitting heavily in the pit of my stomach, just as it had before.

"Thank you," I whispered, kissing her on the cheek.

She nodded and withdrew from me the moment we reached the main floor.

I looked around the house. It was beautiful; decorated from top to bottom in white! There were alabaster toned garlands and snowy toned wreathes adorning nearly every nook and cranny of Ambrose House.

"Finally!" Eva said, spotting me at the foot of the stairs. "Everyone is waiting!"

I smiled.

She eyed the sparkle radiating from beneath my dress. "What's that?" she asked with intrigue.

I swished my gown to the side and showed her my glass slippers!

"Wow!" she shrieked.

"Rosa loaned them to me," I grinned. "Something borrowed!"

"Are you ready?" she asked, eagerly.

"Absolutely!"

She took my hand and led me through the front door and outside to the porch.

"There's no turning back now," she teased, fluffing her shiny, red hair.

"Good," I replied. "Let's do this!"

"Well Cinderella, your prince is waiting for you on the other side of the house."

I smiled.

"So get out there and marry the shit outta him!"

I laughed. Eva smiled and led me towards Richard.

"Hope," Richard said, suddenly taking my arm. He was dressed in a classy, black suit. He was cleaned-up and neatly groomed. He looked distinguished. His hair had been freshly trimmed and his skin even looked tanned.

"Richard," I whispered. "I'm glad you could be here."

"I'm your father," he said, proudly. "I wouldn't miss this for the world."

I smiled and we stepped foot on the grass.

"Bouquet!" Eva panicked. She suddenly thrust an elegant, bulbous bouquet of white roses at me.

"Thanks!" I exclaimed, grasping them. They were perfect and pallid and sat in my hands like a beautiful symbol of my new life with Christian.

"*Now* you're ready," Eva smiled.

I nodded at her before rounding the corner.

BOOM! The tone of my heartbeat was like thunder inside my chest. Christian! He was gorgeous, like an angel in a black suit sent from heaven above just for me! And as he stood at the end of the aisle realized how *real* this actually was! He was my groom—and I his bride. We were about to get married!

"*You are a vision,*" he whispered, with his feathery inner-voice.

"*And you ain't so bad yourself,*" I replied, silently.

Our eyes locked and I could feel myself falling helplessly in love with him all over again. *This* was our moment of happiness together—right here, right now! And it amused me knowing that we didn't even need to rely on magic or our gifts to make it happen!

The soft sounds of an enchanting piano began resonating from Henry's iPod.

I looked ahead; to the ornate altar at the end of the aisle of white rose petals. It had been crafted into a picturesque archway shaped of thorny, rose stems. It was truly magical and I wanted nothing more than to marry my Christian.

Guests were few in number, but huge in significance. Eva and Baptiste flanked baby Stromboli on the right, while Rosa, Henry (in humming bird form), Marco and even his father were on the left. Out of the corner of my eye I noticed Alex standing behind her seat next to a woman with dark hair.

My eyes widened as I neared. "Ryan?" I whispered, as I walked past.

She grinned at me and waved. I had no idea how Alex had found her, but I was glad to see that she had! I couldn't wait to catch up with her, but at the moment I had more important things to do!

As I continued walking I spotted Cindy—my air-brain step-mother, standing to the side. She was snapping photos with her fancy phone—more selfies than pictures of me, but that didn't matter. I supposed it was nice that she even bothered accompanying my father at all. She smiled at me as I passed and gave me the thumbs up on my dress. I smiled back and laughed.

As I moved ahead I noticed a young couple on the other side. They were surrounded by three smiling children; two girls and boy that took great pleasure in running up and down the aisle around me!

"Eradan!" I exclaimed, misty-eyed. It was him—really him, and he looked as strange and spectacular as always!

He nodded at me and grinned, before pushing his spectacles atop his head. His green eyes were radiant and still the spitting image of his father's. Maddy was by his side. She was already in tears! She smiled largely as I passed by and reached for my hand. I reached out and touched her. We smiled together!

As I continued walking I realized that this day—my wedding day was quickly becoming the happiest day of my entire life! I had never been so elated before. I felt beautiful and confident and surrounded by so much love that I wanted to burst with joyfulness! I was in love and in control of my power! My body swelled with icy currents of energy as I walked toward my Tin Man when suddenly I realized that I was walking on ice!

With every step I took, I'd been freezing the petals and the ground beneath me! The children giggled as they slid along the aisle of ice behind me. Like angels tickling each other's wings, the sweet sound of their laughter made me melt inside. I smiled when all of a sudden one of them slid right into me! I stopped and turned around.

It was the smallest of the three children. She was adorable; with golden curls in her hair and incredibly big, blue, eyes. I felt as though I was looking at a reflection of myself as a child! I kneeled down to face her, at her level and grinned.

"Grandma," she whispered. "You look pretty."

My heart swelled with happiness at the tender sound of her tone! I wanted nothing more than to hug her and kiss her and remember that tone forever. I was worried however, that my overzealous affection would frighten her, and so I decided to give her something instead. I extended my hand and summoned my power. I created a singular, spectacular snowflake made of ice within the confines of my palm. I handed it to her and beamed. Just then the other two children approached me! I summoned my power once more and created two additional snowflakes for them. As I passed the snowflakes to them, I envisioned what amazing potential the future had in store for us. I radiated with true happiness and rose to my feet again.

With my eyes fixed ahead, I continued the walk towards my Tin Man. The officiant was standing next to him. He was tall and dressed in a suit. He was relatively normal looking and thankfully not a hoodoo priest as Christian had teased!

The officiant nodded and opened his mouth to speak. "Who gives away this bride?" he asked.

"I do," Richard replied, lovingly.

I withdrew my arm from his and smiled. He leaned in and kissed me on the cheek.

"Thank you," I whispered.

"Thank you too," he replied.

I turned to Christian. He looked so happy. I beamed from ear to ear as I stared at him.

The officiant continued speaking. And as he talked about the significance of marriage and the sanctity of its union, all I could think about was how damn much I loved Christian! I remembered seeing him for the first time again when I returned to Perish and I how much I couldn't keep my eyes off him when he was still human on the HMS Ambrose. I thought of how irresistible he was back in 1957 and how passionate he was in that cemetery in Mexico. I remembered the feeling of him saving me from the water in the mangrove estuary when I was just a little girl. I also recalled the time he took me in his arms and bestowed me with everlasting immortality on the black sand beach in Hawaii. I remembered all the fighting and the countless rescues, but mostly I remembered the feeling of love—his love. And that was a feeling I wanted to feel forever!

This was it—this was our wedding; the day we would officially relinquish our old lives and forge a new one together. And I knew in my heart that things would be different from now on. We'd be blessed with love and family and friends and the feeling of home that I so longed to have.

Not a moment too soon we were already at the declarations!

"Hope," the officiant questioned. "Do you take Christian to be your husband?"

"I do," I insisted. "I really, really do!"

Christian smiled.

"And Christian," he continued. "Do you take Hope to be your wife?"

"I do," he said, eagerly. "Forever!"

I beamed!

"Then by the power vested in me I now pronounce you husband and wife. You may kiss your bride!"

Christian quickly grasped my waist and tilted me back. He ran his hand behind my neck and slowly leaned into me. I closed my eyes. I felt his lips against mine. Our mouths exploded in the most magnificent of kisses! It was tender, yet passionate and entirely perfect! My body tingled ardently and I could feel my power swelling within me. And when he withdrew and returned me to my feet again I realized that I had left an ice-studded halo of frost on his lips!

Christian touched his mouth and grinned while we were met with a shower of applause and cheers!

I turned to Christian and winked before suddenly compelling a beautiful blanket of snow to fall from the sky! Tiny trickles of icy snowflakes descended upon everyone right there in the middle of the humid Florida weather! It was wonderful! And as our family reveled in the undeniable remarkableness of the enchanting snowfall, I delighted in the fact that the deed was finally done. We were married at last!

39. True Love's Kiss

"Couldn't we be, be happily ever after?
We could be strong together for so long.
Couldn't we be, be happily ever after?
Leavin' you never 'til forever's gone."

Happily Ever After - Case

The sky came alive with color. It was pink and purple and blue and yellow! It was beautiful and was comprised of virtually every tone in the rainbow. It was first light and this was our first sunrise together as husband and wife!

"It's so beautiful," Christian said, eyeing the sky ignite with color.

"I know."

"Think we'll ever get tired of watching sunrises together?"

"Never."

I took the opened bottle of rum from his hand and drank.

"Are you drunk yet?" he teased.

"Never."

He smiled. I smiled back.

"Did you enjoy your wedding Mrs. Livingston?"

"Definitely, Mr. Livingston!"

He smiled.

"Did you enjoy *your* wedding Mr. Livingston?"

"Definitely, Mrs. Livingston!"

We laughed together. Christian leaned forward and uncorked another bottle of blood.

"We've been out here all night, Hope." His voice was soft.

"It's still our wedding day as far as I'm concerned. We can do whatever we like!"

He grinned and took a sip of the blood.

"Are you implying that we should change our clothes Mr. Livingston?"

"No," he replied. "I'm implying that we should be getting out of our clothes Mrs. Livingston!"

I laughed. I knew exactly what he meant. And it was kind of funny still cavorting around in our formal attire as we sat beneath the tree in the centre of the yard.

"I really did enjoy the wedding," I added, smiling.

"Me too," he said.

"I really liked the officiant."

"You weren't even listening to him!" Christian exclaimed.

"How would you know?"

"I was reading your thoughts!" He smiled.

"Well I guess it's no secret how I feel about you then."

He laughed and ran his hands through his hair like usual.

"Too bad we had to veil him," I lamented.

Christian grinned. "You made it snow! Did you see his face?"

I shook my head.

"He was breathless!"

"I'm breathless," I said, leaning close and kissing him. "Are you looking forward to the honeymoon?" I whispered.

"What honeymoon?"

"The one I'm taking you on."

"You are?"

I nodded. "It's my gift to you. Baptist and Eva have agreed to cover shifts at the shop for you while we're gone. And since we're an artist short now—after that whole Gabe running the underworld thing, we took on a new apprentice!"

"What?" he exclaimed.

"Don't freak out," I assured. "He's totally cool and knows art and is really eager to learn tattooing."

"Well who is he? And why wasn't I involved in any of this? You can't just trust anyone off the street. We still have to be careful. We still have a huge secret to keep, Hope."

"I know," I said, kissing him on the cheek.

The sky was beginning to intensify with color. It was much more golden and vivid now.

"Well who is he?" Christian persisted.

"Marco," I said, smiling. "After the whole Gabe thing went down, he jumped at the chance to help us out."

"He did?"

"Yeah. And I know that you and Marco are like total BFFs."

Christian laughed.

"And just because he'll be working with us at the shop doesn't mean that you two have free reign to do whatever stupid thing you want!"

"What's that supposed to mean?"

"Like create a cure that nearly destroyed our lives!"

Christian bit his lip and smirked.

"Anyway, everything's been taken care of. We can go away and relax this time...like real people do!"

"Where are we going?" he asked, excitedly.

I cracked a smile.

"Where Hope? Tell me or I'll get inside that pretty head of yours and find the answer myself!"

"Mexico," I asserted. "We had fun in Mexico...well at least I thought we did between kicking evil vampire ass and rewriting history!"

"I love you," he whispered, kissing me on the forehead.

I smiled and stared out at the sky again. The sun was nearly up.

"Hope," he said, hesitantly.

"Yeah."

"Who was that couple?"

"What couple?" I asked, taking another sip of rum.

"That couple with the kids at the wedding. Who were they?"

I shrugged.

"Hope," he persisted.

"It was some girl," I uttered, vaguely. "You know. The one that gave me the present."

"The worms?"

"Yeah," I laughed.

"And the guy," he continued. "You got all teary-eyed when you saw him."

"I did?" I lied.

"Yes!"

"Can you just forget it, Christian?"

"Forget it?"

"Please?"

"Hope, there were barely a handful of guests at our wedding in the first place, and five of them I haven't the faintest clue as to who they even were!"

I rolled my eyes.

"But *you* seemed to know exactly who they were!"

"Christian," I chided.

"Why won't you tell me?"

"Because," I said, finishing off the bottle or rum. "They're not from here."

"What's that supposed to mean, they're out-of-towners?"

"They're not from now!" My voice was animated.

His expression blanked.

"They're from the future—*our* future."

"Future," he muttered, confused. "What do they have to do with us?"

"Let's not talk about it anymore. Let's not make any unwarranted residuals, okay?"

"Okay," he agreed.

I looked him in the eyes and shook my head.

"You can't give it up, can you?" I said, knowingly.

"I just want to know who the hell they are and then I'll shut up. I promise!"

I reached for his hand and brought it to my belly. "Feel," I said, eagerly as I pressed his hand against me.

I focused on my power. I concentrated my energy on my elemental connection to earth and tried desperately to summon some sort of response from the baby inside of me.

"My god!" he exclaimed.

I watched as his hand suddenly jolted, as though he was being nudged from the inside out!

"I'm still pregnant," I whispered.

"You are?" he exclaimed.

I nodded.

He smiled the biggest smiled I'd ever seen.

"I had Richard examine me again and it's real. He used to treat pregnant vampire women at HQ. He knows how help me through this Christian."

"That's amazing!"

"I know."

"But I thought you lost it. I thought that when you—"

"Me too," I interjected. "I guess I just got lucky."

"This is wonderful," he said, elated. "I'm so happy. I'm so happy for you and for us." He kissed me on the lips. A moment later I felt him withdrawing. "Hope," he asked, skeptically.

"Yeah."

"What does all of this have to do with that couple?"

I smirked.

"Hope," he continued, impatiently.

"You wanted to know who they were and I'm telling you."

His brow furrowed. "When you told me you thought that you'd lost the baby, you said *him*...you said *our son*."

I smiled.

"Was that tall guy, the one with the green eyes...was that our—"

"Shh," I purred, interrupting. "Don't say it! We've caused enough damage to the whole time-space continuum already!"

His eyes widened. He was overwrought with emotion.

"Every family has issues," I whispered. "Ours just happens to have some really, really freakin' weird ones!"

I smiled and ran my hands though his hair. And with the tenderest of touches he brought me to his lips. He gave me another kiss. My body heaved with bliss at the feeling of him against me. Life for that moment was the epitome of perfection!

"You did it again," he said, withdrawing.

"What?" I asked, concerned.

"Froze me," he laughed.

I eyed the peculiar halo of ice that studded his mouth and smiled. "Guess that's what you get for marrying an ice-queen!"

He licked the ice with his tongue and grinned.

"You know I'm still changing, Christian." My tone was serious. "I'm not fully in control of all this power inside of me yet. Who knows what I'll become."

He wrapped his arms around my shoulders and smiled. "I love you no matter what."

"I was hoping you'd say that!" I sifted through the grass and roots beneath me until I found a jagged rock. I held it in my hand and showed it to Christian.

"Oh no!" he groaned.

"What? It will be fun! Like old times."

"A blood pact?" he claimed, wide-eyed.

"Yes! And now that you're my husband I want to do something to signify the beginning our new lives together!"

"Because that whole wedding ceremony thing didn't do that for you?" His tone was teasing.

"Christian!" I said, swatting him in the arm. I took the sharp end of the rock and dug it into the flesh on the inside of my left palm. Blood pooled instantly.

"Mmm," he grinned, inhaling the scent of my blood in the air.

"Now you," I insisted, tossing the rock at him.

He grabbed the rock and dug the sharp end into *his* flesh on the inside of his left palm.

"Mmm," I moaned. The smell of his blood was divine as it hit my senses!

I reached out and pressed my hand to his. We laced our fingers together and let the blood from our cuts unite.

"That's it?" he whispered.

"That's it," I replied.

"I love you," he said, laughing.

"I love you too!"

I looked him in the eyes and smiled. Christian really was all that ever mattered to me. He was the Tin Man of my dreams, the dark prince of my childhood, the forlorn sailor of my escapades, my savior, lover, husband and best friend for all time! He was the one who always knew how to take my breath away.

This really was the end of my old life, and the beginning of my new one. I was a witch and a vampire, but still only just a woman—a woman deeply in love with her man.

"Hey," I said, suddenly. "You never read the inscription on the inside of *your* ring."

"You had my ring inscribed?"

I nodded.

He slipped the ring off his finger and eyed the inscription.

"It's us," I said. "It's our love story!"

His eyes narrowed. "You fit our entire love story on the inside of this ring?"

I laughed and grinned.

He held the ring in the centre of his bloody palm and we read the inscription together.

"Once upon a time, we lived happily ever after!"

Christian looked me in the eyes and smiled. He slipped the ring back on his finger and held me in his arms. And with all the passion and tenderness he was capable of, he gave me the most amazing kiss—a kiss so incredible I felt like I was suspended in mid-air! It was the kiss of a lifetime and the true beginning of our very own happily ever after.